GLASGOW BOYS

MARGARET McDONALD

faber

Content Warning

This novel discusses trauma and abuse. However, it never explicitly realises or relives these moments for the characters. When they are described it is through the characters' own words. Other sensitive topics that are depicted include anxiety attacks and substance abuse on the page, as well as an attempted suicide off-page. These topics are handled carefully and responsibly, however please be aware if these topics are personally challenging.

First published in the UK in 2024 by Faber & Faber Limited,
The Bindery, 51 Hatton Garden, London, EC1N 8HN
faber.co.uk

Typeset by MRules
Printed and bound by CPI Group (UK) Ltd, Croydon, CRO 4YY
All rights reserved
© Margaret McDonald, 2024

The right of Margaret McDonald to be identified as author
of this work has been asserted in accordance with
Section 77 of the Copyrights, Designs and Patents Act 1988

A CIP record for this book is available from the British Library

ISBN 978–0–571–38297–2

Printed and bound in the UK on FSC® certified paper in line with our continuing
commitment to ethical business practices, sustainability and the environment.
For further information see faber.co.uk/environmental-policy

4 6 8 10 9 7 5 3

For Caitlin

When they turn to each other in the middle of the night, they whisper to keep quiet. They twist on to their sides and face one another at either end of the room, muffling their words into the pillows. They put a hand on the wooden dresser that sits between their beds. The room is small enough that this is the only thing that separates them. It's their way of touching each other without having to touch each other. It's their way of saying *I had a nightmare* and *are you there* and *I am here*. And it's their way.

Chapter One

BANJO

Banjo kicks the wall and spins to fall against it. *Fifteen minutes.* Basically on time. And why send him into the hall? What's the punishment – missing class? Some genius.

He's given detention for after school. Banjo would rather have it on Christmas Day.

After that, he manages to get into a fight. It happens like this: Banjo feels a dampness on his leg and stops walking. He pats the back of his knees and finds them wet.

'Whit,' he states, right in the middle of the corridor. People look. Banjo looks back. Nobody's exactly holding a bottle of water. He turns around. There's a wet trail behind him.

He feels the bottom of his rucksack. It's his bottle.

'Aw, yer *kidden*'!' Banjo rips off his bag and crouches down. Everything's soaked. Jotters, textbooks, PE kit. All of it. Banjo slaps it on to the floor, but the need to punch something burns inside his hands. He takes a breath, gathers it all up, and stands.

'Urgh!' Banjo stomps a foot.

Everyone within a mile radius jumps.

The short story is that his new school is the same as any other small-time school in East Kilbride, way off the coast of Glasgow. Way off the coast of anything. Same grey corridors. Same smell of dried sweat. Same washed-out sense of despair. He gives it a month, maybe two, then he'll be out. Not because he's such the troublemaker, but because Banjo has some wild kind of karma. It's his first day here. He needs some form of a *fucking break*.

He's not got a locker yet, so Banjo goes into the courtyard with his stuff in his arms and thinks about what to do with his dripping bag.

He spots a group of guys milling about. They look about his age. That's not the reason Banjo notices, though.

He notices because one of the guys drops his crisp packet. Just takes it out his pocket and drops it on the ground as if the world is his own individual bin. The guy grins with all his teeth, like he doesn't even care about the dying oceans. The prick is blond, tall, and probably popular in that smug-shitebag sort of way. He's even got a bit of a tan despite Scotland's version of sunshine, whereas Banjo's a pasty, red-topped milk carton.

Unfortunately Banjo walks over. First mistake.

'Hoi.' His voice is curt.

They all turn.

'Ye gonnae pick 'at up?'

The prick blinks. 'Sorry, *what*?'

'Ye no' gonnae pick up yer litter?'

Prick looks to where Banjo points and back up. 'What's it to you?'

2

Anger rises, clenching his gut in a hot clammy fist. 'Can ye no' pick it up?' Banjo manages. 'Bin's, like, two seconds away.'

Prick grins. 'Seriously, you part of the environmental committee or something? You go about asking people to *pick up litter*?'

The other guys laugh.

Banjo's nails bite into his palms. It dulls the rising hysteria. 'I saw ye drop it,' he grits out, forcing his vowels. 'Can ye no' be a prick and jus' pick it up.'

'Where'd you get that accent? The *bowels* ay' Glesga?' He pitches his voice high and nasal, even though Banjo's is deep. There are shouts of laughter now. Banjo feels his face flood with heat. As if East Kilbride is in any way *posh*. Might not be the city centre, sure, but it's the Central Belt of fucking Scotland.

'Oh aye.' Banjo flashes his teeth in a grin. 'Pure pick'd it oot fae they gutter.'

He can see he's losing Prick just by the way his ear tips forward to catch Banjo's words.

'Bin.' Banjo speaks clear, pointing to the litter.

'*Ahh*, I get it now,' Prick says, widening his eyes like it's all some big revelation. 'You're working on commission?'

A few of his friends snicker. Irritation prickles across Banjo's skin, sweaty and stifling.

He speaks slow and steady: 'Pick. Up. Your. *Fucken*. Litter.'

'You kiss your mother with that mouth?' Prick raises his eyebrows. 'I'm doing charity here. If I didn't litter, I'd put janitors out a job.'

Something wild explodes across Banjo's body. It's a rupturing of all his organs so strong and sudden it goes black. The world, his vision. All of it. When Banjo returns to himself he's got Prick's face pressed against the pavement, a fist in his hair, knee on his back, screaming: *'Pick it up, ye wee prick!'*

He doesn't feel the hands on him, the people pulling him off; doesn't hear the shouts, the taunts, until a no-nonsense grip on his arm cuts off his blood pressure.

Banjo's wrenched upwards.

'What in God's name do you think you're doing?'

Banjo stares at the face of the headmistress, hair scraped back into an unforgiving bun. Her eyes bulge like a dead fish at the supermarket. That's all Banjo can see when he looks at her. Fish.

'He just went crazy!' Prick scrambles to his feet. There's dirt smeared across his cheek, his hair tufted to one side. 'I didn't do anything!'

Banjo rips the litter off the ground and chucks it at his face. 'If ye fucken tae God *picked it up*!'

He's yanked backwards by the arm so hard he might dislocate an elbow.

'Both of you, my office,' Headmistress says. 'Now.'

She stares at them. Her white face is now red, which somehow makes her pastiness worse, odd splotches appearing here and there.

'I want an explanation, and a reason why I shouldn't suspend you both.'

'Me!' Prick glances around like this is the end of a five-part drama.

'I'm sure there's no reason why he had you pinned to the ground.'

'Right, he didn't have me *pinned*—'

'Kyle,' Headmistress interrupts, 'this isn't the first time you've been here. I told you next time would be your last.'

'Okay, what the—' Kyle laughs.

'He didnae start it,' Banjo cuts in before Kyle bursts a blood vessel. Because it's true. Banjo's no coward.

'Finally!' Kyle throws a hand to the sky.

'Enough.' She looks at Banjo. 'Can you tell me what happened?'

'Wouldnae pick up his litter.' Banjo lifts a shoulder.

'Yeah, you've saved the planet, well fucking done—' Kyle claps his hands.

'Very thin ice!' Headmistress booms. 'None of that language or you're both expelled.'

With that information, they both shut up.

'Are you telling me you started this over litter?' Headmistress stares.

Kyle is silent. Banjo nods.

Headmistress sighs. 'Banjo, I'm aware things might be difficult at home.'

Kyle gives him the side-eye. Banjo's whole body burns with shame.

'But that's no reason to be picking fights. It's your first day here.'

Banjo's jaw is glued shut.

'Right, please leave my office while I call your parents.'

'Whit?' Banjo sits up fast.

'Go wait in the reception.'

They leave.

'Who they callin'?'

'Fuck off.' Kyle pushes him.

'Aye?' Banjo spins around, rises to his tiptoes right into Kyle's space. 'Wannae try it?'

'I'm not scared of someone who looks like a wee first-year—'

'*First-year?*' Banjo barks. He's fucking seventeen. He's almost finished school. A new, bitter anger takes shape; Kyle's clearly taking a dig at his height.

'Boys!' Headmistress calls after them.

They both sit outside the office. The walls are a weird scrambled-egg colour, and the harsh flickering of the artificial yellow lights makes it worse. The seats are brittle plastic, fraying apart at the sides and melted in the middle by the heat of everyone's arse cheeks.

Once Banjo's heart slows down, the anger drains like someone's flushed the toilet in his stomach. The bruise blooming on Kyle's cheek doesn't make it any better.

The only thing that makes it worse is Kyle's mum coming in.

'Fed up with this, Kyle,' she hisses, trying to be quiet. Banjo keeps his gaze low as though he's the one being scolded.

'It wasn't me!' Kyle hisses back. Banjo feels like mouldy cheese forgotten in the cupboard.

Kyle stands and they start walking out.

'He might *look* small, but he—'

The door swings shut.

Banjo blows out a breath, falls forward and rests his elbows on his knees. He stares down at his hands. They're throbbing, knuckles red and swollen. The skin isn't broken. Banjo flexes them, and a familiar tight pain rushes up.

He closes his eyes.

Someone stands over him, smelling of antiseptic, a bit sweaty, warm, alive. Ready to patch him back up. Never rough, even when Banjo did this to himself.

Banjo sometimes thinks that's why he does this in the first place.

Paula's not been too impressed with Banjo, obviously. Despite the fact Banjo knows this placement is temporary and he really has fuck all to prove, he still hates the little disappointed, pursed-mouth looks he gets. Truth be told, Paula's been a bit better than most: doesn't bring it up, doesn't want to discuss it, just lets it be. He can still tell she's not overjoyed she's been handed him. He's not even sure how much they get to pick – any child in need goes, it seems.

He waits outside when she texts him: *on way*. He'll miss the detention he got this morning by being sent home now. That probably means something. Fuck if Banjo knows. He scuffs his trainers to try and keep the heat inside. It's just turned September, and the bitter chill stings his nose, the crisp autumn night invading every one of his senses.

He's quiet during the car drive home. Paula too.

Banjo puts his head against the glass and his breath fogs up the window. He wipes it with his sleeve.

'Jus' goin' a run,' he tells Paula when they arrive at her house.

'Back for dinner,' she instructs, as if Banjo even eats with them instead of taking his plate up to their son's old room. The guy's not dead – he's just thirty.

'Yeah,' Banjo says. Then he runs.

Banjo pushes himself further than usual. The air has gone harsh and the wind whips against him. He gets lost and has to circle around before he finds a familiar street.

He misses dinner. It's waiting for him on a plate.

'Put it in the microwave if you need to!' Paula calls from the living room.

'Help yourself to the extra!' her husband, Henry, adds.

'Thanks,' Banjo calls, but avoids the open living room and trudges upstairs. They're so nice it scares him. It makes him soft, want to be soft, but he'll never survive if he is.

He washes his dishes, though. He's not a slob.

His knuckles are still throbbing. At night, Banjo focuses on the pain to try and distract him from the supermassive black hole in his chest, but it doesn't work. The hole sucks him in as it always does.

Thing is, Banjo's been wrung through the care system since he was ten. He used to know how to shove things down and lock them away. But now he carries it everywhere: this rancid regret that bloats inside his gut and swells it raw. He lets the tears stream backwards into his ears to itch his jaw. He lets all the crying happen inside his mouth and releases it in slow, even breaths, the way he's used to.

Sometimes he thinks he's finally getting over all the mess that happened three years ago, and then it slams into him as if it's been no time at all.

Chapter Two

FINLAY

As soon as Finlay arrives in Glasgow Central Station, he steps off the train and looks around in wonder. People rush back and forwards as if they've memorised every route and scheduled every second of it. He's never travelled by train before. The bus is cheaper. But he's carrying luggage with him now: his whole life stuffed into a duffel and a backpack.

He slides his ticket inside the machine and squeezes through, only to be greeted with shops, flower stalls, cafés, pharmacies, Marks & Spencer, Boots, Costa, a barrage of overstimulation.

Finlay knows he should feel excited. This is everything he's ever wanted.

But all he can think about are the streets and the buildings that theoretically stand between them now. Somehow the distance feels smaller than the width of a wooden dresser. It's been almost three years since they lived in Glasgow's city centre. It's difficult not to imagine bumping into him.

Thinking about that is pointless, though. Finlay pushes it aside. He uses the maps on his phone to locate the subway station. He finds it at St Enoch Square and descends a pair of escalators into a dark, damp underground that smells like wet newspaper and urine. He's swept into a queue and frantically searches for the West End on the ticket machine before he gives up.

'Where?' The admin tips her ear closer to the plastic divider.

'Uh, Glasgow University.' Finlay goes up on his tiptoes. His cheeks sting when he realises there's not a stop for that.

Somehow he's still given a ticket alongside some vague instructions about how to find the campus. He descends even more stairs.

There's a platform at the bottom that drops off like a small cliff into a railway, with posters plastered across the wall for constipation remedies and comedy shows. The subway clatters in like a world-weary bullet. Finlay steps on with everyone else. He grips the pole with both hands, holding his duffel locked between his shins.

When the doors sigh open and set him free, Finlay falls out. He's pushed and pressed, hemmed in and shoved against until every single one of his nerve endings feels rubbed raw.

The first thing he needs to do is collect the keys to his flat. They're being held hostage in a building nowhere near it, just to be fun and confusing. Finlay shuffles up the queue of students, keeps his head down, and presents all the correct information at the desk once it's his turn.

Keys secured, Finlay makes his way to his new place. By some miracle he arrives just in time for his phone to die. He watches his small moving dot on the map blink out of existence and go black.

Then he lifts his head.

A glossy plaque engraved with the words **GLASGOW UNIVERSITY STUDENT ACCOMODATION** stands tall, an arrow pointing towards the block of brown-grey flats directly in front of him. Despite their crammed-in appearance, they look clean and habitable.

He yanks himself and his luggage up the set of concrete steps and buzzes the button. He waits. The door unlocks. Finlay peers inside. Nobody is there. There's another set of stairs.

Once he's up them, he walks down a winding hallway and eventually finds his assigned door.

Finlay twists his key in and opens it. And ...

In hostels there was never a quiet moment. People constantly appearing and disappearing, talking, snoring, laughing, whispering. He's lived in six-bedroom, eight-bedroom, twenty-bedroom.

But when Finlay steps into the room, he's greeted with the sensory overload of silence.

He frowns. Glances around. There's a small desk in the corner, a bookcase along the wall. That's when Finlay realises there's only one bed. One modest little bed tucked up against the side of the room, practically shy.

He's got his own room.

Did he read the website wrong? How did he miss the fact he applied for a single room?

It's not even small. The room has enough space to store a bike and not bump into it. There's a bathroom. Finlay sets his stuff down and steps inside. It has a sink, a toilet, a shower. It's his.

Finlay walks around in circles as though he's a simulation

and his player is still getting used to the controls. He can't stop opening and closing the shower door. Turning the tap on and off. Everything works.

'What the fuck,' he whispers. The words shape his mouth in the bathroom mirror; his wheat-blond hair now limp with sweat, light brown eyes unblinking behind thin-wire glasses, cheeks flushed wind-red.

He waits for the happiness to come: to explode inside every one of his organs like he expected.

Finlay's never settled in one place for long. Since he aged out of care and left high school a few months ago, he's just bounced around hostels and worked the odd temp position, biding his time before university. He applied for his degree well before he aged out, of course – frantically finishing scholarship forms alongside final essays. Finlay made sure he was accepted early, that everything would be ready. The safety net of social services pulled apart at the seams when he hit eighteen, but even during his time in care he never allowed himself to rely on it. Finlay planned his freedom meticulously, down to the second.

And here it is, at long last.

This is what he's suffered for: studied, sweated, wept and worked for. Everything that happened three years ago in St Andrews should be lost to the wind now, a memory fading into the dust as his new life stretches ahead of him.

But Finlay feels exactly the same as always.

Shock. It's just shock. Change is slow, and maybe he needs to make it happen rather than expect it to occur.

Finlay exhales to shake the heavy pressure sitting on his chest and heads outside for the Freshers' Fair.

Being a second-generation Polish immigrant as well as a care leaver, Finlay's always struggled with his identity. The two things that complete a person are missing for him: culture and parents. There's a gaping hole where his history should be. Finlay's tried to fill it for himself, but it only ever creates a sense of loss when he attempts to learn Polish and fails. Shouldn't it come easily to him? Shouldn't his mother tongue make itself at home in his mouth?

Of course, he remembers shopping in the Eastern European grocery stores where they sold pre-made pierogi, pickled herrings, yeast buns and potato pancakes with soured cream – but those things never really felt like a part of him, the same way Italian pizzas and Indian curries don't. They're simply the foods of the world.

He doesn't feel Polish because nobody ever sat him down to teach him that aspect of himself. His mother would avoid the questions or tell him to stop asking. It must have been a painful topic. But it meant he never got the photos, the recipes passed down, the second-hand clothes. He's never met anything resembling a father, so he can fill that space with movies, with books, with his own imagination. But with his mother it's different. Nothing fills her space.

Finlay tries not to think about her. Sometimes he thinks about Poland. He's never even been. Yet Finlay feels more Scottish than anything. He's the corner shops and the cobbled streets, the smog in the bus lanes and smell of the oversalted fish and chips. But feeling Scottish and being Scottish are two different things.

Sometimes Finlay wonders why his mother named him Finlay. If she stumbled upon it on a baby names website or if she was actively looking for the most Scottish thing she could find. *Fionnlagh*. Scots-Gaelic. 'Fair Warrior.' She clearly wanted him to fit in.

His mother's name was Kasia.

Chapter Three

BANJO

When Banjo returns to school after The Incident Involving Kyle and the Litter, word has got out. There're notes in the boys' bathroom, in the corridors, just everywhere like he's a princess in disguise.

This is it, to make matters great:

> Avoid the ginger in the hallways. Don't look directly at him, and if spotted – remain calm, keep still, and hold your territory.
> Triggers include:
>
> 1. Littering.
>
> 2. Insults towards janitors.
>
> 3. Older men.

Banjo's been getting 'ginger' as an insult since primary. Hardly fucking original.

But it turns out he's in Kyle's class, and has to sit through the jeers and the taunts. People are now calling him Litter Kid, or That First-Year That Beat Up Kyle Simmons. Everyone knows he's not a fucking first-year. But it's a joke about Banjo's height, because he's about half the size of everyone, clearly.

It's something called stunted growth, the doctor said, *which can be caused by lack of sleep or poor diet—*

Banjo grits his teeth at the memory, his chest sore.

He passes Kyle in the hallway, who obviously veers to throw him against the lockers. For all the bad schools he's been to, this one takes the cake.

Which is why when Banjo sees the poster he stops.

Athletics Try-outs

Monday 4pm

Fourth Year – Sixth Year

Running. All right. He knows running. He picks up the pen.

'Okay, sixth year, line up over there.' Their PE teacher, Mrs Anderson, gestures to the side, hair up in a high ponytail, her face all business. Banjo's not exactly had the pleasure of being introduced, but two seconds of athletics try-outs and he already has a feel for what she's like: firm, stiff, unfriendly.

They line up along the rubber-red track outside. Kyle is here, because of course. He ignores Banjo and everyone takes his lead. People shuffle away to avoid touching him; a mile on either side. He's an infection now.

'Name?' Anderson asks her clipboard, not even glancing up.

'Banjo,' he mutters.

'Is that Litter Kid?' 'What's his name?' 'That made up?' 'Isn't he in the year below?' 'Did he not just move here?' 'Think he's in care or something.' 'His parents dead?' 'Nah, heard they were dealers.'

Banjo stares straight ahead.

Anderson ticks his name and moves on.

They get into position. Banjo ends up pressed between two guys who clearly know Kyle and think it's the funniest thing in the world to jostle him out of place when Anderson blows the whistle.

But then he's running. The cold air feels so good against his skin that nothing else matters but the smell of ice stinging his nose, the damp grass, the dirty rain. He closes his eyes as his feet smack the tarmac. Running is Banjo's personal brand of therapy. No talking. No questions.

But running is a form of anger, too. A furious, forceful moving of every part of his body. Sometimes when Banjo runs he feels as if he could fly straight out his own skin, as if he could leave his body and the restless pit of rage and feel something fucking different for once.

There're two people in front. Banjo clenches his muscles and propels himself ahead.

He sprints across the chalk line. Everyone rushes in afterwards like a gust of wind at his back.

'Fifty-four seconds,' Anderson says, eyebrows up, impressed. Banjo's panting with his hands on his knees. 'That might be a record.'

'Bullshit!' a familiar voice shouts. 'That's bullshit! He cheated!'

Banjo looks up.

'I was in the lead the whole time! He must've taken some shortcut!' Kyle waves a hand, flushed and blotchy. Sweat drips along the sides of his jaw, beetroot skin contrasting horribly with his light hair.

'Kyle.' Anderson's voice goes stern. 'Enough.'

Kyle grits his teeth, chest heaving. He sends Banjo a look so sharp it's laughable. Christ. What a sore loser.

'Do you train?' Anderson asks, focused on him.

Banjo blinks, thrown. 'Uh, jus' whenever.'

Never for a team. Never with a school.

Anderson cocks her head. 'You've never been with a club?'

Jesus, Banjo's getting all hot under the collar at these compliments. 'No.'

Break the fucking news: there might be something he's actually *good at*.

As Anderson walks off, Banjo wipes the sweat from his forehead and hides his grin inside the crook of his elbow. When she calls who made the team, Banjo's name comes first. Kyle is short behind, obviously. But Banjo is part of the club now.

Excitement feels weird. He doesn't know whether he's happy or sick.

The locker room is fogged with the heat of about twenty guys, panting sweating showering laughing farting. Banjo tries not to catch anyone's attention, least of all Kyle's, and rummages through his backpack stained with all manner of shite and a squashed banana he forgot about.

There's a hot grip on his arm.

Kyle crowds close. 'Hey.' His fingers go tight, pinching Banjo's skin. 'Let's do a rematch. No cheat—'

Banjo rips his arm free in a violent motion, the unexpected touch like rubbing alcohol into a wound.

Kyle blinks, surprised at the vehemence.

'Sure,' Banjo states. 'Now.'

Kyle lifts his eyebrows all mocking, but he nods to some other guys. Truthfully the guys sigh, exasperated, but they all head out once they've collected their things. Athletics is over. The track is deserted.

Kyle's wee mates stand at the bottom of the track while Banjo and Kyle line up at the start. There's even one with a stopwatch.

'Go!' the guy shouts.

They're both off like a shot. It's over in about four seconds. Banjo wins.

Kyle's panting by the end, but he smiles in mock-grace, upper lip curling with the force of it. 'Litter Kid's got moves.'

Banjo cringes at such a cheesy line. 'Right.' He tries to push past.

'Aw, don't leave!' Kyle holds out his arms. 'Teach us your ways, wise one.'

'Hilarity,' Banjo huffs, irritation buzzing through him.

'I bet it's that litter picking,' Kyle carries on. One of his pals laughs; the rest look bored. 'Gotta keep in shape.'

'Look, whit in fuck d'ye want?' Banjo snaps. 'Lunch money or some'hin?'

Kyle grins wider. 'If you're offering.'

'Christ,' Banjo says. Nothing quick-witted comes to mind, which just pisses him off more. He tries to move again. Kyle jumps in front. He wants to provoke Banjo. He wants a fight. Banjo knows the feeling.

He shoves Kyle back so hard he stumbles and falls flat on his arse. His mates give a surprised snicker.

Kyle's glare is a wild, crazed thing. He stands up fast, the veins bulging in his neck.

'Leave it, Kyle.' Someone puts his hand on Kyle's shoulder.

'C'mon, he's in foster care or something. Let's just go,' another one adds.

They're talking as if Banjo's not even here. As if he's just empty space. The great mouth of a wave is ready to swallow him whole. Banjo can see it on the horizon.

Kyle shoves him with sharp fingers, jaw tight.

Banjo's two feet are planted firm on the ground. He's not rising to it. 'Move.'

'No.' Kyle crowds close again, lips pulling away from his teeth like a dog.

'Awk, just fucken *move*!' Banjo screams.

Kyle punches him in the face.

Banjo doesn't see it coming. His head snaps back, neck whipping painfully. It's the force of the blow that comes as a surprise.

He collapses, the breath knocked out of his lungs as if both his back and his chest have smacked together.

Kyle kicks him in the side while he's down.

Banjo curls up, defenceless.

'Kyle!'

'Fuckin' hell!'

There's nobody around. Kyle lets loose: jumping on top of him in a mirror of their first fight. Banjo's jaw snaps down in a bite. Blood erupts inside his mouth. Pain radiates all the way into his fucking teeth.

Banjo doesn't move. His body just locks. Maybe it's memory, *trauma response*, some nonsense jumble of words a counsellor would say. Or maybe it's because he wasn't hungry for it today. Banjo suddenly realises these punches are meaningless. Seeking them out is meaningless. He needs to be touched in some way, but this way doesn't count. He doesn't feel it.

Banjo's eyes roll up to the sky. The endless stretch of sky. He keeps focusing on that.

'Kyle!'

Kyle stares down at Banjo. There's blood across his knuckles. On Banjo's tongue, in his mouth, up his nose, down his throat. Banjo's eyes roll away from the sky and he grins up at Kyle. His teeth are smeared wet. His mouth is full of metal.

'Fuck *sake*!' one of his mates shouts, two hands fisted in his black hair, his brown skin oddly grey.

'Idiot.' Another one shoves Kyle.

They all run.

Banjo curls up around himself slowly. He spits out the pool in his mouth. He tests how much he can breathe. It aches to inhale but nothing is broken, experience tells him. He lies there while the air grows cold and the sky darkens. The only thing that pulls Banjo off the ground eventually is his shitty curfew. Such is life.

Chapter Four

FINLAY

When Finlay enters campus it's a buzz of noise and people, volunteers floating around with the purple GU logo printed on cotton hoodies, flyers at the ready. Early September in Scotland is not exactly bitter, but there's definitely an overcast chill.

There are rows of white stalls arranged in squares with banners above them. Leaflets for societies lie on top, alongside cards advertising free pizza plus the smallest can of Coke ever created. 50ml. Still, it's free, and Finlay spends a ridiculous amount of time in the queue – which he still feels is time well spent when he secures said pizza and Coke. He drifts mindlessly with no real objective. He's stopped by club hopefuls every few minutes. *Join this, sign here, donate please, come tonight.* Finlay nods and smiles.

He signed up to do a four-year nursing degree because he's a masochist. No, that's a lie: he wants to be a nurse, to help other people, to contribute to society. Actually, that's the real lie. The truth is that nursing is a stable job. It was either nursing or a career in shovelling chips. But despite the fact undergraduates don't pay tuition in Scotland, Finlay's hopes and dreams and entire future depend on the scholarship he managed to obtain. It's a yearly one-off payment, which he's just received and now needs to ration.

All he needs to do is keep himself floating above the pass mark: 40 per cent. Less than half. No pressure.

Although nursing is a stable job, Finlay still needs to actually find employment until he's qualified. At least something part-time. He was working and staying in Hamilton for a while, a short gig at a chippy and a temporary accommodation unit to tide him over until university started. Now he has to search for work nearby, then calculate the hours he'll need to both stay alive and work around his nursing schedule.

But that can wait for today.

Finlay quietly wanders around, his eyes passing faces, and then—

Finlay stops, looking down. His cheeks sting. *Christ in Heaven.*

There's a boy at one of the stalls. He is absolutely beautiful.

Finlay's wearing baggy jeans. The kind of baggy people save for travelling or when they're doing nothing because of how shapeless and worn they are. Holes gape at the knees, threads loose and trailing. He's painfully aware of the location of each sauce stain on his hoodie, but the T-shirt underneath is frayed, the once-bright logo now barely legible.

Finlay can't help himself. He glances up again.

It's like a punch to the solar plexus, somewhere between the gut and the lungs.

Perfect Boy is tall and lean, with deep brown skin, long shoulders, and this careless way of holding himself. Only his profile is visible, sleek black hair just a little on the longer side, curling at his nape but falling in swept-back curtains at the front. He lifts a hand to run it through with fingers. Dark eyes, thin hooked nose, sharp jaw. His smile is like daybreak. It changes his very nature.

Finlay is frozen. Then he spins on his heel and bolts away. He finds safety behind the rack of potted plants awaiting homes. When he braves the stalls again, Perfect Boy is nowhere to be seen.

Someone forces a flyer into his hands as they pass. Finlay looks down.

9.30 a.m.–11.30 a.m.: Welcome and Introductions, Nursing and Healthcare School.

Shit. Was he supposed to know about this? If he went now, he could just about make the last hour. It's not that far.

Finlay finds the building in minutes. He creeps into the back of the room and takes a seat three rows behind anyone, next to the aisle so he can get out at any time.

Two VP students stand at the front with badges down their denim jackets, colourful hair and huge smiles that strain as they speak.

'This is your chance to find out what's so incredible about Glasgow!' One gestures around. 'To make friends, to try new things; yes, you're here to learn and the course is intense, but you're looking at the best years of your life—'

'Hello.' A voice appears at Finlay's ear, soft and gentle.

Finlay turns.

The sun beams through the windows. Perfect Boy is standing in the aisle. Right beside Finlay.

What kind of twisted act of fate is this?

PB is wearing charcoal-grey trousers, a wool coat, a white polo tucked into his belt and a satchel bag strapped across his chest: clearly posh-boy preppy. His brown hands hold the strap: long fingers, square nails, a ring on his thumb and silver watch on his wrist.

When their gazes touch, Finlay feels this shock wave jolt through him like static connecting. He feels weirdly, eerily, as though he *recognises* this person.

That obviously can't be true.

'I'm not sure if I'm meant to be here,' PB continues, speaking low.

Finlay's brain has unfortunately short-circuited from the overload of stimuli. It doesn't know whether to focus on his mouth, his eyes, his hair, or pass away.

'Is this the Induction for Medicine?' PB asks, eyes optimistic.

Of course.

He's a med student.

Finlay manages a short shake of the head.

Perfect Boy puts a fingertip to his mouth. 'Ah.' He nods. 'I'm in the wrong place.'

Finlay swallows. Say something. *Say something.*

(Stop staring at his mouth.)

'Happens,' Finlay croaks, which is nothing, so adds, 'I was almost enrolled into selling my kidney once.'

There's this moment. This stunned slackness that settles over Perfect Boy. Then laughter booms around the room.

Everyone falls silent.

The students, the VPs, Finlay.

Everyone.

Perfect Boy realises. His eyes blow wide as they dart around the room. He looks at Finlay.

'Sorry,' he whispers, face so theatrically apologetic. 'Sorry!' he addresses the room at large, holds a hand up in a lofty wave, and leaves.

Finlay stares after him. His presence has a lasting effect, like the warmth of a sunspot.

'Okay.' One of the VPs clears their throat very pointedly.

Finlay ducks out after a few minutes to avoid further embarrassment. None of it was vital to his learning anyways.

Perfect Boy is standing outside the building. He's peering down at his phone, one hand cupped above the screen.

Finlay stalls long enough that PB spots him.

'The problem I'm having –' he begins, as if they're already friends. *But why does he feel so familiar?*

'– is that my maps are quite sure it's here,' PB finishes.

Finlay squints over PB's shoulder, but not for the excuse to bask in his heavenly heat. He actually does want to help this lost person. He points to the building across from them over said shoulder.

PB stares at Finlay, their heads close, and grins a smile so disarming it could topple monarchies.

'I'm Akash.' He thrusts out an open palm.

Akash. Something is niggling at him: burrowing deep and taking root.

But Akash hasn't said anything, so Finlay takes the hand.

Akash's touch is warm and dry. He's so sure when he shakes Finlay's hand. That kind of surety is infectious.

'Finlay.' Finlay smiles helplessly.

Akash blinks. He squints. His head lists to the side and studies Finlay for a beat. 'Wait. That wouldn't be Finlay *Nowak*, would it?'

Finlay's heart stops. 'Yes?'

Akash grins even wider, if that's possible. 'Finlay! Oh my God, it's Akash. Akash Singh!' He bumps fingers to his chest.

Finlay does nothing. He was right. Somehow, he does know Akash. But he doesn't know how, or more terrifyingly *where from*. He feels something try to force its way in, but his barriers are iron-clad. He locked everything out.

Finlay stands there, silent, staring, while his entire body reels from the impact.

'Um.' He pulls away and scratches his eyebrow. Their handshake is broken. 'I'm sorry, I don't—' he stutters. He can't say *remember*. He does remember. But it's buried, alongside his childhood, St Andrews Residential Home, and everything else Finlay threw dirt over.

'It'll come to you!' Akash starts walking across the street. 'Sorry, I really need to go, catch you later!' He gives that little wave, spins around, and runs away.

Finlay walks back to his flat. He doesn't go to any more events lined up that day.

*

The vague outline of a memory tugs at Finlay. It's a memory he's often thought was a dream, because those two things are one and the same sometimes.

There's the fuzzy shape of a house. There's a kitchen and it smells like spices and flavours and feels like the sunshine that shines on the walls and turns them a dappled yellow. It smells like a pot of tea and a basket of clean linen, sounds like the freezer door being yanked open, *we're just getting ice lollies!* The feeling of grassy, mud-stained trainers kicked off at the doorway, *can Finlay stay? Finlay's here!*

The walls of his accommodation are painted with bright, colourful geometric triangles amidst a slate-grey background, probably to create a funky atmosphere. Everything feels like luxury. Finlay has to remind himself that his standards are barbarically low: a cot and a working roof suit him.

Somehow Finlay takes a wrong turn on his way to his room, down another hallway, and before he knows it he's inside the common area.

It's a small room. There's a kitchen complete with a stove and a dishwasher, a short wooden dining table with basic wooden chairs tucked underneath. Two people stand over a pizza box on the counter, the microwave door ajar and wafting the scent of melted cheese into Finlay's nostrils.

'Because the risk of food poisoning, especially from takeaways, is—'

The girl pauses when she sees Finlay, a slice of pizza aloft in her hand. The other girl turns around too.

They all stand silent and blinking.

'Hey!' The girl who was discussing food poisoning beams wide. Her hair is cropped short, ashy blonde melting into pink tips. She's wearing a thick-knit jumper, beige trousers, and heeled boots. 'I'm Derya.'

Finlay can't make himself move.

Derya, still smiling, gestures to the other girl. 'This is Jun.'

Jun stands beside her, sleek black hair a curtain across her shoulders, East Asian features warm and welcoming. She's wearing a grey blazer with a ribbed yellow turtleneck, boot-cut jeans, and a yellow beret. She's beautiful. 'Hi!' Her voice is light.

Finlay does nothing. He hasn't even properly stepped inside.

'Did you just get here?' Derya asks.

Finlay looks at these girls. They're clearly lovely, trying to invite him into their small circle. But his social battery has run dry, completely depleted from moving into his dorm and having a very brief encounter with an incredibly beautiful person from his past. Right now, Finlay would much rather be alone than spend another second in public. It feels as though his skin has been scrubbed off with a scourer. It's not that Finlay doesn't want to make friends here – he desperately wants to, with a physical ache below the ribs, but he's just as desperate to retreat into the safety of his room, where he can't get any social interactions wrong and have to beat himself up for it later.

When he stayed in hostels, everyone was there to make friends. They were backpacking through Scotland, having a wild stag do, on a cheap holiday or off to a rave. Instead of making Finlay more sociable, it had the opposite effect – he boxed himself in, completely intimidated by people who could introduce themselves at random, crack jokes that made everyone laugh, and strike up a friendship in the span of a few seconds.

'Um, no.' Finlay smiles, nods, and ducks out the room.

He goes out into the soft carpeted hallway. He's about to leave, but stops.

There're murmurs from the other side of the wall. Finlay listens.

'Was that too much?' 'No, you were absolutely fine! I think he was busy.' 'True – God, I am *so glad* we're across from each other, I'd literally have nobody if—'

Finlay walks back to his room, lies on his bed, and hugs his teddy, Mr Black. He closes his eyes and spreads an arm out to press fingertips to the wall. He pretends he's touching a wooden dresser: that there's another person touching the other side.

Chapter Five

BANJO

Banjo gets up off the ground and has no idea what to do next. He can't go back looking like this. He doesn't want to give Paula early-onset whatever-the-fuck. Banjo knows this would be one hell of a let-down. The stab of guilt only adds to his difficulty breathing. For lack of anything better, Banjo heads to East Kilbride Community Hospital.

'How did this happen?' the nurse asks, acting as though she's about to buzz the police in. When Banjo lifts his shirt to reveal his battered ribs, her mouth drops open.

'Do you need to call somebody?'

'Naw – no, 'hanks.' He shuffles on to the bed. 'Jus' need cleaned or whut.'

She blinks. 'Were you in a fight?'

'Uh. No.'

'Were you attacked?'

Banjo grimaces. Technically. But it's fucking embarrassing. 'No.'

She doesn't look as if she believes him. Obviously the one

33

explanation left is that a building fell on top of him. Banjo offers nothing.

She tilts his chin to the side and presses the cut with an alcoholic wipe. Banjo winces.

'I'll need to stitch this up,' she states, annoyed at him because she thinks he's Britain's next delinquent. 'It's too deep. Are you allergic to anything?'

'Codeine,' Banjo answers instantly. 'No painkillers.'

The nurse won't know he's lying. Because who the fuck turns down free painkillers? Banjo, that's who. He never wants to see another one in his life.

She jots it down. Then she injects something into his mouth before she starts, holds him still and pushes it into the side of his face. Next she pulls her equipment out and starts stitching him up. The sensation feels alien, his skin tugged to one side. When she's finished Banjo touches along his upper lip, the flesh all fat and fuzzy. He moves his jaw around and hears it crack inside his ears.

Then he leaves with an ice pack for his side and a lollipop for his ego.

Banjo's got some change in his pocket, so he goes over to the vending machines 'cause he's thirsty as shit but not for water. He needs some sugar, pronto.

It's as he's pushing the coins in that he sees a girl. On the row of plastic seats near the exit. She's got a small face, thick brown hair in a messy plait, ripped jeans that show patches of bronze-gold skin. In short: she's fucking gorgeous. Her eyes are focused on him.

Banjo pauses, half-bent.

She smiles. It's small, sure, but it's there.

Banjo blinks. Slowly, very slowly, he turns to see who's behind him. Nobody. She's smiling at *him*.

Holy fuck.

Banjo whips around, dumbstruck, doing some three-sixty on the floor like it's disco night. By the time he looks back, though, she's on her phone.

Probably just being friendly.

Only the next time Banjo sneaks a look, she smiles again.

Right. That's it.

Banjo swallows, grabs his lemonade from the vending machine, and puts on some fucking balls. He almost talks himself out of it twice. But by that point he's halfway there and he can't just upside-down himself in the other direction.

'Ya' aw rih'?' His words come out jumbled and slurred with the fat lip. Christ, he meant to say hello. He might've actually spat on her.

'Hey.' She smiles up with hazel-gold eyes. 'How are you?'

'Yeah, noh' bah'.' Banjo nods. He tries to swallow. It takes a few attempts. He probably looks like a dog in hot weather. He's still wearing his PE kit, silly wee shorts showing off his gangly legs.

'What happened?' She nods to his face.

'Jus'.' Banjo waves a hand. 'Goh' in a figh'.'

He sees the way she nods, dropping eye contact for a second, afraid of him now.

Banjo needs to fix it.

'Fur char'tay.'

No idea. He's got no idea what he's saying.

She blinks when she looks at him. 'You got in a fight for *charity*?'

He nods. 'Yeah.'

She stares. 'With who?'

'Uh. Ye' know. Governmen' stuh'. Top secreh'.' He taps his nose.

She stares. Then she starts laughing.

Banjo stiffens up entirely.

She stops, sensing his reaction. 'You're joking, right?'

'Oh,' Banjo says. She was laughing at the joke. His face is hot in a new way. 'Right.'

She laughs again. 'I'm Alena, by the way. But you can call me Lena, if that's any easier.' She points to her face. 'On the tongue.'

'Righ', 'hanks.' Banjo laughs too, which really hurts his mouth stitches. 'I'm Ban-joh.'

He can't even say his own name. Is there any hope?

He's about to repeat it when Alena says, 'Hi, Banjo.' She gets it right first try. It twists his gut into a knot that can never be undone. 'Do you go to St Triduana's?'

Banjo frowns and looks down at where her gaze is fixed on his shorts, with the school logo stitched into the fabric. His heart leaps. 'Eh – yeh, you?'

'I'm St Bride's,' Alena says, as if that means anything to Banjo. He's not got a clue.

'Right.' Banjo bobs his head. 'D'ye wan' lema'nade'?' He holds it out awkwardly.

'I'm all right,' she says.

He retracts his arm. 'Uh, yeh.' Why on earth did he just try to give her his lemonade? The whole fucking can?

'Want to sit?' Alena points beside her.

Banjo nods and takes the seat.

'So. Why 'ou 'ere?' He rests his elbows on his knees and turns to her.

'I've got Crohn's disease,' Alena says. 'I was in for some treatment, but I'm going home. Just waiting to get picked up.'

'Oh righ',' he says, as if he knows anything about what she just said. So of course, like a complete idiot, Banjo says: 'Cool.'

Alena raises her brows.

'Noh! I jus' never meh' someone wae a disease before,' Banjo stutters. Then he hears how that sounds and basically becomes radioactive. 'Crap, no – it's no' *nice* or anythin'—'

Alena laughs.

Banjo's stunned speechless before it bubbles up. He needs to join in. He's powerless to the sound of that laughter. His own laugh is deep and rough, unpractised compared to Alena's light, effortless music. It hurts, rattles his chest and makes him feel as if he's splitting open. It's the first time he's laughed properly in ages. Maybe the first time since Finlay.

Chapter Six

FINLAY

The short weekend passes in a blur of solo walks around the city and trips to the Sainsbury's right outside his flat for instant noodles before he attempts to scout out the nearest Eastern European grocery places. It's peaceful, despite the small twinges Finlay feels when he spots groups of fellow young people gathered in cafés. Classes start on Monday and Finlay assumes someone will be forced to speak to him. This should fix the issue of his social skills and hopefully there won't be a repeat of what happened with the girls in the common room. He wonders if he'll be in one of their classes. Finlay resolves that he'll actually talk if he sees them again.

There's only one small problem. Monday arrives and his alarm doesn't go off.

Let Finlay repeat: Monday morning, his *very first day* of university, his alarm doesn't go off. He cannot stress enough how cursed his phone is.

Finlay rushes like his life depends on it, like he's being physically *hunted*. He throws things into his backpack and shoves on his shoes unlaced. The combined nerves-nausea have created a cess pit inside him.

The building is a maze. It takes Finlay two flights of stairs to find the right room. When he barges in, the students stare at him.

Hellish. Worse than hell.

Finlay sits at the back. The lecture hall is massive, with rows of red-velvet seats and the ceiling towering high above him. The front is dedicated to a desk with a huge whiteboard behind it.

Everyone seems to have brought slim, sleek laptops. Clicks resound throughout the room. Finlay pulls out his notepad.

It seems as if being late is the university standard. Finlay is about to check the time again when somebody slides in beside him.

'Hi!' Derya pants, a little out of breath, as though they're old friends. Jun follows behind, shrugging off her jacket.

Finlay blinks at them. He's wary to believe or accept this cosmic good luck. They pull out their things but don't speak. Come on. *Come on.*

'Hi,' Finlay manages after a solid minute.

Derya looks up with a smile.

A rush of relief and pride floods Finlay. He grins back.

At that moment, the tutor walks in. She's maybe in her forties, with an NHS lanyard around her neck.

'Hello!' she begins to the room at large. 'I'm Nora, one of the lecturers here at Glasgow. For today, we'll have a run-down of the structure of the course, and what to expect with the programme.'

She opens a slide show: **Introduction to BSc (Hons) Adult Nursing**:

Adult Nursing at Glasgow University:

- *Range of Courses*
- *Electives*
- *Clinical Placements*

Finlay starts scribbling amidst the roar of pressed keys.

'Now, a major feature of our programme is that we're based in the medical school, so we'll share our learning spaces with the medical, pharmacy, and physician associate students.'

Medical. Finlay's heart jolts in his chest as his cheeks suffuse with heat. Akash. He'll be near *Akash*. A strange euphoria trickles into his bloodstream, polluted with the dread of actually talking to Akash.

'While you're out on clinical placement, you'll be getting assessed as well,' Nora carries on. 'You'll be given certain learning outcomes, and while you're there you'll have someone called a mentor who'll assess your overall performance.'

Nora keeps talking. Finlay is descending into *barely legible* and *basically another language* categories of handwriting. He covers his notebook with his body so nobody sees how absolutely unfit he is to be a nurse.

'I know that's a lot of information to take in at once.' Nora pauses for a moment to allow them to catch up. Finlay wonders if she's obligated to do that every year. 'It's nothing that won't be repeated and you'll pick all this up as time goes on.'

Finlay breathes out a shaky exhale. Nora moves on to the next slide.

Derya turns her laptop to him. Finlay peers down and snorts. **HELP** is written in caps.

As soon as their introductory lecture is finished, it's on to the next: which is in an entirely different building, in an entirely different part of campus. Finlay walks with Jun and Derya and manages to introduce himself this time. Nothing explodes or collapses. The left-over adrenaline of saying *I'm Finlay* lingers long enough for him to strike up a conversation and actually formulate replies.

He only has three classes this semester, but clinical placements start from October, which is less than a month away. Plus he'll have to keep up with assignments in the meantime. The degree basically works the same way the ocean shore does: a gradual easing in before a sudden cliff-drop down. His feet can feel the oncoming descent, but the top half of him is still floating.

When they're done for the day, Jun turns to him. 'Coffee?'

Finlay is paralysed for a beat. He should say yes. It's all been going so well thus far. And he *wants* to say yes. They're so sweet, so amiable. Yet his first instinct is to say no. Go back to his dorm and lie down and call it a day. It feels blissfully appealing, so comfortable and safe. But he thinks about them laughing in the kitchen. And him listening from the other side.

It's coffee. It's an hour. And he can leave at any point.

Finlay nods.

Derya is from Bursa, Turkey, but she's lived in Scotland for ten years, and Jun is from Daegu, Korea, but moved to Scotland with her family when she was three. They make Finlay feel welcome in every sense of that word.

'Ugh.' Derya takes a seat beside him, her toastie and coffee on a little tray. Her arm briefly brushes against Finlay's as she sits, a warm moment he tries not to focus on. 'It's over.'

Finlay laughs. 'It wasn't terrible.'

He's trying not to look for Akash. It would be absurd if they happened to stumble into the same café. They probably don't even have the same timetable. But every dark-haired boy that breezes in sets Finlay's stomach fluttering.

Jun's eyes are closed, her head resting on a propped-up fist. Her coffee and sandwich sit untouched, hair cascading across her shoulders.

'I can't hack early mornings,' she murmurs.

'I'm also not smart enough for this,' Derya adds.

Finlay hums in agreement, scrolling the reading list for this semester on his phone. Derya hasn't pulled away. There's a warmth in his chest. It's nice. He's not been this close to someone since – well, St Andrews. Finlay blinks the thought away.

'Right, your turn.' Jun straightens.

Finlay looks at her in polite confusion. Jun nods to the queue. Oh. They thought he was saving their table while they ordered.

'Right.' Finlay stands.

'Where did you get those jeans?' Jun asks. 'They're really nice.'

Finlay huffs a disbelieving laugh and glances down. They're his loose-cut pair with paint spatters at the bottom. 'Honestly?' Finlay asks. Here goes nothing. 'Oxfam.'

Jun clicks two fingers. 'I love that! You can always find good stuff there.'

'Yeah, it's really sustainable too,' Derya adds. 'There're meant to be loads in Glasgow.'

Finlay nods back. For some reason his heart twists with the memory of someone else. Everyone is so kind. Jun and Derya have no ties to Finlay. No reason to be nice. But Finlay's forced proximity to the people at St Andrews still felt more sincere. Or maybe just one person in particular. Banjo would never feel the need to justify charity shops.

Finlay goes to stand in the queue. He searches for the cheapest thing in the glass cabinet because he still desperately needs to secure a job. Mozzarella and sun-dried tomato. Tuna, lemongrass, and black pepper. Everything makes his mouth water. Nothing is cheap.

When Finlay collects his single latte, the girls wave him back over. A sense of being wanted rushes in. Finlay knew that feeling once. He's not felt it in a long time. He knows how destructive it can be.

Three Years Ago

The new boy comes into Finlay's room unannounced. Finlay's been here a few weeks; it was bound to happen eventually.

There's a duffel bag clutched to a bony chest, expression blank as the boy's eyes skim the surroundings. His features are thin and sharp, a wild landscape of freckles across his face. Most noticeable, though, is the hair. It's got to be the brightest shade of orange Finlay's ever seen.

Lucy, the manager at St Andrews Residential Home, isn't far behind: smile wide, friendly, and superimposed over her stress.

'Finlay, this is Banjo. He'll be staying with you for a bit. Banjo, this is your new roommate, Finlay.'

Banjo studies Finlay curled up at the top corner of his bed, back pressed to the wall. Finlay meets Banjo's gaze before he pushes his glasses up and goes back to his book.

'Finlay,' Lucy calls. Finlay looks up. 'Dinner in an hour. You need to sit with everyone. No excuses.'

Finlay nods. Lucy leaves them to it.

Banjo hovers at the door, as if waiting for Finlay to do something – drop the silence, jump up and dance, punch him in the stomach – but when Finlay ignores his existence, Banjo seems to take it as his cue to come inside. He sets his things down, back to Finlay as he unzips the duffel. He pulls out some clothes and toiletries.

Then Banjo sits on the bed and looks at Finlay dead-on. 'Right, Ah've aboot a ragin' bladder infection so Ah'll be up aw night.' His voice is much older than his face, hard and cold, but the problem is his Scots. It's so thick it takes Finlay a full beat to understand him.

Banjo can clearly tell. He sighs. 'I *have* a bladder infection. I'll be using the *toilet* a lot.'

Finlay feels locked in place, but he forces a sharp tip of his chin, not looking up from his page. He doesn't see Banjo's response but hears him storm off. Finlay assumes to the living room to watch TV.

But the bathroom door in the hallway slams shut. Perhaps he's telling the truth. Finlay's never been informed on meeting somebody that they have a urinary infection. He almost smiles.

Chapter Seven

BANJO

Banjo laces up his shoes for athletics, a nervous tremor in his fingers, which is fucking stupid because he already made the team. He's on the bench at the side of the track, trying to get his pulse to shut up.

Somebody sits so close to him that their sweat wafts off their body.

'Hey,' the random guy starts, breathless and sweaty in his face, which is very fucking nice this late in the day. 'We came back yesterday but you were gone, I don't – I didn't – *fuck*.' He runs a hand through his hair.

Banjo looks up. Right. One of Kyle's wee minions. The one that went berserk while Kyle was kicking; that pure gripped his hair and shouted *fuck sake*. His eyes are a bit crazed, to tell the truth, but his face isn't pulp. Unlike Banjo, who can feel the sun against his stitches.

The guy flinches when Banjo meets his gaze.

'Get tae fuck,' Banjo states.

Somehow, Mr Minion takes the biggest offence to this. '*What?* I didn't hit you.'

'You tell it yersel, mate,' Banjo states.

To be matter-of-fact, he's not really bothered. Kind of glad Kyle took yesterday to beat the living shite out of him. An enjoyable experience from start to finish.

Missing curfew and coming back to his foster parents with a busted face was not, though. Went a bit like this:

'Just want to chat.' Paula knocked on the bathroom door.

Banjo was scrubbing the blood out his clothes. He sighed and opened up. 'Am a bit knackered, Paula.' He focused on his toes.

There was a beat. 'All right.'

Another knock an hour later.

'All good?' Henry clung to his bedroom door.

'Yup.' Banjo nodded, fiddling about on his phone. The next time he looked up, Henry was away. Banjo stewed in it all night.

Now, however, Minion scrubs his face and huffs. 'Look, I told him yesterday he took it too far. I've stopped speaking to the guys.'

Banjo looks back, face flat. Totally unimpressed.

Minion swallows, stands, and starts running.

It's fine. Banjo's had a lot worse, but he can't run great because of the pain throbbing over every inch of him. He's still got a rotten wheeze coming from that bruise blooming on his side. Somebody can sure as shit *wallow*.

Banjo learns Minion's name is Devlin Marques. He's been kicked out the group, it seems. Banjo knows this because Kyle makes it so obvious that anyone would think Devlin some carrier of bird flu.

Devlin's not slow. Banjo still beats him. They're not even fun to beat, is the problem. The whole team are an utter shambles.

'Where did you train?' one of the guys asks in the locker room.

'Yer maw,' Banjo replies, because he feels like it.

'Shut up, wee fag!' someone yells back.

Banjo wants to chuck a grenade into the room and lock the door.

At the weekend, Banjo decides he needs a job. Now that he's legal and settled someplace he hopes to stay at least a full year, he needs to start thinking about the future. Especially since he'll be chucked out of care at eighteen. Not that Banjo's been smart about that fact, mostly ignored it until now, since it's looming nearer and nearer.

He manages to land a trial shift at a crummy little café called East Kilbride Bistro and Barista a few streets down from Paula and Henry's. He walked in, asked if they're looking, and told them he can do weekends and nights.

The girl behind the counter offered him 9 a.m. Saturday morning.

Paula rolls them up at 8.30 a.m.

'Good luck.' She smiles.

Banjo stares at his phone. 'It's no' fur another half hour,' he mutters.

'Always good to be early.' Paula lifts a hand, maybe to give him a pat, but thinks better of it and sorts her hair.

Banjo nods and jumps out. He grimaces, turning back.

'Thanks,' he says. It's her Saturday morning as well.

He shuts the door before she replies.

The girl at the counter is the same one who offered him the shift. She's maybe mid-twenties, with a dirty apron tied around her waist and a T-shirt underneath. Her blue hair is thrown in a messy bun, wisps curling around her temples.

'Hello!' she beams when he arrives, looking up from her open notebook.

'Eh. Hi.' Banjo scuffs his foot. 'I've got a trial shift the day.'

The girl frowns, checks her notebook, and clicks her fingers. 'Right! Yes, I thought we had someone coming in. Well, my name's Morag.' She places a hand on her chest. 'I'm the manager here, so if you need anything, just come to me for it.' She pulls something from under the counter and holds it out. Banjo takes it.

'This is your apron. We'll get you a name tag, don't worry.' Morag frowns. 'What's your name, sorry?'

'Banjo.'

Morag's head tilts. 'Benji?'

'*Banjo.*' He tries harder.

'Ban*jo*?' Morag asks.

'Banjo,' Banjo repeats. His name is turning into an optical illusion.

'Right.' Morag reaches underneath the counter again, scribbles on something, then slaps it on to Banjo's chest. 'This is just for today until we get you a proper one.'

Banjo looks down.

Banjoe.

Well. Not much he can do about that.

He's quickly introduced to a place called 'the back room', and just as quickly learns he should make himself at home here, 'cause he'll be spending most of the shift and what feels like the rest of his life in it.

'So you stack the dishes sideways because you'll get more in.' Morag's hands move effortlessly as she piles plates into the dishwasher. 'Make sure you scrape all the food off first because it'll clog it. If you can give them a rinse as well that's great, if not just shove them in.'

If not? Why wouldn't he give them a rinse? Isn't that his whole job?

'You put all the rubbish in this bin, and put the clean dishes here so someone can lift them.'

Morag looks at him expectantly. Banjo looks back.

'Get all that?' Morag prompts.

Banjo nods quickly. 'Yuh, yep.'

'Good.' Morag pats him sharp and leaves.

Then all holy hell breaks through the back room.

Banjo's never sweated this much, and he does *running*. He's *athletic*. The steam from the constantly opening and closing dishwasher turns the back room into some kind of sauna, and his apron sticks to just about everywhere on his body, hair turned wet and plastered to his face. He's also never touched so much food: gross, soggy, moist food, chips stuck to the plate in a puddle of sauce, melted cheese crusted around the sides, lettuce. Christ. *Lettuce.*

Banjo will never eat lettuce again. He doesn't even think he'll *look* at a leaf after today.

He accidentally lets some slip his radar. It gets into the dishwasher.

Banjo opens up and is met with a gust of toxic fumes.

'*Huu*—' Banjo turns away to gag.

It only gets worse. The pots come with some breed of congealed, burnt soup welded to the bottom. Banjo has to go in armed and scrape it out. He's dealt with a lot of smells, not half from today, and the smell of the burnt soup at the bottom of this pot is the worst.

'No!' someone shouts.

Banjo whips around.

'That's not how you do it! You have to do it *quick*, see, scrape fast—'

Banjo stares, dumbstruck, because Alena has her brown hair up in a ponytail, apron tied around her waist, hazel-green eyes fixed on him.

Alena from the hospital.

Alena, who Banjo laughed with and hasn't stopped thinking about since.

'Benny!'

Aw, fuck.

Alena bursts out laughing. 'Oh God, Banjo, your face!'

Banjo can't really see his face, but he can feel his cheeks burn to some unholy level of hellfire, mouth stretching.

'Hi,' he says, full-out grinning now.

'Hi!' She grins back, all teeth on display. God but she's beautiful, even in work clothes. It hurts a little to look at her.

'Whit – how're ye doin' here?' Banjo stutters out.

'I think I should be asking that.' Alena grins, crosses her arms, ponytail swishing. 'Hm, *new* recruit? You been following me?'

Banjo's eyes bug out. He shakes his head so fast his own sight blurs. 'No! *God*, no, I looked – I *wus* lookin', and this place only hired – it wus the only one tae hire—'

Alena waves a hand. 'I know, we've been trying to find a replacement for weeks.' She laughs. 'Don't worry, I'm winding you up.'

For whatever reason, when Alena laughs it makes Banjo want to laugh too. Even if he's not in on the joke. Even if he *is* the joke.

'Aye, wonder why.' Banjo raises his eyebrows, trying for the air of coolness. 'Got some lettuce stuck tae the dishwasher and been breathin' in they fumes fur the past—'

Alena shakes her head. 'Rookie mistake, my friend. I see you're not getting along with the pots either?'

'That. *Pot*,' Banjo starts, ready to go on a three-day bender explaining the horrors, but Alena laughs again.

'It's no' funny, Alena, I cannae even – *talk* about it, fucken trauma.' He laughs as he speaks though, pink-cheeked and utterly charmed.

'It's a test,' Alena whispers like a secret, leaning all close. 'We have to see if the new recruits can hack it. But, hey, you've lasted longer than most.'

Banjo blinks. 'Serious?'

Alena nods. 'Oh, yeah. We had someone crying about an hour in, and last week this guy passed out. You made it.' She pulls her phone out and checks the time. 'What, four hours? Four and a half?'

Banjo gapes. 'It's been *four hours*?'

Alena's eyes shine as she grins. She's so unfairly pretty. 'I think we'll keep you.'

Banjo knows she's talking about the job, but still can't help blushing. He must be a neon stop sign at this point. 'Whut, I – I've got the job?'

'Oh, you had it like an hour ago.' Alena waves a hand.

Banjo stares. 'I got it? Really?'

Alena smiles wider. 'Of course.'

'Ha!' Banjo laughs. He wants to jump around this fucking back room. He actually *got* the job.

'Shh, shh!' Alena waves. 'Act surprised when they tell you!'

Banjo nods quickly, but he knows his face is a dead giveaway, and Alena's smile is sparkling.

'Anyway.' She makes a finger gun towards the door. 'I should get back to work.' She crooks her thumb as if firing. Banjo even finds that dorky move somehow phenomenal.

Once she opens the door to leave, though, she swivels around. 'How's the –' she gestures to his face – 'charity work going?'

'Oh.' Banjo laughs, touches the sensitive scar. ''Hink I'll stick tae washin' dishes.'

Alena laughs at that. Banjo's stomach bursts with butterflies. She raises a hand to her forehead.

'Good luck, comrade!' She salutes, back stiff and straight. 'It's been an honour!'

Banjo laughs. He gives her an awkward salute in return, but she's already away to deal with the customers.

Chapter Eight

FINLAY

Over the next week, Finlay settles into a routine of early morning lectures, insanely expensive coffee with the girls afterwards, then a dinner consisting of 80p noodles and microwaveable pierogi ruskie from a little corner store a ten-minute walk from his flat. He's got enough money from the scholarship payment to keep himself afloat, but his rent just came out and his job hunt is a total disaster. It turns out the entire West End has about three vacancies. Of those three, two of them require a degree. For retail.

He'll be here for the next four years, though. Employment is the bare-minimum requisite for survival. He can't accept any below-minimum-wage hourly rates when his hours are already so precious, either.

He needs something for stability, for security, but nowhere wants to take him. After his fifth rejection, Finlay curls up in his bed and decides not to move for the weekend.

The girls have messaged their new chat with plans to catch a movie. Finlay tries to think of a way to say he's busy without sounding rude for so long he gives himself a headache. Not that he *is* actually busy – just skint and socially inept. Finlay imagines joining them. Being a normal student with friends for a day.

In the end he gives up replying. Hopefully by Monday he'll have an excuse.

An ache forms in the base of his spine after an hour. It doesn't subside no matter how much he fidgets. Finlay decides to get some air and go for a jog. He'd normally take a walk, but there's a knot of anxiety about work in his chest that he wants to physically expel. When Finlay shoves on an old pair of trainers, a memory surfaces.

Goin' a run. Clear ma head. Banjo jogging restlessly on the spot, shaking himself out like a dog. *Need some air.* The words sitting heavy on Finlay's tongue. *I'll come with you.* He could never push them out.

Finlay kicks his toe into his shoe, trying to dispel the image. His body is screaming for movement.

It's difficult not to think every passer-by is judging him. He starts too soon and his foot goes wonky. He stops to stretch it for a minute. He looks up *how to jog* and scrolls the images online. He copies the correct posture, shoulders back, and tries again.

Finlay's going a speed barely considered jogging, but once his limbs are warm and loose it gets better. The West End is nice. There's not as much traffic as the city centre: vines crawling up the sides of the expensive tenement buildings, trees growing crooked out of small front gardens, cobblestones down small residential roads.

Finlay associates Glasgow with exhaust fumes and grease, with an amalgamation of a thousand different takeaways and the wetness of rain when it mingles with the concrete to create this foggy smell. But now he realises Glasgow sprawls out in every direction. The Southside, the East End, River Clyde. There's so much he's not seen.

On his third lap of Kelvingrove Park, however, a stitch develops. He bends with both hands on his knees, trying to get it under control, but every inhale—

'Hi!'

Finlay glances up *what the fuck.*

Akash stands in all his athletic glory. He's wearing a long-sleeved black zipper, little thumb holes at the hands, grey shorts with thermal leggings underneath. He looks effortlessly windswept and at ease, clothes hugging every inch of his frame, hair falling in perfect curtains.

'I've been looking for you!' Akash beams wide. 'You okay? You look a bit sick.'

'Nope,' Finlay gasps, pinching his side. 'Just – swallowed it.'

What.

What.

Finlay did not just imply he literally swallowed his own vomit.

Akash blinks, mouth open, before laughter bursts out. '*Gross*, Finlay.'

Finlay stares back, body locked in place, face radiating the energy of a small sun. 'Sorry. I—I am so sorry. In my head it sounded sort of funny—'

Akash laughs, dark eyes creased at the sides. 'Look, I've just started.' He throws a thumb over his shoulder. 'You want to run together?'

Finlay gives him an incredulous look. 'After I just told you I've swallowed my own vomit?' The question pops out unbidden.

What the ever-loving fuck?

'I'm choosing to ignore it,' Akash confides.

'Seriously, I need to make sure you heard it.' Finlay's absolutely *babbling* at this point. He's lost his mind.

Akash nods seriously. 'Of course, it's information people need.'

Finlay barks a laugh. He surprises himself with it; feels as though a pressure is lifted off his chest as it gallops free.

Akash joins in. It makes his entire face transform from chiselled divinity to most precious thing on the planet.

'So, how do you normally run?' Finlay asks: assumes a crouched stance, both arms out, about to bolt.

Akash *giggles*. It makes Finlay quietly implode. 'Not like that. We can just walk for now.' He tilts his head. 'Why are you wearing glasses?'

'Well, it's actually so I can see,' Finlay explains as they begin.

Akash's face glows. 'No, I mean – why are you wearing them out a *run*? You should wear contacts, like me.' He points to his eyes, as if Finlay needs the visual cue.

Finlay, however, is smiling. 'You wear glasses?'

Akash nods. 'That's basically why we became friends, remember?'

Finlay's heart jolts, caught off guard. Akash smiles simply, so easily, confident that Finlay will remember. But something inside Finlay repels doing so; shrinks away from it.

'Uh . . .'

Akash groans to the skies as if searching for religion. 'You still don't remember!' He tilts his head to catch Finlay's eye. 'We went to St Mary's Primary, I know it's been a while, but ...' He waits.

Finlay's feet slow. 'St Mary's ...' he murmurs. Memories start to trickle in. He knows that name ...

'Right, gimme the glasses.' Akash holds out a hand.

Finlay passes them over.

Akash puts them on and pulls his hair away from his face.

It slams into Finlay with the force of a comet.

He's back in Akash's house. Chasing Akash around the playground, laughing with him at night, diving into sleeping bags, picking each other for every team. His best friend, his terrible influence, his backup for everything, his lookout when stealing snacks, who cupped spiders with gentle hands to save them, who raced Finlay everywhere and smoothed bandages over Finlay's knees when he lost.

Finlay thought Akash was somebody from one of the various high schools. Somebody who knew about Finlay's foster homes and his family life. That's why Finlay wanted to keep it blocked out: because he assumed if he remembered Akash, he'd only remember something unpleasant.

But no. Akash is from *primary*. From a small moment in Finlay's life when he had something, *someone*, to look forward to.

Finlay feels something build in his stomach and well upwards until it booms out his chest. *'Akash!'*

'Now he gets it!' Akash beams.

'I forgot!'

'Fuck you!' Akash laughs, good-naturedly.

'It was so long ago!' Finlay says defensively, but he can hardly speak around the grin splitting his face.

Because the memories of Akash surround Finlay like the school jumpers Akash lent him, the soft balm of cotton across Finlay's skin and the warmth of Akash's body heat. The way Akash wordlessly tipped his packet of sweets towards Finlay, or stopped running to shout at Finlay's feet *shoelace!* The way he poked his head out of assembly line to give Finlay the thumbs-up.

And now he's here. He's solid and taller and older but as beautiful as always. They found one another again.

'*So?* I didn't forget *you!*' Akash gives him a light punch, barely felt. Finlay gives one back, until Akash lunges at him and Finlay's enfolded in a warm embrace.

He goes stiff.

Akash's arms are solid and sure, chest to chest. It's an intense explosion of pleasure, achingly wonderful. Finlay feels tears sting his eyes. Akash laughs against him as though it's the most natural thing in the world.

He's never been hugged like this. Never so crushingly. It's been years since he was touched at all. Because how could anyone ask for this?

Akash feels like sunlight heating him from the inside. Finlay's arms come up and return the embrace. It's such a beautiful thing to hold somebody.

Chapter Nine

BANJO

Once Banjo finishes his trial shift, he comes out the back room drenched in sweat and stinking of cheese. He's sure he's absorbed it into his pores by now.

'Well?' Morag asks when Banjo's finally done with all the dishes. 'What did you think of that?'

Hell. Torture. Worse than death.

Banjo shrugs. 'Wus aw'right.'

'Well, then. If you'd do the honours.' Morag gestures to Alena. She grins.

'Uh.' Banjo takes a step back warily, glancing between them. 'Yous gonnae gimme a wedgie or somethin'?'

Morag and Alena look at one another. Then they both smile.

'No.' Alena shakes her head. 'Come here.'

Banjo takes an uncertain step, but she leads him outside the café.

'Stand.' Alena takes both of his shoulders, setting him somewhere near the entrance. She touches him for a fraction of a second. It's still too long and too short. 'There.'

Banjo stands stiff as Alena jogs away, pulling out a camera from her apron.

Then she lifts the camera to her face. 'Smile! You're officially our newest member of staff!'

'Aw, *naw*.' Banjo laughs and turns away, tucking his hands into his apron pocket. He has the most absurd urge to cover his face. He's not used to this feeling, or doesn't know how to feel it. It's not shame. It's warmer. He's *shy*.

There's a whirring click, a bright flash. Alena grins and pulls it from her face.

'Wh – *wait*, I wasnae ready!' Banjo shouts. 'That's no' fair!'

Alena raises a playful eyebrow. 'You want another?'

Banjo straightens his shoulders and does his biggest, cheesiest grin. He clenches all his teeth and pulls his lips away from his gums. He knows it's ridiculous but Alena laughs, shakes her head, and *doesn't take the picture*.

'Alena!' Banjo feels his face break apart as he laughs. 'Whit ye waitin' fur!'

The flash of the camera catches him off guard. He's mid-laugh and half-twisted away, and the light catches him right in the eye and blinds him for a second.

'Authenticity!' Alena says.

She shows him the photos.

Banjo looks at the big, handwritten *Wall of Employees!* banner. He looks at all the strangers he doesn't know, grinning and pulling faces, covering their eyes and hiding. He sees

Morag among them, with a bored expression and the middle finger up.

Banjo huffs, looks over at her currently wiping down tables. Alena's been here longer than the manager, it seems.

'It's tradition,' Alena says. 'I take a picture of everyone after they pass their trial shift.' She gestures with a flourish. 'Most of them are gone now, though.'

'So ... am gonnae be up there?' Banjo blinks in wonder.

Alena taps an empty spot on the wall. 'Immortal. Once I get it printed.'

Banjo's cheeks are hot. He doesn't own any pictures of himself. He doesn't even have any from when he was a kid. It feels a bit weird.

'Where's you?' Banjo asks, to distract himself.

'I'm the photographer,' Alena explains simply.

Banjo frowns. 'Yer no' there?'

She shakes her head. 'These are my subjects.'

'But ye should be up 'ere too,' Banjo protests.

'Not this again!' Morag shouts from where she's wiping. 'I've tried it, pal!'

Alena crosses her arms. 'It's not happening. If I see myself up there, it'll ruin it.'

'Th—' Banjo chokes on his own tongue to stop from saying, *The fuck? Ruin it? You'll* make *that wall.* 'That's shite!'

'Look, I know where you're all coming from, but this is art,' she insists. 'This is my exhibit. You don't see an artist sticking themselves into their own painting.'

'That's bullshit, artists draw themselves all the time!' comes Morag's high-pitched cry.

'I'm talking about *landscapes*, not self-portraits,' Alena says, and gestures to the wall. 'This is a *landscape* of employees.'

'Shut it with your arty-farty shite.' Morag waves a cloth.

'I'll shut *you*, lob that mop bucket right over your head,' Alena replies.

'Try it, skinny!' Morag shouts, but she stumbles when Alena takes a step.

Banjo laughs, watching them.

Alena turns to him with a secretive grin. 'You'll get used to us.' She bumps an elbow into Banjo's side.

Banjo winces and doubles over.

Alena's eyes go wide. 'Oh God, I'm so—' Her hands flutter but don't touch.

Banjo breathes through his nose. 'Is fine.' He waves a hand, opening his mouth before something else catches his eye. He peers close. 'This their names?'

'It's, in my humble opinion, the *essence* of the photo,' Alena states.

Beneath Morag's feet, in small print, reads *bold*. Banjo snorts, because okay. He'd have written something a little stronger. Underneath someone's covered face, it reads *self-conscious*. But underneath someone else, hand out to the camera and turned away, it reads *embarrassed*.

Then there're the smiling ones. So many people, all smiling, but all with a different word. A woman standing with her hands behind her back, beaming, is labelled *kind*. Another one grinning straight at the camera, hands on hips, reads *confident*.

And there's more. So many more. Two thumbs up gets *excited*. One thumb up is *positive*.

Happy. Funny. Bored. Tired. Confused. Nervous. Flattered.

Banjo pulls away. 'Whit am I?'

Alena gives him a soft smile. 'You'll find out.'

A job. A club. A new life. Banjo tries to imagine the word Alena will use for him. For some reason he has a better time picturing Finlay in that apron, striking a silly pose.

Finlay's word would be something like *good*.

Chapter Ten

FINLAY

When Finlay buzzes himself into his flat, it's almost dark. He'll have to go down to the common room if he wants any dinner. He's still got some eggs that aren't out of date.

When Finlay opens his dorm room door, all his things are as he left them. Clothes on his bed, toothbrush charging on his nightstand. Even the air hasn't shifted, stale and stuck in place.

Akash forced his number into Finlay's phone and instructed him to text. Finlay drafts a million things and doesn't send anything. He stares at Akash's contact, the little smiley Akash added beside his name. He wants to reach out, but instinct makes him shrink back. The instinct that yanks him away from the edge whenever he finds himself getting too close to someone. It warns him of the pain to come.

Finlay is intimately familiar with the terrible, dark feeling that washes over him sometimes when he's not been touched for a while. The one that makes him feel as if he's slowly disappearing. His own hand on his arm becomes foreign.

What an experience to have a body. This thing that needs

watered and fed and rested, is yanked around all day to various places and into various poses. The unreality of it all overwhelms him sometimes: that it's only a collection of cells and tissues and electrical synapses.

I don't exist, the waves would come. He wanted to run out into the street and shout to anyone *please just touch me, tell me I'm alive, make sure I exist*. He was sure if just one person did that he would be cured.

But now Finlay stands in his room after being bodily squeezed and realises there is no cure. It's an incessant need inside him, this hunger for other people. But at least with the girls Finlay can erect levels of separation. He can be physically distant, can avoid spilling personal details about himself, can excuse his aloofness by pretending it's his natural state.

With Akash there's not enough distance. Akash sees everything. He'll soon see Finlay's naked, desperate hunger. Finlay is too much himself when he's around Akash. Better to avoid him and the inevitable mess.

Three Years Ago

Group homes are fine, but Finlay prefers foster placements. Quieter. Not to mention group homes are stricter mealtimes, chores, curfew. Everything run on military precision, no matter how cheery the staff are. They're good stopping-off points, though. Jumping from carer to carer can hurt a little, each family unit a separate knife. It's nice to feel no attachments for a minute.

On Banjo's second day at St Andrews, he starts a fight. Finlay has no clue what it's about or how it begins, only that he's reading in bed because it's the summer holidays when Banjo storms into their room, Douglas just behind him.

'Ah dinnae even—' Banjo starts, a harsh pen mark down his cheek and a slightly swollen left eye.

'Don't want to hear it.' Douglas holds his hands up. 'Cool off for half an hour in here.'

Banjo's eyes widen, mouth opening ready to release a tirade, but Douglas shuts the door pointedly behind himself.

Banjo crosses his arms, throws himself on to his bed and huffs loudly. 'Fucken prison.'

Finlay doesn't look up from his book, holds it over his nose so he's invisible even though it forces him to squint behind his glasses.

'How ma 'ae know there's a *rota* fur the pens—'

Finlay has no idea why Banjo wants to use the art supplies, but there's a schedule for them. As evidenced by Banjo's face, they can still be used as weapons. For some reason, the image of Banjo doing art is so absurd Finlay has to bite his lip against a laugh.

'Fuck aw else tae dae,' Banjo finishes, but his voice grows soft as he realises he's speaking to himself.

Finlay wants to say something. He should say something. Maybe he was meant to tell Banjo these things. Don't take the pens away, sign in and out when going anywhere, check the cleaning chart every day.

Everybody here has so little that what is theirs will be fought for. And Banjo seems more willing to fight than most.

Banjo's sullen and bored, sprawled across his bed, blowing out air and hitting the walls at random intervals.

Finlay stares at the words on his page.

'Where'd they keep the painkillers?' Banjo breaks the silence first. There's a forced casualness in his voice.

A second passes, then another. Finlay is stuck. He clutches his book, willing himself to speak. This is usually the part where people repeat the question.

Banjo doesn't. The silence reigns on.

Finlay's struggled with being quiet his entire life. But silence is safe. Silence is nothing. And Finlay is safe and nothing in the silence. Yet sometimes he resents it. Struggles inside its hold. Finlay closes his eyes, swallows, and forces his breathing to slow. Counts backwards, *eight, seven, six ...*

'You need to ask.' He carefully selects each word.

Banjo swivels around to sit up on the bed. He looks at Finlay even though Finlay focuses on his page.

Interest acquired. *It speaks!*

But Banjo surprises him. 'Ye cannae jus' go an' get some?'

Finlay shakes his head.

'They're locked away,' Banjo realises.

Finlay nods.

Banjo throws himself back with a huff.

Finlay lifts his eyes above his page. 'They'll give you them if you ask.'

Banjo is quiet this time. Finlay is unfamiliar with the role reversal. He studies Banjo for a moment.

'Ah dinnae fucken feel like askin',' Banjo mutters eventually, because silence will out.

Finlay fiddles around in his pocket and finds a granola bar he was saving. He chucks it across. He doesn't really know why.

It lands beside Banjo's head. Banjo jerks, bony shoulder blades up to his ears, a startled animal. Then he looks down. He makes a soft sound.

'Thanks.'

After three days at St Andrews, Banjo goes to the bathroom. It's 2 a.m. Finlay decides to leave him to it – clearly this is why Banjo mentioned the bladder infection – until he hears the sound of vomiting. Finlay's up and at the door before his next breath.

'Banjo?'

There's no reply, only a ragged gasp and more retching.

'Banjo, I'll go get somebody?'

'No!' the croaky shout comes. More vomiting. Finlay runs a hand through his hair.

'I need to get somebody,' Finlay decides, forcing the words clearly. His voice is raspy with half-sleep and disuse.

Banjo sounds closer to the door when he speaks again, but his Scots is thicker too. 'It'll fucken stoap, jus' pleese don'.'

Finlay presses his forehead to the door. It's easier to speak with the barrier between them. 'I can come in?'

Don't fucken come in, Banjo demands, voice so dark that Finlay pulls away from the door. After a beat there's the sound of violent diarrhoea. Banjo runs the taps, but groans as though he's dying. Is he seriously sick? It could be food poisoning. People die from that. Or a concussion; maybe he hit his head during his fight yesterday.

Eventually the rushing taps are the only noise.

'I can get *medicine*,' Finlay tries. He'll ask the staff, but he can tell them it's for himself.

'No,' Banjo rasps, then quieter: 'Don' go.'

Those words are the thing to make Finlay pause. One foot is poised to run, but he can't make himself move. Banjo holds him in place.

'All right.' Finlay makes himself speak. 'I'll stay.'

The toilet flushes. Sounds filter through. Washing hands. Splashed cheeks. Drying hands. Harsh breathing. Feet shuffling. Finlay waits awhile but nothing else happens.

'Are you okay?'

'Yes,' Banjo croaks, but sounds oddly low down.

Finlay frowns. He crouches. 'Are you on the floor?'

'. . . Yes.'

Finlay goes on to his hands and knees and peers underneath the gap in the door. He can just about make out Banjo's mouth.

'Why?'

''S fun,' Banjo's mouth says.

Finlay lies flat on the floor, cheek pressed to the carpet. 'Yeah.'

'Why ye breathen' so loud?' Banjo asks, even though he's also panting.

71

'I thought you were dying,' Finlay explains.

Banjo laughs, a deep sound, unusually old. It makes Finlay laugh too. Banjo doesn't speak again, and his breathing slows. Silence falls. They stay there, lying on opposite sides of the door.

'It's ... withdrawal,' Banjo confesses after a long time.

Finlay is silent.

Where'd they keep the painkillers?

I have a raging bladder infection.

Of course. There is no bladder infection.

'Okay,' he whispers back, because he can't think of anything else. There's no reply.

Finlay feels his eyes grow heavy as the time draws on. But he promised Banjo.

When the door opens, Finlay jerks awake.

Banjo looks down. His hair's a mess, the shock of orange up every which way. His eyes are puffy and his T-shirt has two huge beach balls of sweat under the arms. He looks terrible.

'Ye a'ight?' he croaks.

Finlay sits up. His glasses have created a dent along his head, and he pulls them off his aching ears. The lining of his throat is dry. 'Mm.'

'Ye gonnae move?' Banjo quirks an eyebrow.

Finlay stands. His muscles ache. He twists his neck side to side, wincing in pain. Banjo watches, dark sunken circles underneath his eyes, ugly and exhausted.

Finlay doesn't say anything. He stands up and goes back to

bed. His eyes slip shut again, but after a while he hears Banjo do the same.

They fall asleep to one another's breathing. It's the first time they both sleep through until morning.

Chapter Eleven

BANJO

Banjo takes to work a little less like a duck to water and more like a cat off the street, but it's something to look forward to – well, seeing Alena, more specifically. Plus Paula and Henry are pretty happy he's got something to do at the weekends. School has settled but it hardly matters he doesn't have anyone to spend lunch with. He can just come here. It's a bit of a trek from Triduana, but the food is free as long as Banjo cooks it himself. He's practically never out the fucking place: even on days that Alena doesn't work.

Morag has been letting him out the back room to try a bit of serving. Banjo's quick to discover the two are pretty much an orange and an apple. A bit different, yeah, but still *fruit*.

'What do you mean, there's no chips?' The guy blinks at Banjo with the same level of disgust Banjo knows is on his face when he looks at lettuce.

'We've run oot,' Banjo repeats.

'Have you checked?' the guy insists.

No. Banjo hasn't checked. He's just standing here spewing total shite.

'Yeah,' Banjo states. He's got three plates on one arm and two on the other, that – believe it or not – are so hot they'll probably rip off some skin when he goes to set them down. He's got sweat itching his armpits and the nape of his neck, he's got two separate tables waiting for these plates, and he's been in the same spot for ten minutes, because for about the *tenth* time today, someone is asking him about *fucking chips*.

'Well, then,' the guy says. 'Better try somewhere else.'

'Bye, then!' Banjo calls. 'Come oan in soon!'

Some of the customers glance at him with lifted eyebrows and hushed whispers. Banjo clenches his jaw and heads towards the tables.

'Sorry fur yer wait.' Banjo tries to hide his bitch face and unsticks the plates from his arms.

'Um, excuse me,' the woman begins. 'I thought the sandwiches came with chips?'

Banjo about combusts. Once he's patiently explained, *We have none left and if you take issue with it I'll stab myself with a fork*, he stomps over to the front of the café.

Morag is off today, so Lizzy – their part-time cook – is manning the café. She's been rushed off her feet the whole day doing two people's jobs.

That also means Alena is serving at the tills, chatting to a customer.

Banjo's so focused on her face, it's only when he goes to squeeze around the counter that he gets a look at said customer.

He near chokes on air.

Kyle stands half-bent over the countertop, hip cocked out, smile in place. He catches Banjo's eye and his grin falters for less than a second. Then it's back up, same as always.

'I said they'll need to look into their pension fund—' Alena chats while she makes a latte.

'Banjo!' Kyle booms out, lifting an arm. 'Fancy seeing you here!'

Banjo and Alena look at each other like cartoons.

'You guys know each other?' Alena asks.

Could ask the same. Banjo's jaw is stuck.

'We're in athletics.' Kyle jerks a thumb between them.

Alena's face opens up in curiosity, eyes intent on Banjo. Banjo feels like there's a brick in his gullet.

Kyle won't say anything about their fight. Why the fuck would it come up? Even as Banjo tells himself this, he's so utterly unhinged his mind floods with visions of Kyle spilling everything: that Banjo's a complete liar that never fought for charity, even though that was a *joke*, and that he's in foster care, and has no friends, and eats Paula's pre-made sandwiches in the toilet.

He's so hyper-aware of Alena she becomes static pulling at Banjo's arm hairs.

'Uh, yeah,' Banjo states. He knows there's this deer-in-oncoming-traffic expression plastered across his face.

'Me and Kyle grew up on the same street before I moved,' Alena explains, her beautiful cheeks bunched in a smile. Kyle's eyes linger on her.

Banjo wants to sink straight through the floor. Of course Kyle likes her. Of course Kyle has history with her. Banjo has no chance. Not even the hope of one.

'Right. I'd better—' Banjo nods to the kitchens, foot inching backwards.

'Banjo! Hold up.' Kyle pushes off the counter. 'I said to Alena I'm having a party tonight. You're more than welcome.'

Banjo stops. He gives Kyle a bug-eyed *be serious* look. They're not buddy-buddies.

Kyle gives him a raised-eyebrow *up to you* response.

Banjo has no idea what's happening, but it might mean more time with Alena. He looks at her, hope blooming in his lungs like fresh air.

'I also said I can't make it.' Alena's bottom lip juts out.

Banjo can't hide his disappointment. Alena doesn't hide hers either. They hold each other's gaze. Banjo wants to take her chin between his fingers and touch her pout.

'Most of the team are coming, by the way,' Kyle cuts in, ending the moment, practically swinging over the counter to break them up. 'Dev too.'

Banjo understands the weight of those words. *Devlin, who avoided us after we beat you up.*

So this is an apology? Let's all be friends and dance in a circle? Truthfully, if Kyle has history with Alena this makes Banjo feel far more fucking friendly. Alena is a good judge of people. And she's smiling at them both.

Plus, if Kyle's willing to make the effort Banjo can't exactly spit in his face.

Banjo swallows. 'Okay.'

Kyle claps his hands. 'Great!'

And that's how Banjo finds himself going to the party of a guy who put him in the hospital. Everyone here is just full of surprises.

Chapter Twelve

FINLAY

Finlay doesn't text Akash. It still manages to plague him, even the vague notion that Akash is waiting for Finlay. His insides feel turned out. But if this is Akash's effect after a handful of interactions, Finlay knows it's for the best. There's too much shared history.

Finlay and the girls tumble out of class in the morning, on the hunt for coffee between lectures. He ended up replying to them on Sunday night to say he missed their messages and will be at the next movie meetup. He tossed and turned in bed, terrified he'd be evicted from their small social group even while he told himself he'd be fine by himself.

Thankfully they totally understood. *No worries! Yeah, definitely next time!* The relief was like an instant high. Finlay tries not to think about how attached he is already.

But one good thing manages to happen. Finlay pulls his phone out while walking with the girls and sees an email.

Application for Relief Cleaner (Schools). He clicks on it so fast he almost pulls a thumb muscle.

We are pleased to inform you that your application has been successful and we would like to offer you the position ...

Finlay's eyes scan the words as happiness balloons inside his chest. A job. Which he can start *tomorrow*.

The girls chat beside him and Finlay tries not to buzz out of his skin. He clenches his jaw to hold it in. If he tells them he has a job, it'll only lead to: *Can't you ask your parents for help?* It's not a malicious question. But Finlay's not ready to tell them everything yet.

'Have you started the assignment?' Jun asks as they enter the glass doors.

'Managed about half,' Derya replies. 'Finlay, what about you?'

'Oh?' Finlay blinks. He's hardly thought about it – finding a job is a full-time job in and of itself. 'Yeah, I've started.' He lies to avoid suspicion.

'We can bash it out later?' Jun offers. 'Late-night study session?'

Finlay smiles, but there's no un-evil way to say, *I need to do it alone because I have the social battery of an old lamp.* 'Sure.'

'How do you guys feel about placement next month?' Derya asks.

'I just want to know where we'll *be*!' Jun groans. 'How can they not let us know until a few weeks before it?'

'Do you think they'll tell us what to do if a patient dies?' Derya asks once they're sitting with their cappuccinos. 'I mean, before placement? Because I'd rather know what to do than have to find out if it happens.'

'Okay, now we're really getting into worst-case scenarios,' Finlay tells them, wrapping his hands around his cup to heat himself.

'Do you think if a patient dies on your first day of placement, they kick you off the course?' Jun adds.

'I mean, it depends on if you had anything to do with it,' Derya says. 'I think if they can prove it was your *fault*, probably.'

'Ahhh, sadly this is making the thought of it a bit worse for me,' Finlay tries, sensing that familiar bile sting the back of his throat. Because the thought of actually being on placement – of looking after vulnerable people who rely on him – is making him more than slightly nauseous.

'Do you think it would be some kind of cosmic sign?' Jun asks, sounding mildly curious rather than alarmed. 'Do you think you would be cursed forever or something?'

Finlay opens his mouth, before two soft hands land on his shoulders.

'Boo.'

Finlay knows that voice. His heart bursts. He turns to find Akash smiling wide, wearing another adorable get-up of linen trousers, a sweater vest over a shirt underneath a puffy coat, two books under his arm, and to top it all off – a pair of glasses. It's like being lovingly stabbed in the stomach.

'I was trying to think of something clever on the way over, but I couldn't so I gave up,' Akash explains, glancing at Jun and Derya.

'What!' Finlay says, mock indignant. Every tiny insecurity and argument against this evaporates with the reality of Akash. '"Boo" is a classic! The original before the adaptation!'

He has no idea what he's saying. Something about Akash makes Finlay freer, looser, as though Akash's childlike nature seeps into him or brings out Finlay's own. It's so euphoric in the moment that Finlay forgets he's meant to be limiting how much of himself spills out when he's with Akash.

'Coming to a cinema near you!' Akash adds, because he's a wonderful dork. He looks so different with glasses: achingly familiar and innocent, stirring memories Finlay's buried deep.

'Exactly!' Finlay clicks his fingers. 'Starring – someone good, obviously!' He can't think of anyone on the spot. His face becomes a furnace.

'Critics are calling it good; I've heard.' Akash goes with it.

'The director said, you know, "Yes, I made it,"' Finlay adds.

'It's quickly developing into something mediocre.'

They laugh at the same time. It feels exactly the same as when they ran together. Finlay's lungs expand as oxygen floods through him.

There's a kick to his shin. Finlay turns to find Derya's eyebrow raised.

'Sorry, this is Jun and Derya.' Finlay introduces them with a waved hand, embarrassed and oddly raw. 'Guys, this is Akash.'

'Hi!' Akash beams. 'Nice to meet you. I actually have a class in ten, so I'm just getting coffee.' He points to the small queue. 'But I'll see you later. Message me.' He does a little motion with his thumb to Finlay before he leaves.

'Oh – right, yeah!' Finlay tries not to croak. He watches Akash take his place in the queue, reshuffling the books in his arms to hold them more securely.

'Oh my lord,' Derya murmurs. 'Who's that?'

Finlay blinks. He realises he was just caught staring. His ears are blistering. 'Um. Just an old friend.' That word sounds weird coming from his mouth.

'That boy is obsessed with you,' Jun decides. 'Full-blown infatuated.'

Finlay's cheeks sting with immediate heat. 'What?' *I'm the one obviously infatuated. Akash is just lovely, sweet, beautiful Akash.*

'Did you not just witness what *we* witnessed?' Derya asks.

'No, no.' Finlay laughs, the sound reedy and thin, brittle enough to snap. He wishes he could cover himself with his coat. 'You've got it wrong.' He shakes his head and sips his cappuccino for something to do.

'If you say so.' Jun holds her hands spread. Derya studies him. Finlay avoids both their eyes.

Chapter Thirteen

BANJO

Banjo has dinner at Paula and Henry's because he doesn't want their food going to waste. Then he makes his way to Kyle's house. It's one of those silly little posh-boy estates in Stewartfield, so it takes a good fifteen minutes by bike.

'Banjo!' about six guys cheer when he comes in.

Banjo jumps. Kyle just slings an arm around Banjo's shoulders and drags him through the front door.

Banjo shoves him off, instantly tense and ready for the oncoming mockery, but everyone laughs.

Truth be told, Banjo's never been to a proper party. Never exactly got close enough to anyone for an invite.

He kind of expected smoke and mirrors or something, laser beams and disco balls. Instead it's just like being in someone else's house except with twenty other people. Awkward, cramped, and a bit boring.

He takes the drink Kyle hands him until he finds it's foul.

'Fuck is this?' His face contorts after a sip.

'Never had vodka?' Kyle asks, face all innocence.

'Naw, 'cause am no' *eighteen*!' Banjo shoves the cup back. The terror tightens around him like a hand going for his throat. He mostly avoids that kind of stuff. Maybe he's never had alcohol, but he's known other things. He can't go there. Curled up and shaking out of his mind. He wants to shove fingers down his throat.

'You a wee grass, aye?' Kyle asks with a grin, trying and failing to sound Scots.

'Ha,' Banjo states, dry. 'Got lemonade?'

'Knock yourself out.' Kyle waves towards the kitchen.

Banjo finds some in the fridge, then finds a quiet corner to drink it.

He feels as if he's on display. As if everyone's watching him. There are some girls here, too. Banjo didn't know Kyle had any friends that were girls, but then again he didn't know Kyle knew Alena.

Still, it looks like everyone is standing around in circles, laughing, staring at him. They aren't, obviously, because they've got their own lives and Saturday nights. But it feels like they are.

After a while Banjo wanders into the garden. Of course Kyle has a swimming pool, the idiot. It's not even big. It's sort of pathetic-looking, swallowing up the already small space available, just so wildly out of place beside the shed and the bushes.

There's nobody to talk to out here. It smells like wet grass and salty chlorine, better than sweat and perfume and alcohol. He breathes in, eyelids fluttering shut.

'Found him!' Kyle shouts.

Banjo whips around. He frowns, confused. 'Why ye looken'?'

'Because yar an aggressive *sonovabitch*,' Kyle imitates Banjo as he saunters over. A few other guys follow. This type of grin comes over Kyle's face that makes Banjo uneasy. He's been waiting for the other shoe to drop all night – now Banjo can feel it sinking straight through him.

'That right?' Banjo asks.

'Yeah,' Kyle says. 'Look, I've no issue with you. I've just got two requests and we're gold.'

Banjo cocks a brow. 'Oh, aye?'

'Yeah.' Kyle nods, holds up a fist, and pops a thumb out. 'First, quit the team.'

Banjo scoffs. Kyle doesn't.

Right. This is why Banjo was invited.

'Whit's aw this?' Banjo laughs, gesturing around, even as bitter vines of embarrassment coil in his gut. 'Sweet talk?'

Kyle shrugs.

'The second?' Banjo asks.

Kyle's index finger appears. 'Stay away from Alena.'

Banjo doesn't laugh at that one. He looks at the guys behind Kyle. *Are you hearing this?* his face says.

But they stare back, serious as a heart attack.

'Whut ye gonnae dae?' Banjo's curious now, actually.

'Can do a few things.' Kyle's lip curls back in a smiling sneer, and with everyone behind him it's clear what he means.

'Nice.' Banjo grits his teeth trying to calm down, really trying not to combust. 'So, whut, she yer property?'

'Nah, nah.' Kyle pulls a face. 'She's used goods, mate. It's unhygienic. I'm looking out for you, actually.'

It goes through bone and hits pure nerve.

'Ye utter fuckin'—' Banjo storms up; the rage is in his blood system now.

But Kyle just laughs, the other guys laugh, like life just gets so funny sometimes. More people have come outside. It's basically the whole party here to spectate.

Banjo can only hear the white rush of blood in his ears as he goes to swing.

Yet Kyle expects it; pushes him backwards with ease.

Banjo staggers and trips.

There's this second of weightless nothing before his back hits ice cold. The pool water closes over him: invades his mouth, nose, ears, eyes. Banjo tries to breathe like an utter fucking idiot, because nobody breathes underwater, nobody would even *try to*. The water burns his insides, scorches up his throat and into his head, and he can't move, he can't see, he can't swim.

Fuck. He can't swim. He's never once—

Banjo's stomach heaves. He throws up. But it doesn't *go anywhere*, it stays in his mouth, down his throat and inside his nostrils, burning his brain like acid because it's *everywhere*.

He's going to die. He'll die in this pool with everyone laughing until his body floats to the surface and they realise the thrashing wasn't a joke, and everyone will scream because he drowned, he's *dead*—

Something grips him and yanks him up.

Banjo coughs a ragged inhale when he breaks the surface. It sounds wretched, like a strangled animal. Snot and vomit run down his chin and blister his whole throat. He thrashes his limbs, trying to find something to grab. He can't hear anything but a gaggle of noise, bright lights, voices shouting, he's shivering, shaking—

He's shoved on to the tiles.

'Fucking *piece of shit*!' Devlin pierces his eardrums. 'The fuck you push him in for? You wait to see if he can *swim*!'

'Aw, Christ, he's been sick in the pool,' Kyle babbles. 'Right in the water, my dad will kill me—'

'Think it's funny? He could've *drowned*!'

'Jesus, it's everywhere—'

Banjo shudders and throws up again on the concrete.

They get him a change of clothes. Truth be told, nobody is happy about it. His near-death experience seems to have put a bit of a dampener on the party. It wasn't very funny after all, big surprise. One of Kyle's pals chucks a T-shirt and shorts at him while Kyle tries to fish out the gunk in the pool. The clothes are too big and smell strange, but better than his soaked ones.

Once Banjo's thrown up all the pool water he managed to swallow, Devlin finds him. 'You okay?' he asks outside the bathroom door.

Banjo rests his head against the toilet lid for a moment. The porcelain is utterly pristine. Someone cleans on their hands and knees for the glory of this thing.

'Fine.' He breathes through his mouth because air through his nose feels like a knife to the brain.

Devlin is quiet. 'Well, if everyone knew you from the fight, this'll make the headlines,' he tries. 'Sunday papers.'

Banjo chuckles. 'Fame came too fucken early, I'll tell them.'

Devlin barks a laugh. Banjo half laughs, half chokes on sick. Devlin hovers at the door.

'Am *fine*, Devlin,' Banjo states, because he doesn't want Devlin listening in to this intimate fucking situation.

'Right.' Devlin scampers off.

Banjo presses his forearms to the lid and rides the waves of nausea until they stop. Then he walks down the stairs and leaves out the front entrance, because fuck it.

Three Years Ago

'Banjo? You good?' Finlay's mouth is at the bottom of the door frame, his fingers at either side. Banjo wants to reach up and open the door. He wants to let Finlay inside. He doesn't have the strength, though. His arm drops weakly on the second attempt. He exhales sour breath back into his own face and tries to keep his head still, his cheek to the bathroom floor, because if he lifts it he'll be sick.

He knows he could take some painkillers and stop the nausea, but the cause is hardly the fucking cure.

'Am good,' he croaks eventually.

Finlay stays on the floor. Somehow he can always tell the difference between *good, so please go* and *good, but please stay*.

Chapter Fourteen

FINLAY

Finlay leaves the girls to their study session with the excuse of needing a food shop. While it's true, the coffee he just bought means he can't afford it. Another packet of instant noodles for dinner. He also feels oddly vulnerable that they saw him with Akash – they witnessed that bubblier version of Finlay only reserved for those closest, and yet somehow Akash pulls it out no matter who's around. The thought is terrifying.

Still, considering he starts his new cleaning job tomorrow, it's probably a good idea not to stay out late either. And hopefully he can go back to three full meals a day.

Finlay manages to cram some essay writing in, but can't help getting distracted by the blank message history with Akash on his phone. He feels like he should say something. Give an explanation for why he's not getting in touch.

Message me.

Maybe it would lead to more pain. Akash's embrace has only given rise to the need for it. Ignorance is bliss; Finlay should retreat into it rather than keep discovering the ways in which Akash is wonderful. But then again, he was in too deep the moment he spoke to Akash on his first day.

Finlay goes back to his essay: types and backspaces sentences like it's a new hand exercise. Eventually it creeps into midnight. Finlay vows to finish tomorrow because he must have added a total of five words.

When he settles down to sleep, his shoulders tingle with the memory of Akash's warm hands on them. He fidgets restlessly until he passes out from sheer exhaustion.

Finlay jolts awake at 5 a.m. to the horrendously shrill noise of his new alarm. He looks out his window blearily to see it's still dark. He squints at his phone to make sure he should be awake. 5.04. Why is he awake? Oh, Christ.

He starts his new job at 6 a.m.

Finlay jumps out of bed and is slapped by the cold.

He doubles over. 'Mother of Christ.'

He hobbles like an old man to his drawer and finds socks, putting on two pairs for good measure. He quickly discovers that he can't straighten his spine without the cold piercing his skin, so he bounces on the spot until he can actually unfurl enough to brush his teeth. After that, Finlay gets dressed.

Once done, Finlay surveys himself in the mirror, flattening down the front of his hair with a finger-comb. He assumes a fighting position: fists raised, knees apart. Nausea coils in his upper stomach. He goes back over to his bed and presses Mr Black against his face for moral support.

Finlay heads for the bike rack at 5.25 a.m. He bought a bike for the express purpose of this job: it turns out he needs to spend money before he can make it.

It stays dark outside, a thick layer of fog coating the air in front of him. It's a quiet ride; the streets are completely deserted, the fuzzy glow from the streetlamps the only thing awake. Finlay passes the cafés and the shops he's lived beside for nearly a month now, dark and empty with chairs upturned on tables, with rails of clothes untouched. It's fascinating, this whole world dipped in quiet.

He sets out on to the main road and pulls his chin out from his jacket collar to breathe in the sharp, stringent air. Cold stings his exposed nose, but it also wakes him up. By the time he gets to where he's supposed to be he's flushed warm.

The only problem is there's nobody else there.

Finlay slows to a stop and checks his location a few times. He checks the time as well: 5.50 a.m. He's early, but only a little. He looks up at the main gate of the building he's been sent to: **Leonards Primary School**.

Finlay cycles around trying to find an entrance. It's sealed tight. Obviously. It's a primary school. Anxiety races through his blood. Finlay pulls out his phone to call the contact on the job advert when a car slides up and a window rolls down.

'Finlay?' A woman's head pokes out.

'Hello!' Finlay forces a beam, back stiff and straight.

'Let me park and I'll let us in,' she states.

Finlay's heart thunders. Is it not a good thing to be early? Is she already rethinking her decision? How much can these things retroactively be withdrawn?

She goes into the small parking lot, puts her car in and heads over to where he stands. Her set of keys all jangle together as she unlocks the gate.

'So, I'll show you how to set the alarm, where things are kept, and then I'll be off because I've got another place to get to,' she continues.

Finlay thinks this is the manager, Janet, but he can't be sure because he's only emailed her.

'Sure,' Finlay says, his voice thick with nerves. 'Um ... *Janet*, right?'

'Yes.' Janet smiles. 'What age are you, Finlay?'

'Eighteen,' Finlay replies. Even though he's pretty sure he gave his date of birth on the application.

'Awk, you're just a wee baby.' Janet opens the door. Immediately an alarm blares. Janet quickly presses a code into the box and it stops.

'4312,' she tells him. 'Don't forget.'

Finlay starts typing it into his phone.

'Just joking, I'll text the code whenever I send the location,' Janet replies.

Finlay smiles weakly. He's afraid if he speaks he'll burst into overwrought tears.

Janet switches on the main reception lights, which briefly blind his sleep-deprived eyes, and then takes him through to the blissfully dark classrooms with their tiny desks for tiny people, their play areas and multicoloured carpets. The bookshelves are all stocked to the brim, whiteboards that can be flipped over to chalkboards, small seats all tucked underneath group tables. Janet shows him where the supplies are kept, where the bins get thrown out, all the basics.

'So, if you just hoover, sweep, mop, change the bins, check the toilets, check the kitchen, and wipe down all the tables and counters,' Janet states, 'that should be us. I'll be back about quarter to eight to make sure everything is all right. You've got my number if there's any problems.'

Finlay nods the entire way through her speech, mentally writing the list inside his head. 'Great. Sounds good.'

'Well, here's your keys.' Janet then hands him a set of keys. On his first day. Day Zero.

Finlay stares down at them within the circle of his palm.

Janet laughs. 'Don't look so worried, we've all got them. Right, I'm off!'

Her legs practically become a cartoon blur she moves that fast. Finlay doesn't have the time to even wave goodbye.

After that, he's in an empty primary school, alone, with the whole place to clean in two hours.

First, the bins need to be changed. Finlay's used to that from a lifetime of odd jobs. He finds fresh bin bags in the supply closet and gets to work.

Next, the hoover. Half the primary is covered in carpet. Once that's done, he wipes the sweat rolling along his jaw before he starts on the bathrooms. Janet pointed to a few cleaning products to use; Finlay gathers them all up in his arms and heads in.

When he comes out, sleeves rolled up and significantly sweatier, it's lighter than before.

Finlay pauses. He was content to work in the darkness to stave off the eye strain. Do the classroom lights come on automatically?

No. A glow spills across the classroom. Finlay glances out the window. The small point of the sun is climbing its way up the sky, streaks of orange and yellow bleeding across the clouds. He checks the time: 7.06 a.m. He's been working for a full hour.

It's strange to see the sunrise for the first time. He's never stopped to watch it. Finlay sets his bucket on one of the small group tables and breathes in. It touches his face like a warm hand, soaks through his clothes into his skin.

In the darkness, Finlay never spotted the little things. It just looked like an empty classroom. Now he sees the paper plates decorating the walls.

There are all different drawings: blobs of people, stick figures, splashes of colour, cartoon faces. He walks up close until he notices the banner above them written in huge block letters:

MY FAMILY IS ...

Finlay's eyes scan the words written by small-fisted hands: *Mum and Dad, LOUD, at work, loving and kind, a good family, my two mums, my little sister and my cat, happy, annoying but nice, all my aunties and uncles and cousins, THE BEST!*

Finlay smiles at the little private jokes, the innocence of the answers, the parents captured in their crude essence. He tries to imagine having this. He must have, once. The memory is foggy: the warmth of school, the promise of food, the freedom of playtime. Akash is there too, big beam and shared sandwiches.

But no. That's not what Finlay's answer would be. It would be *someone who lies on the other side of a bathroom door.* That was, and still is, the prevailing definition. The ache comes as it always does. It's no longer a nerve-collapsing spasm, but from the pain comes: *where is he now, is he all right, is he healthy, is he happy?* Finlay will never have an answer to those questions, though. He pushes them away as he always does, gathers up his cleaning supplies, and makes his way to the other bathroom.

Chapter Fifteen

BANJO

A week later, everyone at school avoids Banjo. He keeps going to athletics and Kyle doesn't kick up any fuss whatsoever. Banjo's near death must have made him re-evaluate some life choices. Or just drop the threats in the first place. Nobody speaks to him, actually, so Banjo goes to work as normal too.

The shift passes in a blur of dirty plates and screaming kids. Banjo's pretty sure Kyle's threats were hollow as a black hole. He's only just settled into a comfortable rhythm of mopping when Morag calls him over.

'Whut?' Banjo pants.

Morag takes Banjo's wrist, palm-up, and slaps an envelope into his hand.

Banjo blinks.

'Wages,' she says.

Banjo stares down at them. He forgot that was the whole fucking point.

'So . . .' Morag grins.

Lizzy, who only really works weekends so Banjo has been getting to know here and there, comes out holding a plate covered by her hand.

'Congratulations!' they both shout.

Lizzy's hand falls to reveal a cupcake with a lit candle.

'Just a little ceremony for your first month,' Morag explains.

'This ... fur me?' he asks.

Lizzy laughs. 'Of course!'

Banjo takes the plate from Lizzy. Nobody has ever given him a cupcake, or made a ceremony over him. His ribcage tightens. They're so nice it hurts. It's like the Paula and Henry Effect.

Morag jumps up and down on the spot even though she's sweated her entire weight today and is still red in the face. 'Go on, blow it out!'

Banjo blows it out, pretty badly, but it gets the job done.

'What you wish for?' Morag grins.

'Uh, nuthin'.' Banjo frowns.

Morag covers her face. 'Oh God.' She laughs. 'Banjo, you're a special something.'

They watch him, though, so Banjo takes a bite. His last break was about three hours ago, and he hasn't eaten since. Horrifically, a familiar sting presses against his eyelids. Banjo's seriously about to start crying over a *cupcake*. He swallows quick before he can. 'Brill'ant,' he warbles.

Lizzy laughs.

'Hmm.' Morag puts a finger to her chin, looking over his head. 'I wonder what that new addition to the *wall* is ...'

Banjo nearly drops the entire plate.

'Whut – did Alena put – do the 'hing?' His cheeks burst into flames.

'Well, you've *yet* to look.' Morag lifts her brows.

Banjo feels paralysed.

The idea that there's a photo of him on a wall makes his stomach shrivel up and die. But another part of him wants to rush over and see what Alena's written about it.

Banjo sets the rest of his cupcake gently on the counter.

The Wall of Employees is still where he remembers it. The closer he gets, the bigger the wall grows. The more the cluster begins to take shape and separate into individual pictures.

Banjo stands right in front of it. He scans all the empty spaces, but he can't see anything.

'Banjo.' Morag appears at his side. 'It's right in front of you. She put you in the middle.'

Banjo blinks.

It doesn't even look like him. Banjo remembers laughing, standing by the entrance of the café, but it's different to actually see it. His apron is pristine clean – not in its currently knotted, crusted state. His hands are in his pockets, half-bent as he twists away from the camera.

But he's grinning straight down the lens. Straight at Alena.

'Of course she put that one.' Morag huffs over his shoulder. 'Alena makes such a big deal about how people look away from the camera. How the lens is the *window to the soul.*'

Banjo finally looks at the word. It's not written in small print

100

beneath his feet. It's written in bold above his head. His eyes scan it until he beams. *Brave*.

The whole week drags until Friday. Banjo's shift starts in twenty minutes and Alena is working too. They're open until 8 p.m. on Fridays for the late-night students and the friends catching up, and Paula and Henry know he walks straight over from school and eats there.

But it'll be the first time Banjo's seen Alena since the photo. So of course last-period geography runs over. After the bell rings, Mrs Mulley wants to keep discussing the topic.

'Not finished yet.' She holds up a hand. 'I still want to know what we can do to reduce carbon dioxide in the atmosphere. You'll be the ones to figure this out in the future, you know.'

There's a full minute of silence.

'Anyone?'

The whole class is mute, willing the lesson to end.

'Can nobody give me *one* factor in reducing CO_2?'

'Ah dunno, miss.' Banjo's voice is loud in the quiet room. 'Breathe less?'

There's a few snickers.

Mrs Mulley raises her eyebrows. 'Do you think that's funny?'

Banjo scratches his eyebrow. 'Answered.' He's not trying to be funny. He just wants this to be over.

But then he's sitting in front of Headmistress. She gives him a load of eyebrow action, unimpressed, but Banjo doesn't break eye contact. He watched a nature documentary where it worked.

This time it backfires.

Suspended. For one day. They're calling it 'persistent opposition to authority'. Because he *answered*.

Paula arrives soon after that. Banjo's too pissed off to care. He'll have to sit through this speech before he can go to work, obviously.

'Are you listening?' Paula asks him, arms crossed, blocking the exit to the reception area.

'No.' Banjo's sitting on one of the plastic chairs, knee bouncing like it's ready to bolt off without him. 'I wannae go.'

'You're not going until you explain yourself,' Paula says calmly. 'First you're getting into fights, now you're suspended?'

'Oh my *God*, I need tae *go*!' Banjo fists all his hair in one hand: feels as if he's being revved up like an engine on the brink of fucking *explosion*.

'Where? To work?' Paula asks. 'Maybe that's what's interfering with school.'

'No it's not! Jesus Christ, I *need-tae-go*!' Banjo slaps his forehead with the heel of his palm three times, feels as if his skin is being peeled off in small sections.

'Well, I'm sorry Banjo, but you're grounded,' Paula states.

'WHAT?' Banjo jumps to his feet.

'I really didn't want to have to do this, but if work is getting in the way—'

'Oh my God, it's *wan day*! Am suspended fur—'

'And you know what happens next, Banjo, it's expulsion—'

'I answered!' Banjo cries. 'I fucken *answered*! It's no' fair, aw a fucken did wus *answer*!'

'That's not how I've heard it,' Paula starts, 'And I think getting to work after school is too much pressure, I can call them and explain, they can change your shifts—'

'Ye cannae dae this!' He's ready to go ballistic. How can any of this be fair? He can't just change his working pattern willy fucking nilly; he needs to go or he'll lose it – his job, his life, Alena, all down the drain. 'Yer no' ma fuckin' *MAW*!' It comes out paper thin, like the screech of a fucking seagull, and the mortification burns alongside everything else.

'What is this all about, Banjo?' Paula asks, her voice going soft like a cheese grater along his fucking face.

'*Nothing!*' Banjo shouts, desperation clawing at his insides, gnawing with blunt teeth, wanting out. It's literally about *nothing*. Why does there have to be something? Why can't he just want to *leave*, why can't he have a *life* he cares about?

'Is this because—'

'Oh my fuck-*ing* God! *It's aboot nuthin'!*' Banjo cries, takes a chair by its legs and flings it across the room. It clatters against the wall so hard it sounds like a bomb.

Paula staggers back, chalk-white.

He hates that face. It makes him feel sick. His hands are shaking, rage or terror or a mixture of both. He's seen that face. He knows what it can do. No dinner, no internet, new placement, new school. He'll lose everything.

Sweat prickles over his skin like tiny insects.

Paula doesn't say anything. She takes him home in silence.

*

Banjo calls Morag the second he's back at Paula and Henry's – ignoring their offers to do it for him and slamming the door to his room shut. It all spills out his mouth in a nonsense babble.

'Am so sorry, Morag, am absolutely curled up wae the flu, a can barely get outtae bed—'

'Oh no!' Morag's voice floods down the line so understanding, so apologetic. 'Take all the time you need, I heard something's going around.'

Her kindness makes it worse. Banjo actually wanted to get shouted at.

He's 'grounded' for a whole week. Not technically; he's still allowed outside, still allowed to go to athletics, still allowed to do everything he normally does. But Paula tells Banjo to change his shifts to the weekends, she's putting her foot down 'for his benefit', and that means an entire fucking week without work, because they already had staff for the weekend.

He's quiet as he moves around the house. They don't talk to him. Banjo knows he upset Paula. She's well within her rights to return him to his worker, Louise, to call this some type of 'violent incident' and then it's back to square nothing: trying to find him a new place, speeches from Louise about his future, living out of a bin bag.

So Banjo does as told, does all his homework, does all the classwork, puts a date in the margin, acts the star pupil. Prays *please don't throw me away, please don't throw me away.* Not the bin bags, not the bin bags, not the bin bags.

He studies until he has an ache in his back and cramp in his hand and finishes his homework to go to sleep to go to school to get more homework.

He collects his dinner left out for him and lingers by the living-room door. Paula and Henry are watching TV. They don't speak to him. They don't invite him in. His shadow spills across the carpet like some deformed monster. He looks at it and he hates it, this hulking creature he has to fucking live inside.

Obviously Paula and Henry don't like him. Why did he even think he could settle here? Make something here? Another argument and it's over.

He eats alone.

At the end of the week, Banjo wakes up early enough that the sun hasn't even appeared. He goes to sit on their back porch, the damp concrete slab with weeds bursting out the cracks, their tiny back garden with its little patch of grass and stonework and clothesline. It's too cold to be sitting outside shirtless in pyjama bottoms, but there's the wild, restless feeling in the pit of his stomach again like he might tear at his own skin just to get it out. His ribcage feels as if it's shrinking, collapsing in on itself, and he needs to be outside, somewhere with space, somewhere *in space*.

He yanks out his phone and finds Finlay's contact.

It's the closest he's ever come to giving in. For one wild second Banjo thinks he will. Finlay's voice is the only cure to this fucking feeling, but Banjo can't bring himself. *I made a mistake, I made a mistake*, the speech starts up in his head, the words he's practised so long now, *I know there's no way to say sorry but I made a mistake.*

Banjo shoves his phone away. The anger is so strong it seeps through his bones and vibrates his body. It's like acid inside his throat: his teeth ache to keep from crying, his throat stings with the tears, and he can feel it in his gums and jaw, this aching anger, and wants to scream with it, scream so hard his lungs burn and his voice breaks.

Chapter Sixteen

FINLAY

The essay that Finlay promised himself he'd finish after work still isn't complete a week later. Finlay attributes this to two things.

There's construction happening outside Finlay's flat and right next to the university library. It would wake anyone quicker than a gunshot. The first day it started, Finlay thought it *was* a gunshot. It was just the drill accidentally starting up and cutting out.

Now, the familiar sound of concrete breaking splits his eardrums every morning.

The other issue is work. His hours are split over the week: 6 to 8 a.m. Monday to Friday. The locations of the schools vary; sometimes they're a short walk and sometimes they're a forty-minute cycle.

It's not a terrible job. Finlay likes it. Janet gives him a uniform that makes him feel like the regular housewife-slash-janitor. Blue cargo trousers with too many pockets, a stiff blue tunic, and a huge pair of safety boots.

Still, Finlay is happy for the opportunity to make money, and it's peaceful being alone. He settles into a routine of typing in the code, taking out the bins, and making himself tea in the staffroom. Finlay's come to learn that a sweet, strong cup of tea at 6.10 a.m. is the only way he can wake up. He holds it in both hands for warmth and sleeps while standing for five minutes.

The job isn't the problem. The problem is when he comes back to his flat at 8 a.m., the construction work is just starting up. The chance of a nap between now and his 10 a.m. lecture is impossible. Then when Finlay finishes class for the day and goes to make dinner it's *still* going on. There is virtually no time or place for him to focus.

why has it not stopped? Finlay sends into the group chat with the girls.

did u not see? Derya replies, then adds a photo.

Finlay clicks on it. It's a poster at the entrance to their flat.

Extended Working Hours

His eyes scan the words *essential road development work*, and *due to necessity*, and *extended working hours in order to reduce overall site occupation*, and *duly apologetic to any disturbances caused*.

Finlay pushes his thumb into the pressure point behind his eye where it throbs. The deadline for this essay is tonight. He's barely able to think inside his own head, never mind unscramble his thoughts into an academic essay. He gives it a solid attempt, but after another hour, Finlay doesn't have the energy to hold his head upright. He presses submit on what he's got and hopes for the best.

*

'Do you know why I've called you in today, Finlay?' his academic supervisor, Grace, asks.

Finlay nods before he speaks. 'Um, yes, because I failed.' He presses his hands flat between his knees to keep them still. 'The Nursing Care assignment,' he tacks on. His stomach cramps so hard that he has to bend over just slightly where he sits.

'Not exactly. Don't look so nervous!' Grace laughs. 'You're not in trouble!'

That does nothing to ease the stress.

When Finlay signed up for university, there were a few questions on the application. One asked if he was a care leaver. It talked of special provisions and additional support. It seemed like it would just be more check-ins and hassle. And he didn't know who was granted access to that information. He selected no.

'I just want to chat,' Grace assures him. 'I noticed you're one of our recipients of the Talent Scholarship. That's incredible; it was really competitive this year.'

Finlay would not be here without that funding. It's called a Talent Scholarship, but it's not. It's a hardship scholarship. He had to submit evidence of how hard he's been scraping the bottom of the barrel his entire life. That said, surviving a cost-of living-crisis is nothing if not a talent.

'What happened?' Grace asks. 'Half the essay's missing. It doesn't even meet the minimum word count.'

'I know, I know.' Finlay starts bobbing his head. 'I started a new job and I'm doing a bit of overtime while they're short – I thought it would be better to submit something rather than miss the deadline.'

'You could have asked for an extension.' Grace gestures. 'These things happen, but we need to know, Finlay, before we receive half an essay.'

An extension? On what grounds – *I'm busy right now, please just give me it?*

'Um ...' Finlay tries. 'I thought extensions were for illnesses and stuff.'

Grace shakes her head. 'Nope. Anything less than a week, normally a few days, doesn't need a doctor's note.'

Oh. Finlay feels idiocy sweep through him. He never even asked. Why didn't he *ask*?

'I feel I should say, though,' Grace begins. Finlay's stomach starts wringing itself out. 'This course is intense. When placement starts, I doubt you'll manage to do many hours at your job.'

Finlay stares. 'Right.'

'As I said, the Talent Scholarship was competitive, and we can really only offer it to students who are going to give their all. I need to know that's you, Finlay.' She gives him these big, imploring eyes.

It's not a threat. Grace could not be less threatening. But considering the fact the funding is renewed every year, Finlay's kind of depending on it. The knowledge it could be unceremoniously ripped away at any time is not enjoyable.

'Um ...' Finlay murmurs. 'So, next year if I don't manage the grades, it'll be given to someone else?'

'Well, if you keep submitting half essays, Finlay, you might not be here next year,' Grace jokes, but given the audience it falls flat.

She notices. 'Look, I really don't want to scare you, and if you're struggling to meet deadlines there's loads we can do, but we *do* need you to tell us.'

'Of course.' Finlay nods, mouth dry. 'It won't happen again.'

She's just doing her job. She probably enjoys giving this speech as much as Finlay enjoys hearing it. He can't be the worst student ever but it's absolutely impossible not to feel it. He considers dropping out right there on the spot. To stop himself, Finlay collects his stuff and leaves. He just about makes it to the bathroom before he hyperventilates so hard he retches up everything in his stomach. Which is not much, considering his general lack of appetite, money to buy food, and time to eat. One week. He's got one week to finish the essay.

Jun and Derya want to celebrate the assignment being over, and Finlay wants to celebrate for them. He doesn't tell them he failed. They'll only be concerned, it'll only put a dampener on the night, and they don't deserve that. They deserve to have fun.

Over the last few weeks of coffees and lectures, he's grown closer to the girls – close enough to call them friends. That very thing he was terrified and exhilarated by the mere thought of.

But instead of going out like normal students (which would probably cost an arm, a leg, a kidney, and selling some feet pictures on the internet), the girls decide to create their own pub night in Derya's room.

When Finlay shows up with a bottle of Tesco's cheapest white wine, Derya opens her door to a set-up almost identical to his own.

'Welcome, welcome.' She steps aside and takes the wine when Finlay offers.

Finlay quickly regrets that decision when it leaves his hands with nothing to do. He holds them out in front of himself before stuffing them under his armpits.

'Lovely.' He smiles, glancing around with his shoulders stiff up by his ears.

She's done things with the space, of course. Nobody except Finlay would leave their room bare. There's a noticeboard above her desk with random sticky notes, postcards with paintings of cats pinned up by thumbtacks. There's a string of fairy lights along her headboard, throw pillows and stuffed toys strewn across her bed. Her laptop sits open on her desk and plugged into the wall, bowls of crisps and popcorn beside it.

'It looks great in here.' Finlay beams. They've not had much opportunity to socialise outside of lectures: he has no idea what to say.

'Thanks!' Derya sets his wine on the drawer beside her bed. 'It's not much, but it's nice to try and make the place feel lived-in.'

He watches her move around as if she knows exactly where everything is. It even smells like Derya: her light, clean smell. It must be a mixture of her clothes, her things, her sheets, every little piece that makes her a whole person. A wash of fondness comes over him. It feels as though she's offering him an insight into her life.

There's a knock. Finlay finds Jun at the door, dishevelled from the rain, brown parka zipped up to her chin. She exhales in lieu of a hello, dropping her bag, which makes an ominous thud.

'Alcohol,' she explains, jumping on to Derya's bed, her wedge boots dangling over the edge.

Finlay laughs, but something sharp twists inside his stomach at how easily she makes herself at home. He wonders if she's been in here before.

'I *ran* to Sainsbury's before it shut,' Jun explains. 'I'm sweating in places you shouldn't sweat.'

'Oh, sure, lemme just give you the tour!' Derya calls out, pouring Finlay's wine into some mugs.

This is Jun's first time here. What is he even thinking? Of course Jun and Derya haven't been planning secret outings alone. Even if they did, would that be awful? He squashes down his ugly jealousy and tries to remember this is supposed to be *fun*.

Derya hands him a mug of wine. Finlay takes a delicate sip before he wrinkles his nose. He didn't know what to expect, but not a mouthful of vinegar.

'Finlay!' Derya gapes, handing a mug to Jun, who pushes her shoes off and accepts. 'We're meant to cheers first!'

'Oh! Sorry!' Finlay holds up a finger, and feels daring enough to joke: 'I'll regurgitate it, two seconds.'

'*Ew!*' she cries, but she's laughing and smacks him playfully. The joke landed. Finlay's relief and joy are instantaneous. Some of the tension he's holding lifts away. Derya's touch is gentle, resonating through him. Finlay can be oversensitive and raw sometimes, but thankfully today is not one of those days.

'Cheers!' Jun thrusts her mug up to the both of them. They all delicately clink. Derya collects her laptop from her desk.

'Movie?' she asks.

They get settled in. Finlay takes off his shoes and joins Jun on the bed. Derya's just wearing slippers so she hops in too, meaning Finlay is pressed in between them. Their warmth and soft skin surrounds him, their flowery smells, their small bodies. He forces himself not to pull away and tries to appreciate this rare human contact. He dreams about warmth, a kind hand. Now it's here he's too terrified he can't accept it normally. He'll break down or grip on to it. Finlay forces his body to relax.

Jun scrolls Netflix for twenty minutes and Derya disagrees with every halfway decent-looking film until Finlay steals the laptop and clicks on the first thing trending: some romantic comedy that looks appropriately light-hearted and risk-free.

Five minutes in Derya jumps up to get the abandoned snacks, so the movie is paused. After another five minutes, Jun has commented on everything including, 'Why did she just make that face, I thought she liked him?' and 'What a stupid plot device, as if anyone gets homework over the summer.'

Finlay's barely even following the plot. Which is why – when the male lead becomes shirtless spontaneously and Derya says, '*Now* we're talking' – Finlay hums.

He's not thinking when he does it. It's not a disinterested, casual-input hum. It's a *hum*. An interested hum. A *yes-I-agree-that-guy-is-attractive* hum.

He might've played it off as nothing if he hadn't tensed as stiff as a plank. And because the girls are so close, they notice.

Derya and Jun pause to look at him.

'Finlay?' Jun asks, stopping the film, a handful of popcorn midway to her mouth. 'What's wrong?'

Finlay blinks wide eyes at the screen. 'Uh.'

'You know we're totally cool with you being gay,' Jun says.

Finlay ... did not know that. Nope.

Jun covers her mouth in horror. 'Are you not? I'm so sorry, I didn't mean—'

Finlay can't help the laughter that barks out, high-pitched and sharp. 'No, I – I am,' he says, a little crazed, because somehow the words are out. 'I'm gay.'

Derya and Jun physically sag, their bodies melting into him.

Finlay laughs. His heart pounds somewhere in the vicinity of his fingertips, oddly displaced. 'I did not expect this.'

'Why?' Jun frowns. 'Finlay, I'm *bi*, I'd never –'

'No, I know.' Finlay swallows, his saliva thick and pasty. 'This is just the first time, um ...' *I've said the words out loud.*

Gay. *I'm gay.*

There's a beat.

Jun and Derya stare at him.

'What?' Finlay asks shakily. His throat hurts.

'This is the first time you've come out?' Derya asks.

Finlay swallows. He nods.

'Oh my God!' Jun straightens up, eyes wide, expression bright. 'We need to celebrate!'

Finlay blinks.

Derya runs over to her desk and comes back with a bottle of unopened wine.

Finlay laughs, a little tinged with hysteria because he has no idea what they're going to do. 'Girls, really, it's not that important—'

'Finlay, you came out to us,' Jun states, a hand on his shoulder melting warmth. 'It means a lot. We want to celebrate!'

Finlay's eyes sting, abruptly overcome. *Celebrate.* He forces a grin and slaps his thighs. 'Right, then! Let's celebrate.'

Derya opens the bottle and takes a swig before she passes it over, and then they look through a list of cheesy gay movies and fight over the laptop because Finlay is *not* watching the one with two *basically* naked men on the cover.

'Come on, it'll be fun!' Derya laughs, falling over as Finlay tackles her.

'I'm seriously not—' he shouts, but they press it on anyway.

It starts with them *being naked*.

Finlay cries, covers his eyes, and takes a mouthful of wine blindly, but they're all laughing and the movie plays. Finlay feels so light it's as if there's nothing inside him, as if he's completely empty. He ends up so tipsy his fingers feel like small heaters as he blurts out: 'I can't believe I'm gay.'

In that moment it seems ridiculous. It seems utterly absurd coming out his mouth.

Jun stares. Then she laughs, curling towards him. Finlay feels it infect him too, his laughter big and loud. Derya flaps a silent hand.

'I'm really gay,' Finlay repeats, but this time it's warm and true.

'Own it, Finlay!' Jun shouts. 'You need to *own* it—'

'I'm gay!' Finlay beams. 'Completely gay!'

'Louder!' Derya raises her mug.

Finlay jumps up on the bed, tipsy, and holds both arms out. 'I'm GAY!'

Jun and Derya are in hysterics, so Finlay steps up to the end of the bed as though they're in a musical, plants both feet, expands his chest, and sings, slowly raising one hand to the sky: 'I'MA *GAAAAAY*—'

There's a crack: Derya's bed breaks right in the middle. It throws them all together. Finlay falls on his arse, whipping around in terror to apologise. Jun and Derya are howling with laughter, clinging on to one another, clinging on to him. Finlay's powerless to do anything but laugh so hard, for so long, it feels as though he's setting something free.

Finlay walks back to his own room in a sort of daze. The adrenaline of terror washing into joy has frayed his nerves apart. But something else is in there too, an unknown emotion, a sadness for his younger self. The wish for that younger self to see him right now.

Finlay feels both intensely happy that Jun and Derya know and terrified of how this changes things. His distance is crumbling.

The silence that greets him in his room is heavy. He looks around and compares it to Derya's. There're no fairy lights, no photos, no books. Nothing. He brought nothing with him, never intended to, and meant to carry on life that way.

Finlay walks over to his duffel. He pulls it on to his bed and opens it up. He starts to unpack. Puts his rolled-up socks in the drawers and hangs his trousers up in the wardrobe. Once he's done, his bag is empty but the room doesn't feel any less bare.

Finlay stands in the middle and breathes. He tries to absorb this room, this life, this person. He walks over to the wall and touches it. He lays his fingertips down gently, running them along the rough exterior. He touches his bookcase, strokes his smooth desk. He sits on the floor, sinks his fingers into the soft carpet. He lies down on his stomach, presses his cheek to the fabric, smells its musty, fibrous old smell.

He closes his eyes. He's on the floor at St Andrews; he's on the other side of a gap.

Chapter Seventeen

BANJO

Banjo needs to get back into Paula and Henry's good books. Although he's still grounded because he threw that chair, he knows he can butter them up enough to get them to give in early and let him go back to work.

At the same time, though, Banjo can't really stand the icy silence between them. Despite the fact he's rejected their every offer of kindness, niceness, and overall good foster parenting.

At first it just made sense. Soon enough they'll start to realise Banjo isn't the long-lost son they've always wanted, or the perfect helper for household chores. But now, Banjo is willing to pretend: he's got a life here.

He starts with an apology. Because he can't bear their disappointed faces or striking up a conversation in the silence, he writes it on a scrap of paper. *Sorry.* He leaves it on the kitchen counter.

When Banjo comes home after school, there's a note waiting for him. *Thank you.* It has a little smiley beside it.

They're still at work for the next hour. He thumbs the note for a minute, the indent of Paula's handwriting. He cooks the pizza in the fridge and leaves some for them in the oven.

Once the ban lifts, as if being freed from prison, Banjo's allowed to work again. It sounds soppy as all hell, but Banjo wants to see everyone. Fuck it, he wants to see *her*. The weekend rolls itself around and Banjo is flopping about trying to get his trainers on, shoving a jacket over his work clothes and cycling with the speed of Chris Hoy to the café.

He's so excited that it just bursts out as soon as he steps in.

'Alena!'

God, his happiness is all over the space. He's not even got his *apron* on. He might as well be naked for all he's covering his arse.

Alena spots him over the top of a crate of lemonade and beams.

'Banjo!' she cries. 'It's *Banjo*!' She sets the box down on a spare table and starts dancing. 'Banjo's back!' she sings as she twists about all awkward: elbows out, knees wobbling, a complete dork.

Banjo's laughter barks out, weird and unpractised. He can't help himself; comes up to dance beside her, not really any better at it, mostly stiff and unsure, twisting his arms like some kind of chicken. Actually, no, scratch that: he probably looks like a stark-raving lunatic, dancing over the fact he's got an eight-hour shift in a grimy, dirty-dish-infested, cheese-crusted café. Christ if he's not happy about it.

The only problem is that Banjo can't really *talk* to Alena. Not the way he wants to. Not the way she can talk to him. Alena can

120

chatter about anything, but Banjo can't join in; can't share things like where he grew up, what schools he went to, if he's ever had pets, *whereabouts he stays.*

If Banjo confesses any of that, then he tells her everything. Because the questions wouldn't stop, and he's not got any believable lies. It only opens more cans. So it creates this terrible distance between them, every time he answers her innocent conversation starters with another version of, 'Aw, I don' really remember, tellin' the truth.'

Banjo knows almost all there is to know about Alena. He knows her favourite subjects (art, modern studies, history), her least (maths, chemistry), that she doesn't like coleslaw, chews on her thumbnail when she's thinking, plays netball and tennis, loves photography, is two inches shorter than him. Banjo stores the information away as though he's preparing for an exam.

Yet Alena, Morag, Lizzy, none of them know Banjo's in care. None of them know *why* he's in care. And he doesn't want that to change. He doesn't want *them* to change.

At least not right now. He's never been handed the ability to fucking ... *work up to it.* It's always been ripped away from him. It feels as though everyone he's ever met, everyone who's so much as looked at Banjo, has known. And it gives them this control over him, this peering insight that makes his skin feel raw.

Banjo never expected to keep it a secret at St Triduana, so it hardly mattered when word got around.

But it matters now. Maybe because he can do it on his own terms, in his own way. He can have the control for once.

Which would be great if he wasn't constantly on edge, expecting Kyle to waltz back in and drop it like a bomb, or Paula and Henry to swing by one afternoon and let it all slip, and Alena will look at him totally different, she'll look and she'll see a *liar*.

Or maybe Banjo can't have a good thing and not think it'll end in disaster. The last good thing did. Obviously.

But something miraculous happens. Something incomprehensible. Something damn near religious.

Alena asks him round to her house for dinner.

'Ye . . .' Banjo tries, milk jug held over a latte glass. 'Whut?'

'Come to mine.' Alena smiles. Her hair is down today, soft brown all around her shoulders, tucked behind both ears, small jewels in her lobes. She's literally heaven.

'Why?'

Is Banjo actually pissing in the face of this?

'Because it's the easiest way to set up an account,' Alena informs, hands on hips.

'Aw, no' this again,' Banjo groans. She won't quit about the fact Banjo isn't on any form of social media.

'It's happening.' Alena waggles her finger. 'Just accept it.'

'Whit am I gonnae use it fur?'

'To connect to the world!' Alena gestures to the skies.

'Tae who?'

'Me!' Alena spins around to get back to work, but she's smiling. Banjo's face burns the whole fucking day.

*

He remembers to text Paula before she calls the police: *going to a pal's for dinner.* They are pals. That's what they are. It would just be nice if he weren't half in love with her.

Having dinner at Alena's house isn't so much a reminder of the fact that he doesn't have parents, but more like stepping into a life he'll never have.

He cycles over after a shower, while everyone is still out. Alena told him to come as he was – straight from work – but Banjo looked down at himself and decided his first impression on her family wasn't going to include tomato-soup stains.

As it stands, Alena's house is pretty easy to find. It's not too far out. Banjo sets his bike against the terraced building with washed-out cream bricks, front window with the curtains drawn, flat steps leading up to the white door. Some knot eases in his gut to know that Alena isn't one of those random rich people with a mansion in the middle of nowhere, Thorntonhall.

Banjo steps up to the door and knocks.

Alena opens up with a wide grin, a cropped black T-shirt and jeans on.

'Hiya.'

'Hey.'

There's an awkward pause.

'Banjo's here!' Alena turns and shouts into the empty air.

Banjo peers around her, catches a glimpse of a woman in the kitchen, who waves, before Alena takes Banjo's wrist and pulls him up the stairs.

They stamp up to Alena's room. Banjo's heart is beating in his palms, inside the pads of his fucking *fingertips*. Her room is quite plain. There's a white desk filled with paper and pens, an open laptop, a long collection of photos above her bed, a small fluffy beige carpet, and some teddies lined up along her pillow.

'Come sit.' Alena pats the bed. 'I can set it up on my phone.'

Banjo sits.

'So. First things first – name.'

'Banjo?'

'No.' Alena laughs. '*Last* name.'

'Oh. Murray.'

'Nice.' Alena nods.

Banjo wrinkles his nose. 'No' a fan.' His stomach clenches. The memory of their faces as they were called in. *Mr and Mrs Murray, I'm so sorry to bother you, but Banjo has been very disruptive.* The look he got from those words. The tight grip on his arm.

He swallows it down like a sour taste.

'Try Lekkas,' Alena states, pulling him back to the moment.

Banjo frowns. 'But that's cool.'

'It's Greek. Along with half my family.'

Banjo smiles and gives her a nudge. 'See? Pretty cool.'

'We're supposed to be making *your* account, not mine,' Alena reminds him.

Banjo laughs. It's not funny, but sometimes Banjo laughs when he's around her because he's happy. Their shoulders almost touch they're sitting so close together. His fingertips pulsate again. He's not been this close to someone in fucking forever.

'Right. We need a profile picture.' Alena reaches under her bed and brings out her camera. 'I think I still have the ones from the café. They're actually really good.' She crosses over to her laptop and connects the camera with a little wire plug.

Banjo watches her fiddle about. 'How long ye been taken photos?'

Alena shrugs her back at him. 'Picked it up, really. Just always loved it.'

'Yer brilliant,' Banjo blurts, then blushes to his roots.

Alena turns with a smile. 'Thanks. I don't really know what to do with them, though.'

'Well. Plenty ae 'hings tae dae wae them,' Banjo begins. 'Can stick 'em on the wall, fur one—'

'No, I mean in the *future*.' Alena laughs as she comes over, holding a scrapbook she picked up on her desk. As she sits down, something flutters out the pages.

Banjo bends to pick it up.

'What—' Alena scrambles.

Banjo pauses. Because it's him. He's looking at himself.

Hanging up in the café is the one with Banjo grinning wide to the camera. But this one is Banjo hunched in laughter, hands in pockets, body twisted away.

'I just – I make collages with all the photos I take, it's not—' Alena starts babbling.

Banjo squints. There are words scrawled along the edge.

Happiness

Charm

Dignity

Humour??

'I have a hard time naming them, I know it probably sounds stupid but I like to get it right.' Alena laughs again, but she tugs on the edge of the photo with no little insistence. Her face is so red Banjo can *feel* the heat. It makes Banjo go hot and clammy, but a smile unfolds on his face, big and, dare he say, fucking *bashful*. She kept a photo of him. That's something.

'Why'd ye keep it?' he asks, his voice croaky-soft.

Alena's mouth drops open. Banjo's actually making her flustered. Christ but it's a feeling.

'It's not as if there are hearts on it!' she cries.

Banjo's eyebrows go sky high. *'Hearts?'* He's even louder.

Alena grows even more frantic. 'I just mean this looks weirder than it is—'

Banjo laughs, a freer sound than normal. 'Ena, chill.' He doesn't even register the fact he's given her a nickname.

'Ena?' Alena grins, and Banjo goes to explain until she says, 'I like it. Sounds edgy.'

Banjo grins back, glowing at this point. 'Ena it is.'

Then he stands, strolls over to her desk, and snatches a highlighter. He uncaps it with his teeth, holds the lid there, and circles the word *happiness*.

'Got it right the first time.' He speaks around the cap and points the end of the pen at it.

Alena's eyes crease in a smile. Banjo flushes hot and cold like he could run a mile just for the sake of it. He wants to speak. He caps the pen.

The sound of thundering feet startles them both. There's a slam.

'Jace!' a woman – Banjo assumes Alena's mum – shouts.

'*What?*' a girl cries. She sounds young, maybe not even teens.

'Slamming!' Alena replies.

'Need the loo!'

Banjo bites his lip to keep from grinning. Alena turns to him.

''Ello there!' This time the voice in the hallway is distinctly older, and clearly male.

Before Banjo can react, a man pops his head round the door.

'What's going on?' he asks. His shirt collar is undone, tie pulled down. He looks like Alena. His hair is darker, shorter. His eyes are the same. This is clearly Alena's dad. Banjo's pulse kicks up.

'Jace slammed the door,' Alena tells him.

The man looks from Banjo to Alena. 'Right.' He raises his eyebrows.

'Dad, this is Banjo,' Alena starts, as though rehearsed. 'He's a friend from work, we're just.' She turns to Banjo with a grin. 'What are we doing? We were supposed to be setting up your account.'

She laughs, then waits. Does she expect him to answer?

Banjo lifts his shoulders helplessly. 'Dunno, jus' got sidetracked wae the photos—'

'Oh, so *he* gets to see them?' Alena's dad glances at Banjo playfully. 'That's how it is, then.'

Alena groans. 'Dad—'

'No, I'm just saying.' He holds up his hands. 'I mean, Ben—'

'*Banjo*,' Alena interrupts.

Her dad's eyebrows skyrocket. '*Banjo*, right,' he says. 'Very unique. Any Greek?'

Alena covers her face with her hands. '*Dad.*'

Alena's dad pulls all kinds of innocent expressions. 'What! I knew someone called Banjo once—'

'Sure,' Alena scoffs.

'It's true.' Her dad winks at Banjo.

He *winks*. Banjo doesn't even know what to make of it.

'Oh my God, Dad, you can't *wink* at people any more!' Alena cries.

'This another thing that's uncool?' He looks to Banjo for help.

Banjo can't help grinning.

'No, it's just *weird*,' Alena says.

'Well, if that's the case,' her dad heaves a long sigh, 'I suppose I'll just go.'

'*Please*,' Alena groans as if it's killing her.

Banjo's cheeks hurt. He grins at Alena's dad. Her dad grins back before he shuts the door. His chest is warm.

'I'm so sorry about that,' Alena says once he's gone.

'Why?' Banjo laughs. 'I love him. Think he's fucken awesome.'

Alena goes still. She doesn't even blink. 'Literally nobody's ever said that in the history of the universe.'

Banjo laughs again.

Once they're called for dinner, Banjo skips downstairs to the smell of cooked food filling the air: warm steamed vegetables, hot meat, fresh bread, mingled flavours.

Banjo hovers as he takes in the scene before him. There's a table in the middle of the room, chairs lined up neat underneath. There's a lace tablecloth covering it, and in the corner of the room there's a sofa.

And this is where Banjo meets Alena's mum. She's placing bowls on the table: buttered bread, potato skins. There's so much. There's *too much*.

'This—' Banjo swallows.

Alena's mum looks up. She's wearing a soft-looking jumper, her short hair lighter than Alena's. Her skin is a little lighter too, with a thin nose and a kind mouth. There's something of Alena there. She waits patiently.

'Is this all – just. For dinner?' he manages. It looks like a spread at St Andrews where there was twice as many people.

'Of course! I'm feeding a small army.' Alena's mum laughs.

Banjo can't take his eyes off all the things on the table. It's like a restaurant.

'I – I,' Banjo tries, jerks a thumb to the door. It's just them in the room; Alena's in the kitchen. His voice goes low; he's trying not to be overheard. 'I can – I have money? Like, in my bag, if you—'

'What?' Her eyebrows shoot up. 'Don't be silly, it's just dinner! You're welcome any time.'

Banjo's throat is doing that weird thing again. He swallows thickly. 'Uh. Thanks, Mrs Lekkas.'

She smiles. 'Please, call me Julie.'

Banjo's face is probably as red as his hair. 'Rh – right.'

Then Alena comes through and sets three glasses of juice on the table.

'*Careful*, this isn't work,' Julie tuts.

Alena huffs. 'Please, I've carried twice as much in work.'

'Maybe so, but you don't need to here!' Julie calls after her.

'There're only two left!' Alena's voice floats from the kitchen.

Banjo stands in the middle of the room, a bit bereft and not entirely sure what to do.

'Can I – there anythin' tae do?' Banjo says, then edits that whole sentence because he can hear how thick his accent is. 'Is there anything I can *help* with?'

'Nope, you just sit down.' Julie waves.

Banjo scans the table. 'Cutlery!' he shouts. 'I'll do cutlery, I can—'

'It's Jace's turn,' Alena swings around the doorway to say.

Julie chuckles. 'Really, don't feel as if you have—'

'I want tae,' Banjo states, and his voice is clear.

Julie smiles, nods her head towards the door. 'Well then, we'll need cutlery.'

'It's *Jace's turn*,' Alena repeats.

'WHAT IS IT?' Jace cries, tumbling down the stairs and storming inside.

She can't be any older than twelve, thirteen at a push. Just a younger, scrawnier version of Alena. Everything is there: brown hair, brown eyes, light brown skin. Her hair is cropped close to her head, fringe tufted up. She looks a little harassed, and she must play football because she's wearing a school strip with muddy socks all the way up to her knees, grass stains along her front and on her nose.

'Jacintha, get changed; you're not sitting in that,' Julie says.

'I *was* changing, then you started *shouting my name*!' Jace/ Jacintha says defensively, until her eyes round on Banjo.

'Who are you?' she asks.

Banjo freezes.

'This is Banjo,' Julie explains. 'He's Alena's friend. He's over for dinner.'

'What?' Jace pulls a frown so hard it's a grimace. 'Since when does that happen? She's never—'

'Jace, it's *your turn*,' Alena hisses, giving her sister some kind of severe look, but her cheeks are scarlet.

Banjo's heart leaps out his chest and through the ceiling. *She's never had someone over.* It must mean something? *Or maybe it means friends.*

Jace huffs at Alena and tramples towards the kitchen.

Banjo darts in front. The kitchen is cluttered with all the evidence of a good life, a lived life, pots and pans, fridge magnets and mugs hanging on some little metal tree. He yanks open some random drawer and like jackpot finds all the cutlery in trays.

Jace frowns at him. Banjo gathers a pile of forks and nods to the stairs she came down.

Go. Make your escape.

Jace blinks, but slowly she starts to grin, creeping towards the staircase as if she's some vigilante spy.

Banjo smiles, then goes into the living room to set it out.

Alena rolls her eyes when she sees him, but she's smiling. Banjo knows he is too: feels the overworked muscles of his cheeks ache.

They move around one another like they do in work. They could be in that dingy back room right now, sweating with a million dishes to wash and another million orders to sort through. But this is better.

Jace reappears in a matter of minutes, wearing a T-shirt and shorts. Her fringe is damp as if she's just splashed her face. She sits down and reaches for a roll.

'Patience.' Julie taps her hand.

'I'm *starving*, it's *one* roll,' Jace moans.

Julie gives in with a sigh. Jace pumps her fist in victory.

Banjo watches. He tries not to look weird about it, but also can't help it. It's sort of fascinating. He's stayed at a lot of foster homes since he was ten, but most of the dinners were frosty and silent. He was an impostor. Some of them were nice, of course: people just wanting to help out an unfortunate case like himself. An endless circus of Paulas and Henrys. They smiled every few seconds, as if to show any other emotion would make Banjo flee. More often than not, it just made him uncomfortable.

Sometimes Banjo wonders who he'd be if he had parents. Someone better at school? Would it give him a reason, if he had people he wanted to make proud? If he had people that cared whether or not he was getting enough sleep or if he'd brushed his teeth that morning?

Julie runs both hands down Alena's shoulders as they pass

one another, just letting Alena know she's there. Banjo's never had that. Natural, unspoken touch. Even when he had Finlay. It looks so simple. It looks so nice.

'Banjo.' Alena motions to the chair beside her.

Banjo's throat is sore, picturing a pair of hands on his shoulders like that. He nods and tries to twist his face into a smile.

'Right, then, are we all set?' Alena's dad claps his hands as he enters. He's changed too, pristine collared shirt and tailored trousers swapped for a soft T-shirt, joggers, and fluffy slippers. He looks comfortable. Everyone looks so comfortable, as if this is their regular everyday.

Alena's dad gives Banjo this beam. Banjo thinks that's probably where Alena gets hers from. There are so many little things that make up Alena, so many people that created her. It feels a little unreal to watch all the evidence.

Banjo's quiet. He leans close to Alena. 'Uh. Alena, whut,' he whispers. 'Whut's yer da's name?'

'Dad, Banjo wants to know your name,' Alena says.

Banjo near *chokes*. 'Wh—' he splutters.

'Ah, Banjo, the age-old question,' Alena's dad begins, as if he's about to tell a story. 'Unfortunately, I've forgotten. Every dad does at one point. They just become "Dad".'

'Please just tell him.' Alena closes her eyes.

'Carlos,' her dad laughs. 'You can call me Carlos.'

Banjo bobs his head a few times. Then he pokes Alena in the leg. 'Total threw me under,' he mutters.

She just grins.

Julie appears. 'Right!' she says, and starts piling Banjo's plate with food.

First chicken, then vegetables, then potatoes, but then she doesn't *stop*. She's piling his plate for years. It becomes a small mountain in front of him.

'Uh, ye don't – I don't,' Banjo stutters.

Julie stops, spoon mid-air. 'Too much?'

Banjo shakes his head quick. 'No, jus' – I mean, thank you.' He looks at her as if to really show it.

Julie laughs, and then she shakes her head. 'You don't have to keep thanking me, sweetheart.'

Banjo's cheeks explode with fire. He's never been called fucking *sweetheart*. It makes his insides go weird.

Something brushes his leg. At first Banjo thinks it's Alena shifting in her seat, and he shifts over to give her some space.

Alena's knee touches his again. It's not moving away.

He freezes.

She must be able to feel his knee. She must *know* that's his knee.

'Well, then, let's eat!' Carlos starts.

Julie takes a seat, and then everyone's eating.

It just happens. As if on cue, everyone lifts their cutlery and digs in.

Banjo doesn't really know what to touch first.

Most of the food he eats doesn't require cutlery. Pizza, chips, sandwiches. Not a fully *home-cooked meal*.

As soon as Banjo tries a bit of chicken, all manners fly out his head. When he's hungry and starts eating, it's like starting to pee. There's no stopping it. He scoffs it down, one arm leaning on the table while the other shovels food in as fast as possible, until he feels silence descend on everyone.

Banjo glances up, mouth full. All eyes are on him. Alena's fork is mid-air.

He swallows. 'Sorry, jus'.' His cheeks sting, and he swallows. 'Hungry,' he manages.

Julie blinks. She holds up the bowl of wedges. 'Do you want some more?'

Banjo looks down at his plate. It's virtually finished. He nods. 'Yeah. 'Hanks.'

'I think we should have Banjo over every night,' Carlos states. 'He could help with the food waste.'

The tension disappears. Banjo cracks a grin, everyone laughs, and then they're back to eating. *Food waste*, Banjo thinks wildly. *Who the fuck is wasting this?*

'So, Banjo,' Carlos begins. 'What do you want to do after school? Any ideas yet?'

Banjo looks at them: their bright faces, their excited eyes, and for some reason he wants to tell the truth. He wants to give them something more than *I don't know*. 'Eh.' He scratches his eyebrow. 'Always quite fancied racing cars.'

It probably sounds bizarre. But it looks fun. Who the fuck doesn't want to have fun and get paid?

Alena rounds on him because he's never mentioned this a day in his life.

'Really?' Julie lifts her brows.

'No way!' Jace says, instantly intrigued. 'For real?'

Banjo nods, a bit embarrassed now at his left-field reply. 'Yeah.'

It doesn't really matter, though, does it? What he says is all fantasy and make-believe. Banjo will never do anything more than shovel chips into foam boxes or some other minimum-wage gig. What he actually *wants* to do is null and void.

'So how do you do that?' Carlos asks.

'Uh.' Banjo swallows, because truthfully he has no clue. He hasn't exactly thought that far ahead. 'Learnin' how tae drive might be a start.'

Everyone laughs. Banjo feels a warm flush of happiness spread over him.

'Other than that, somethin' tae do wae runnin'.' Banjo jerks a shoulder. It feels strange to admit this. To actually speak the words. Nobody's really asked before. 'Am on – I do athletics. Am oan the team.' It's not a brag, it's just a fact. But it makes his face hot when Alena whistles and Jace goes, 'Cool!'

'Whoa! So, something sporty?' Carlos asks.

Banjo nods. 'Yeah, I – yep.' He grins. 'Gimme sports and Ah'll be happy.'

'You wouldn't think it from looking at you,' Julie notes.

Banjo laughs, surprised.

Alena's eyes widen. *'Mum.'*

Julie shakes her head frantically. 'Oh, no, I just—'

Banjo laughs again. Alena's family are quite funny. 'It's aw'right, I hear it lots. Bit of a scrawny wee— guy.' Banjo just manages to stop himself from swearing and clears his throat. 'But, yeah, kindae the whole point in runnin'.'

'Well, you don't really see many bulky runners,' Carlos adds in support. 'They need to be quite slim, don't they?'

'Yeah, 'sactly,' Banjo agrees.

'So what do your parents do?' Julie asks.

Banjo doesn't know why he didn't expect this question. It's a valid question. It's something people ask any day of the week. Sunday afternoon talk. *What do your parents do?*

But Banjo stiffens. He doesn't say anything.

'Wu—' he waffles, racking his brains. Mortification burns his face like a flat iron. Banjo picks up his glass and swallows down some diluted juice. Everyone is watching. Waiting.

He couldn't tell them the truth. *I don't know. I haven't seen them since I was ten. They were in prison and now they're fuck knows where.*

But nobody can reply they *aren't sure* about their own parents.

'Uh – teachin'. They're teachers,' he croaks. 'Primary.'

Does it sound like a lie? A bald, naked lie? He can't look at Alena.

'Oh, really? That's nice,' Julie says, and everyone hums, and the conversation takes a turn to politics.

And it's that easy. Parents mean nothing. They're nothing.

'Please, am *so* serious—'

'Banjo, you're not washing the dishes!' Alena hip-checks him. 'Get out!'

'Ena, I spend enough ae ma life washin' dishes Ah never even *eat*.' Banjo nudges her back, thrumming with that small contact. 'I 'hink I can clean the ones where I *did*.'

'Don't—' Alena guards the basin, both arms spread.

'If he wants to help, let him!' Julie calls from the living room. She's clearing the table. Carlos is taking the bins out. Jace is upstairs.

It's just the two of them in the kitchen, the soft linoleum glow catching in Alena's hair, the warmth reflecting in her eyes. She's smiling. So is Banjo. He flicks her nose with soapy water. It makes her laugh. They wash up in relative comfort, the same way as always.

Only it's not the same – not really, because in the back room they're metres apart, and both harassed out their heads. Banjo practically flings dishes her way, and Alena stacks like it's an Olympic talent.

This is softer. Warmer. They wash side by side. Her body heat seeps into Banjo: their shoulders brushing with every movement.

Banjo barely knows what to do with himself. He barely knows how to use his *hands*.

Alena's hair smells faintly of flowers, like fields during the summer. Banjo's hair mostly smells of grease and dandruff and *hair*. He'll never know how girls do it. Some magic.

'You have a good time?' Alena's gaze is warm, voice quiet.

I don't know how to have this and not ruin it, Banjo thinks.

Banjo thinks about Finlay almost daily now. That's the problem with opening up a crack, with unsewing a poorly-fucking-done stitch. All the rot and the pus comes out too. All that pain needs to flush out.

Banjo finds himself picturing Finlay at the table. He finds himself looking for the spot where Finlay should be. He's been ignoring that spot – that supermassive hole in his life. It feels as though he's edging closer to it every day.

But Banjo can't say any of that to Alena. He just smiles, and nods, and keeps his balance at the edge.

Chapter Eighteen

FINLAY

Finlay inexplicably *still* hasn't completed the dreaded assignment three days later. It's almost harder not to finish it than just to press submit. Every time he tries to work on it, he remembers the fact that this is his last chance, that if he fails again he could be out of university. And then he can't write a single word.

It's also been nearly two weeks since he saw Akash. Although Finlay knows Akash asked him to message, he starts to think Akash was just being nice. A friendly *see you soon!* It was good to catch up, but there's no obligation to uphold a friendship they had ten years ago. And although Finlay misses him, that feeling is precisely the reason he doesn't get in touch.

He also hasn't seen the girls in a few days either. After he came out to them, this fragile nakedness started creeping in. Finlay feels oddly vulnerable that they know now, as though it gives them a greater insight into him, a more private reach. He needs to keep his distance, at least for a little while.

Plus Finlay has more pressing concerns. Because today is his first shift on placement.

It starts at 9 a.m., so he finishes his cleaning job at 8 a.m. and cycles to his flat to get showered and changed. He's mapped the route there and back. He's packed his lunch. He's set his clothes out. He's ready.

Finlay received his nursing uniform at the start of term. It's a zip-up navy tunic with the Glasgow logo stitched into the breast pocket, a huge pocket at either side, and a pair of navy drawstring trousers.

He's obviously tried it on a hundred times. He likes the fit, but every time he glances in the mirror it's as though he's trying on a Halloween costume. He doesn't feel like a nurse. He doesn't feel equipped to look after people. To put their life in his hands and confidently know what the fuck he's doing. So there's that.

He also doesn't know anyone at this placement. They found out a few weeks ago: Jun is in the gastroenterology ward at Queen Elizabeth University Hospital, the biggest hospital in Scotland, and Derya will be in radiology a bit further afield in the West End Clinic.

Finlay is residential: Silver Lodge Care Centre.

They've been split up. For the next two months. Although Finlay thinks it might be a good thing now, more of an excuse for why he can't see them, but at the time the confirmation deflated them.

'Well, I guess this is the last supper,' Finlay had announced in the common room when they found out, morosely stirring his instant noodles and making the girls laugh until he had to join in.

But even though Finlay tells himself it's a good thing, now he has to do it all over again. Meet people. Make friends.

Outside, the late October air is bitter and biting on the way to placement: winter coming in fast. It's been over a month since he started university, which is still surreal.

The building is short and stocky, brown bricks and low windows, a flat roof and a homely atmosphere. There's a long driveway. He sees a plaque with *Silver Lodge Care Centre* embossed on it, and a few cars in the small car park. The sun hasn't fully risen; the sky's a pale, murky grey. Finlay slides his bike into a rack and locks it. Nerves squirm in his abdomen with the thought of being the newcomer and the terror of being the outcast.

He makes his way through the silent reception area of the care home, with soft armchairs and coffee tables placed around, and hitches his bag up his shoulder.

The receptionist at the desk has short auburn hair, ivory-pink skin and slight wrinkles forming. Her name tag states: *Charlotte*. Finlay files that information away.

'Hi, Finlay Nowak, I'm here on placement.' He smiles wide.

'Oh.' Charlotte blinks. 'You're quite early.'

Twenty minutes, in fact.

'If you just wait there, I'll get Rhonda.'

Finlay follows Charlotte's directions towards one of the plush seats. He sits down for two seconds before he notices one of the coffee tables is a little messy so starts collating the leaflets into a pile. *Dementia, Tinnitus, Ostomy Care.* He picks one up and flips through. He can't focus on the words.

Finlay's stomach is cramping. Will they expect him to

know what he's doing? Do most student nurses know what they're doing?

Once the table is a little tidier, Finlay notices some coffee stains underneath. He sanitises his hands and finds some wet wipes. He's still cleaning when Rhonda appears.

'Finlay?' she asks. Her voice is Scottish, familiar, kind.

He shoots up like a string puppet. 'Yes!'

Rhonda is short, wearing a similar uniform to Finlay's, cluttered with badges and lanyards. She's black, with brown eyes, a tightly curled afro and prominent dimples when she smiles.

'My God!' She raises her brows. 'Workin' already?'

Finlay laughs. 'Just habit.'

'Well.' Rhonda leans in conspiratorially. 'In this job, ye take all the spare minutes ye can get.'

Rhonda gets him a disposable apron and gloves, and gives him a tour of all the important sites: the break room, the toilets, the store cupboard, etc. It's small but clean, smells nice and looks orderly. There's a coffee machine, but it costs a pound to use so Finlay makes a mental note to limit himself to one a week.

Then Rhonda introduces him to the 'team', which consists of four other staff.

Beth's in her twenties, recently graduated, honey-tan with long blonde hair. She says to Finlay: 'You're tiny!'

Leanne's in her early thirties, maybe, with rosy-peach skin and brown hair pulled back with hairclips. She nods silently, quiet and demure.

Somaya is a similar age, with brown skin and small features, and wears a hijab. She smiles and tells Finlay, 'If you need anything, just ask.'

Charlotte is, obviously, on reception.

Next: the residents.

Some are nice, some are not; most are very neutral about his addition. In that Finlay comes into their room with a wide smile and a 'Hello!' only to be greeted with absolutely nothing. Not even the blink of an eye.

For some reason Finlay assumed he'd be doing the unskilled jobs, the does-not-need-qualifications-for jobs, but it's the total opposite. He almost wants each resident to sign a form that says: *Finlay was forced to do this on his first day and is not liable for whatever happens to me.*

One of the first things Finlay has to do is to change the leg dressing on a seventy-year-old man who's hard of hearing.

'Ah don't want him dain it.' Patrick swats Finlay as if he's an annoying housefly.

'Finlay's doing it today, Patrick, and he's more than capable,' Rhonda says firmly.

Finlay has to take Patrick's side on this one and disagree with that. Finlay shoots Rhonda a look. She just nods him along like he's a small child headed off to school.

It doesn't go terribly. It doesn't go *great*. Patrick groans and grumbles and complains as Finlay peels off the old dressing, cleans the area, dries the area, and puts on a new dressing, chanting lecture slides in his head the entire time.

But then it's done, and the dressing is functional. Finlay blows out a long breath.

'Not so bad, eh?' Rhonda bumps him as they enter the corridor. 'So – what made ye pick nursing?'

'Um.' Finlay rubs his nape. 'It's a good job.'

Rhonda raises her brows. 'Plenty of good jobs.'

'I . . .' Finlay swallows. 'I like it.'

He's never admitted this to anyone. It's a weird thing to admit. He likes this. He likes sickness and dirty bedsheets. He likes antiseptic smells and human waste. He likes pain, pus, blood, urine. He likes holding somebody's chin to pick out small pieces of gravel, their knees pressed and breath close: trusted and trusting.

Wanting to be a doctor is normal. The healers of the world, the pride of their family. But normal people don't want this: to be overworked, underpaid, overstressed, undervalued.

'Me too.' Rhonda nods. 'You'll meet people, you'll love them, and you'll help them. But you'll touch death, too. It's good to know that first.'

Finlay's mouth is dry as he nods again. Rhonda's gaze holds him in place, and then she smiles. 'Ready?' She somehow manages not to shatter the moment, voice gentle and calm. Finlay imagines that voice at the edge of his bed when sick, and knows it would soothe the same as the cool touch of a hand.

'Yes.' Finlay smiles.

'Good.' Rhonda nods again. 'So, I'm no' throwing ye into the deep end—'

Dread curdles in Finlay's stomach.

'But I'll let ye handle the others yourself—'

Finlay opens his mouth in panic.

'Trust me, you'll be fine.' Her hand lands on his shoulder. 'And if ye need anything, just shout. Don't be scared to say I'm a student, I'm no' sure. We're always here to help.' She smiles.

And then she hands Finlay the medical files of all the residents he's overseeing today.

'Baptism of fire,' she tells him. 'Only way.'

His residents today are Patrick, Alice, Harry, and Edith. Finlay reads their information, steadies himself, and enters the belly of the beast – their bedrooms.

Alice has dementia, but she also has a colostomy bag that needs care. Finlay's never dealt with one before. So of course when Finlay touches it, it explodes. Everywhere. All over Alice's clothes, legs, stomach, bed, everything.

Finlay literally doesn't care about how bad it smells or the fact he's up to his elbows in it, but Alice is so confused and upset she starts shouting for help. Because who the fuck *wouldn't* shout for help if a random stranger barged into their room and burst their stoma bag?

Leanne comes in, takes one look at the scene, and immediately intervenes. 'It's all right, Alice, you're all right.'

Finlay hides in the disabled toilet and cries.

Leanne finds him.

'Finlay?' She knocks gently.

Finlay stiffens. He opens the door an inch. 'I'm so sorry—'

She comes in, takes his hands, and puts them under the tap. 'You need to make the water *hot*.'

Finlay is silent as she scrubs, clearly more familiar with this than him.

'The smell passes,' she murmurs. 'I know it's a shock, but you'll get used to it.'

Finlay shakes his head and sniffles. 'I'm so embarrassed. I literally can't believe I burst her bag. That must've been *awful*.'

Leanne looks at him, but her eyes soften. 'These things happen.'

Finlay reaches for the paper towels. 'She must've been terrified. I completely forgot to introduce myself. I just barged in, said hello, and started changing the bag.'

Leanne turns the tap off and stares at him. She lets out a laugh, sharp and sudden. Finlay adjusts his glasses, a little affronted.

Leanne waves a hand. 'I'm sorry,' she manages. 'It's not funny. I just imagined you rushing for her stoma as if you wanted to steal it.'

Finlay wants to be very serious right now, but that is objectively hilarious. He snickers. Then Leanne starts really laughing, and Finlay joins in. He laughs so hard he has to double over, the absurdity of the moment rushing through him.

Eventually, Finlay meets his two other residents.

'Where are ye fae?' Harry immediately asks.

'Scotland.' Finlay frowns.

'Whereaboots?' Harry leans forward. 'Ye dinnae sound like it.'

Finlay clears his throat. 'Uh, Glasgow.'

He can't pinpoint a specific location because there isn't one; he's moved around too much for that. And Finlay doesn't speak Scots either. He was too secluded and unsociable and his tongue never unravelled enough to learn. His mother spoke with a Polish accent, and Finlay spoke to her every day.

Maybe he overenunciates English. Maybe that's how his voice will always be now. That's why they're called formative years. They mould a person into a shape they can't melt out of.

'Well, I dinnae agree wae this relaxin' the borders and lettin' in anywan.'

Finlay nods silently, gives a hum here and there as he sorts Harry's many medications and Harry rants some more anti-immigration rhetoric. Finlay doesn't point out that the NHS wouldn't exist if it didn't recruit foreign staff.

Edith is quiet and calm. She's in a wheelchair with Parkinson's. Finlay helps her to eat and wash. This is the kind of job Finlay imagined doing, so it's about the only thing that goes smoothly.

And then the day is finished. It's over. It was literally not good. Finlay was actually very terrible.

'Shush, you were fine!' Beth laughs.

'Honestly, I've done it before too.' Somaya nods. 'The bags are really tricky, you need to make sure the flap is sealed—'

Finlay groans and puts his head on the reception desk. 'What's my nickname?'

'Still being decided,' Rhonda states, and they all laugh.

Finlay leaves them with a wave and pulls out his phone. He bites his lip, hesitating, but takes the plunge before he can talk himself out of it.

Coffee?

IM FREE, Derya texts, *I need to rant*

That was awful, Jun adds, *I almost left*

It cannot be worse than mine, Finlay replies, smiling. The thought of seeing them lifts his entire mood. *Meet you guys in an hour.*

When Finlay gets back to his flat, the sensation of looking after someone is still in his hands. He remembers this feeling. Making his fingers gentle, making his voice soft. The memory has clotted in his chest to form a strange, heavy pressure. There was fear and nausea with Banjo, plus this strange transferred pain, a wince for every black-and-blue bruise. Now Finlay can unpeel dressings from mottled wrists and feel nothing.

It's a good thing, this distance.

Three Years Ago

After Finlay sleeps outside the bathroom when Banjo is sick, things are easier. Banjo is calmer. Finlay's not about to call them *friends.* They'll be moved out of St Andrews soon, considering it's only a temporary housing solution until the longer placements with proper carers are secured. Most of the kids here have behavioural or other issues, which is what makes finding a placement for them even harder, and probably why they land here in the first place. But it also means nobody is really here to make friends.

Then something unthinkable happens to Finlay.

He goes into his room one day after therapy, lies down

149

and frowns. Something feels off. His skin itches. Finlay reaches underneath his pillow. At first he only uses one hand, then both. Then he rips up the pillows, the duvet, the sheets, throws his mattress off, flings his drawers open, searches and searches and—

'No, no, no, no.' He's only aware that he's speaking as he gets louder. 'No, no, NO!'

He tries Banjo's bed, Banjo's things, Banjo's drawers. Nothing.

Finlay tries the bathroom, the kitchen, throws himself into the hamper of dirty clothes, pulls everything out, pyjamas and underwear and—

'Finlay! Finlay, what's happened?' Lucy appears at his side.

Finlay keeps searching.

'Finlay, please,' Lucy tries. More staff surround him.

'Just give us a wee idea, mate,' Douglas tries. 'We'll help ye find it.'

'It can't have gone far,' Sophie adds, as if she even knows.

Finlay shakes his head, moves into the living room where everybody is watching him. He throws up the cushions, looks under the couch, scatters the magazines and books and snacks and toys.

Marco and Calum and Lewis and Sonny are all shouting, complaining, shoving him, saying things, but Finlay can't *find him*.

It doesn't even matter, nothing even matters, because Mr Black is *gone*.

Finlay screams. It's an ear-splitting, shrieking noise. He slaps his face with both hands, rakes nails down his skin. People start restraining him. Finlay thrashes wildly, but he's not strong enough.

'Whit the fuck!' Banjo crashes on to the scene. He's wind-bitten and sweaty, eyes crazed. He must have been outside. His eyes meet Finlay's before he takes a step forward.

But the walls collapse. Finlay sobs and falls to the floor. Because it's all gone. He's lost everything. His only companion, his one comfort in life, the only thing that smells familiar, that feels like home.

'Jesus!' Marco – a boy a year younger than him – cries. Mr Black is ripped out from the couch cushions, floppy and crushed. 'Thought it would make you speak, I didn't think you'd go *ballistic*.'

Finlay freezes. Every part of him goes still. Everyone in the room holds their breath. Banjo stares.

'Marco, that's your TV privileges revoked,' Lucy informs him, but they're still on edge. Sophie and Douglas say nothing.

Finlay walks over. Marco holds Mr Black out, bored. He's bigger than Finlay, shoulders wide. Finlay should let this go. Allow this to have been a simple mistake, a prank, a nothingness. But everyone is watching him. Every single person in St Andrews knows now that Finlay's one weakness is a worn old teddy. And they'll come again. They won't stop.

Finlay flies at Marco.

He gets both hands around Marco's throat before Marco throws Mr Black at Calum. Finlay doesn't lose focus though, tightens his grip, because Marco has clearly never known the frantic animal pain that overtakes the body when you reach for the last something you own in the world and discover it gone.

There's so much commotion, so much noise: Banjo's jumping between Calum and Lewis, who are tossing Mr Black around,

Sonny has his hands over his ears, the staff are trying to split Finlay and Marco up and comfort Sonny and stop Lewis and Calum and pacify Banjo.

Finlay's soon ripped off Marco, who takes a ragged inhale, staggering backwards to the couch. But then Finlay sees Mr Black being pulled between Banjo and Calum, about to be ripped in two.

'*No!*' he screams.

A change comes over Banjo. He abandons his mission of retrieving Mr Black and punches Calum three times in quick succession, arm diving in with almost blinding speed. Calum sways but Banjo keeps going: this new, horrific brutality in every line of his body.

'Banjo, Banjo stop, right now—' Douglas tries to interfere without getting hit, but Banjo's too quick. It's only when Calum stumbles that Douglas steps between them.

Banjo doesn't notice. He picks Mr Black up off the floor.

Lucy and Sophie are holding a struggling Finlay by both arms; Douglas is tending to Calum, Marco is coughing, Calum is shouting, 'My *nose*!'

Banjo holds out Mr Black with a bloodied hand and smiles. 'Here.'

It's the greatest act of love Finlay's ever known.

Finlay is allowed in the quiet room with the cuddly toys and the cushions for however long he wants. He lies in the middle with Mr Black protected in the concave of his body. He doesn't want to face anyone or anything.

After a couple hours, there's a noise outside his door. Finlay doesn't move. He assumes it's the staff.

'Oi,' Banjo states, voice low as if he's pressed to the gap in the door.

Finlay doesn't move.

'Ye oan the floor?' Banjo asks.

Finlay wants to say something. *Life is hard. Sometimes it puts you on the floor.* They already know that, though.

It sounds as if Banjo sits down and presses his back to the door. 'D'ye ... wannae talk?'

Finlay curls into a smaller ball.

'Ah, fuck it, I'll talk. Eh ... Said sorry tae Calum. But staff made everyone say sorry in a wee sorry circle so it wasnae like it mattered. 'Hink they're jus' givin' us time tae cool aff an' that. Don' 'hink anyone'll try that again.'

There's silence.

'Is it ... special? The teddy?'

Finlay is silent. It's a teddy. He's fifteen. He doesn't know how to explain it without opening up his insides.

Banjo doesn't repeat himself. He's content to wait.

'His name is Mr Black,' Finlay manages, voice hoarse. He lifts Mr Black up to his face, strokes his floppy ears and presses their noses together. 'He says "thanks" for saving him.'

Banjo is quiet.

'I found him in the bin,' Finlay rasps. 'He only had one eye. It would be so easy to fix, but someone threw him away. He's shy because he's not from here. He doesn't know anybody. And he

153

doesn't speak because people make fun of his voice. So he's sad, because no matter where he is ... he can never be home.'

They breathe for a minute.

'I get that,' Banjo murmurs. 'I fucken get that, Mr Black.'

Chapter Nineteen

BANJO

After Banjo's shoddy peace offering of oven-cooked pizza and the *sorry* note, he's back friends with Paula and Henry. They come home all smiles, asking about school. It didn't take much. That thought burrows into him.

Banjo's had a few carers, but he's never let himself settle with any of them. He knows the people who take him in are looking for a nice kid, a new addition to the family, but that'll never be him. They want too much, ask too many questions, crawl under his skin. They never give him any *space*. Banjo's not looking to join anyone's fucking family.

But for some reason, he wants to settle here. With Paula and Henry.

Maybe because he's got too much to lose now. They don't shout, they don't pry; they just trust. They just let him *be*. Plus there are other things. Alena. Work. Athletics. Microwave pizza. His own room. *Alena*. He's sinking deeper by the day. He wants to pull back, but he's so tired of pulling back. His feet are so fucking sore. He's ready to sink.

That's the whole problem, of course.

Anderson finds Banjo after athletics lets out.

'Hiya. Just need to chat. Come to my office when you're ready.' She tips her head in that direction and walks away.

Banjo frowns. He gets ready in seconds. He throws Kyle a look, who just smiles and waggles his eyebrows.

Banjo's stomach becomes a boulder and drops right through him.

'Look,' he starts as soon as Anderson closes the door, already pacing a new groove. 'I dunno whit he's said, aw'right, but it's pish. Am the best on the team so unless they're aw gonnae walk out, ye cannae jus' kick me aff cause some'dae doesnae like me.'

'I think it's a bit more than that, Banjo,' Anderson informs him, her voice grave. 'I've had complaints coming in from a lot of the boys—'

'*Who?*' Banjo barks, throwing his head back with a hard laugh. Because he knew this was coming. Something is always fucking coming. It was just getting too calm, too comfortable. 'Aw, this is classic! Cause am the best? By *more* than a mile?'

Anderson bows her head, arms crossed, leaning on her desk. 'Banjo,' she begins. 'I know about the fight with Kyle. I know about the party. I know you were suspended last week. There's a pattern here.'

Her disapproval hurts worse than a sharp slap. His whole face stings as he stands there, legs vibrating, made to submit to the punishing force of it.

'This isn't a team sport, I know that.' Anderson nods, head

bowed and arms crossed. 'And I can understand it hasn't been easy for you, coming into a new school in your last year. But I can't have this kind of behaviour among my athletes. I've seen how destructive it is.'

Fuck.

'Please,' Banjo tries, because he can see it happening. He can see the words forming in her mouth. It's why she can't look at him.

'This is only a warning,' Anderson states, and meets his eyes. 'All right? But I'll need you to take next week off. I want the other boys to know I take their concerns seriously. That I listen when there's a problem.'

Banjo is stiff, stunned. The fuck. *The fuck.*

Kick him out for one week just to show the *other boys*? He's not done anything to the other boys. Clearly this is all Kyle. And just how the fuck has Kyle wound the *other boys* around his finger this much? Some pack mentality shite?

Rage erupts from every corner inside his body. He wants to rip up everything in the room including himself, and he's going to do it, every muscle prepared, until he randomly starts gasping for breath.

He just can't breathe any more, for some fucking reason. Every time he tries to reach for it, the air speeds away from him, and everything feels fuzzy, even his own skin.

'Banjo, Banjo—' Anderson's in front of him. What the fuck? Did he collapse? His forehead is to the floor, mouth open on the dirty carpet, wheezing hard.

Why does this matter so much? So he's not on some pish-shite team – he ran his whole life before this, he can do it again. But the butter-smooth track on the soles of his feet and Anderson's surprise when he beats his own time slips from his fingers the way everything always does. Alena's whistle of approval. Jace's *cool!* Carlos and Julie and *what do you want to do?* Paula and Henry and *come back before dinner gets cold!*

He always makes one thing too important, always makes it the only thing he's got, the only thing that makes him worthy of anyone or anything in life, and it always makes it hurt worse when it's gone.

'Banjo, you're all right.' Anderson's voice is calm, her palm warm on his spine. 'That's it. You're doing well.'

Banjo nods against the carpet, his breath still unsteady.

'Just breathe. You can do it.'

It would be patronising if not for her hand rubbing small circles on his back. Instead, it's actually working.

'There we go. Can't lose my star.'

It's clearly just to make him feel better. Banjo still chokes a garbled laugh.

Anderson goes away and passes him a bottle of water. He gulps it down, gets to his feet, and brushes his trousers for something to do. Mortification is starting to trickle in: that shocked humiliation that hasn't really accepted the situation as reality yet.

'Banjo ...'

He can hear it in her voice. She wants to ask. But he doesn't want the concern, the prying questions: *Is everything all right at home, have you been under any stress lately?*

He turns away. It's subtle, but it's enough.

'Okay,' Anderson murmurs. 'You don't have to talk to me if you don't want. But I'm here if you need me.'

Banjo nods at the floor.

'It's one week,' she promises. She's trying to catch his eye but he won't let her. 'Take some time, come back, and we'll put it all behind us. I'll tell Kyle and the others to do the same. I know you can turn this around. I *know* it.'

He gives Anderson a rough jerk of his chin and heads for the bathroom. He clatters inside and slams the cubicle door shut twice.

When he makes it to the bike rack, Kyle and a few others are milling about. Waiting on him.

Banjo wants to kick their teeth down their throat. He wants to grab the back of Kyle's head and smash his nose into the stone pavement. It frightens him. No wonder Anderson wants him off the team. *I've seen how destructive it is.* It feels as if someone has peeled him open and found him disgusting.

'Ah, Banjo!' Kyle calls when Banjo gets closer. 'You'll be missed. Honestly. But it's for the best.'

Banjo stands in front of him. Kyle is taller. A lifetime of green vegetables and nice mattresses. But Banjo would win in any fight right now. His jaw could bite into something and tear it off.

He lifts a hand and claps Kyle's shoulder.

Kyle flinches. Banjo just gives him a light squeeze and unchains his bike. He salutes them all with two fingers and cycles off.

Saturday eventually shows up after a sluggish, slow week of no athletics. Banjo is thrumming for work: for the opportunity to use his muscles, the opportunity to let his mind go blank with washing dishes, the opportunity to *see Alena*.

She's not there.

'Where's—'

'She's off today,' Morag replies without straightening up from wiping the counter. 'Just us, pal.'

Christ. Really couldn't make it up. If his life was scripted, Banjo wouldn't even have this much bad luck. He slumps before he can even stop himself, like a sad cartoon. And then he frowns as a trickle of worry creeps in. 'Is she ... *sick* or something?'

He can't pick out a time Alena looked or seemed it, plus she would tell him if she was – she told him she had Crohn's when they met. There's not much else for Banjo to know, surely.

But if Banjo thinks about it, she didn't look sick then, either.

'No, she's just got some holidays to use up.'

When Banjo blinks, uncomprehending, Morag clarifies, 'Annual leave.'

'Oh,' Banjo says. Swallows. What's so special about this weekend, then? Does she have plans?

It's not his business or whatever, but surely she wouldn't take a holiday for nothing.

160

He goes to message her, but he can't think of anything to say. *Why the fuck did you take a day off?* Hardly a good look. *I want to talk. I want you here. I want you something fucking awful.* Banjo leaves it.

The message comes at the end of the day: *I hope you survived :'(*

It's weirdly serious for Alena, who would normally make a joke. Banjo types back in seconds: *barely.*

He has to restrain himself from sending, *what were you up to?* She'd tell him if she wanted him to know.

Alena sends some kind of stick figure. Banjo has to tilt his phone sideways to see it. He thinks it's meant to be dead. He writes, *me without you*, but deletes and just sends, *me.*

By the time he's allowed back to athletics, he's miserable, pent-up energy buzzing out his skin. He's ready for anyone, but it turns out nobody cares.

Because there's a competition in a couple days.

In the week that Banjo missed, they got invited to 'represent' Triduana at the Schools Athletics Association in Glasgow. Supposedly they never made the cut last year.

It's all the boys can talk about. Kyle yammers on like it's the Olympics, and everyone else is too preoccupied to notice him even come in. Devlin nods when he sees Banjo, so Banjo tips his chin back. That's all the ceremony he can expect.

'So I want us all to push today!' Anderson finishes her speech about the competition before warm-ups: when, where, what to bring, etc. Banjo waits a beat, but she nods for him to join in so he does with little complaint.

Once practice is over, Anderson catches him before he goes into the locker room.

'How you feeling?' she asks, but she peers into his face. Banjo knows what she's really asking.

'Fine.' He nods, shoving a hand into his hair.

'You know, there's some great mental health services available through the school,' Anderson says softly. 'You could chat to your guidance counsellor – I think it's Mrs Gibson for sixth year, right?'

Banjo gives a jerky nod. He's not got a clue.

'And my door is always open,' she adds.

Banjo manages to mangle his mouth into a smile and moves around her.

'So you up for it, then? The competition?'

Banjo stops. He turns.

Anderson is smiling.

The surprise rips through him in this searingly good way. He's been waiting for her to tell him the opposite all day. For *sorry, Banjo, I just don't think it would be a good idea right now.*

But she wants him to come.

Banjo's muscles buzz like static, sweat marches down his face, and the roof of his mouth tastes like blood. He fucking loves it. 'Sure.'

Banjo shows up on competition day with spare clothes, a ham sandwich, and a bottle of water. It's cold and bright at 7 a.m., so he's still scrubbing sleep out his eyes when they're shuffled on to the bus.

'Nervous?' Devlin stops at his seat with a raised brow.

Banjo pulls his rucksack away to make space.

'You better be,' Devlin tells him, throwing himself in and pointing a finger. 'This is your last chance.'

'Right,' Banjo states. This is probably Devlin's hottest attempt at friendship. Somehow he's halfway to succeeding.

It turns out the competition is in the city centre. Banjo hasn't really been near the city since his stay at St Andrews – he's had placements around Glasgow, but not so much the city centre. The further in they travel, the more things start to look familiar. Streets, shops, parks. Banjo's stomach knots. Fuck, he can't think about Finlay. Not now. Not again.

He clenches his hands, blunt nails biting into his palms, and focuses on his breathing. Three seconds in, three seconds out.

'Christ, you *are* nervous,' Devlin notes.

Banjo grits his teeth.

Eventually, they leave the streets and neighbourhoods Banjo used to stay in and enter another part of Glasgow. The area is clean, the houses immaculate. The closer they get, the more Banjo realises today is a big deal. They pull up to a huge, dome-shaped stadium with **GLASGOW SPORTS ARENA** at the front.

His pulse jumps into his throat, but warmth also starts to pool in his stomach, the same way it does before he sees Alena.

Thinking about Alena only makes him nervous right now,

though, because he's not seen her since the family dinner, and what if he did something wrong?

'Now, this is a friendly competition in the name of team spirit,' Anderson begins once they've piled out of the stuffy bus and into the icy October air.

'I don't want any nonsense.' Anderson points to each of them. 'You're representing the school today. There will be other schools here, other teams.'

Every single one of them stands to attention. Banjo flexes his hands to stop them trembling.

'Now let's have fun.' She nods.

They all head inside. Banjo glances around at the enormousness of the place, the sleek floors, the long banners, everyone in expensive tracksuits stood in clusters. He imagines this as a life and it pricks hotly in his chest. The desire is so strong it hurts a bit.

'Private-school wankers,' Devlin mutters at his side, nodding to the ones in matching jackets. Banjo grins.

What he didn't know is that parents were invited too.

This woman runs up to Devlin, and for one wild second Banjo thinks it might be a *fan* until she opens her arms with a smile. Devlin throws himself back so violently anyone would think she was radioactive.

'I'm *fine*,' he hisses.

'Oh, come on.' She squeezes his skinny arm. 'I just want a nice photo together before you're all sweaty.' She's shorter, plump, but her face softens when she looks at him.

Right. This is the mum.

Devlin rolls his eyes, but Banjo wordlessly holds out a hand. The mum smiles at him.

He snaps a few pictures and leaves them to scrutinise. He floats about, picks up a free water bottle and copies some stretches from the private-school coaches. They head outside to where the track is, a long ring of blue asphalt around a field. Banjo's feet, so used to potholes and uneven tarmac, can already feel how smooth the run will be. He wants to bend to his knees and kiss it.

It's difficult not to notice all the families, though. He feels like a lost toe. Banjo snaps a front-facing picture of his paper number and sends it to Alena.

He bounces on the spot as he waits for her to reply. She doesn't. Why isn't she replying? Normally Alena gets back within seconds. But her replies have been getting fewer and further between. They've not spoken since she texted him at the weekend about work. And even then it was short.

Unless she's trying to put distance between them? It's the only thing that makes sense. Banjo didn't get another invite to family dinner. He's put her off, clearly.

Banjo ignores the sharp, stinging wound of that. It is what it is.

First, there're the events before the sprint. It's jumping and skipping and all that shite. Banjo doesn't really try, not because it's embarrassing, but because it's fucking *hard*. Only thing Banjo can do is run in a straight line.

But he participates, does nowhere near good . . . and then the sprinting starts. Those stupid jitters Devlin was yapping about come on full force. There're rows of seats for all the families to sit, cheer, eat, wave down at everyone.

Banjo looks up at them for something to do. Suddenly this terrible heavy pressure comes over him. It starts slowly until it becomes the weight of the world. He knew he hadn't asked anyone to come, but the proof is different. There's absolutely nobody up there for him.

Even Kyle's family showed. Banjo's family would never be here, sure, but he knows one person would've come if things had been different. If he hadn't ruined it.

The whistle blows. Banjo's off easy, already warm and loose-limbed. People close in at every angle, far more fucking motivated than they are at practice.

That's the point, right? That's why schools have competitions. That's why people invite their families.

Fuck that. Running is all he's ever had so who cares if people have parents watching because this is *his*, and he's as good as won—

Someone passes his side.

Kyle's eyes are forward, expression grim: so totally determined not just to beat Banjo but to beat everybody.

Banjo wonders how many good sleeps Kyle's had. How many cooked meals, packed lunches, small touches, birthday parties, drop-offs, pickups, bedtime stories, holidays abroad, photo albums, framed pencil drawings. All for this pathetic show.

Because Kyle's pushing himself to the brink. His whole face shows it. Banjo could beat him again. He's been the best for a long time, maybe even for his whole life. And it doesn't even fucking matter. Because nobody cares.

Here's the choices:
1. Win and take a little medal away.
2. Lose and watch Kyle take it.

It's over in four seconds flat. Much the same as their first race.

'You all right?' One of the attendees rushes over.

'Hamstring's away.' Banjo rubs his thigh, hobbling off to the side.

'Let me get the physio, stay there and don't move.' They shove a water bottle at him and force him to sit on the ground. Banjo does, even though his hamstring's fine.

Out on the track, Kyle is looking about wildly. The guys are all slapping his shoulders and jumping about as though the victory is theirs. Devlin has his hands on his knees, panting for his life. Banjo didn't even notice him. Poor sod.

Kyle's face breaks into a grin. His mum is rushing down. He starts giving it all this, puffing up his chest, but when she gets close he opens his arms. She laughs and hugs him. He really wanted this, the idiot.

Kyle pulls away and starts looking around again. He only stops when he sees Banjo.

He frowns, points, mouths *okay?* Banjo gives him the middle finger. Kyle grins, pretends to sucker-punch him in the air. Banjo rolls his eyes until the physio comes over.

He's washed, dressed, and getting on the bus when Anderson halts him with a hand. She gives him some eyebrow action. Banjo gives her a flat look.

'Not what I had in mind, but . . . point taken.' She pats him on the shoulder.

Banjo just nods, sharp, and steps on. Hoots go up as though he's told a joke. Kyle shouts over them: 'Happens to the best of us!'

Banjo ignores them all the way to the back of the bus, where Devlin is sulking.

'Please tell me that wasn't deliberate.' Devlin glares out the window.

'Please tell me that fucken *was*,' Banjo retorts, good-humouredly though because he can tell Dev needs it. 'State ae that performance.'

Devlin snorts a laugh. The bus starts off in silence.

'I told her not to come,' Dev murmurs. His knee is jittering.

Banjo knocks it with his own. 'She loves ye, ya prick. Course she came.'

He leaves his second-place medal on the kitchen counter for Paula and Henry.

'*Whoa*, what's this?' Henry's voice booms all the way from downstairs. Banjo creeps down and ducks his head into the doorway.

'You win a race?' Paula holds it up with a grin, Henry crowding around her to take a look.

'Second place.' Banjo shrugs and scratches his arm.

'That's fantastic!' Paula beams.

'Takeaway tonight,' Henry decides.

Banjo chuckles. He feels it seep through him and rubs a hand over his head, self-conscious.

He has two missed calls from Alena. His heart slams into his ribs and pounds harder than it did when he was sprinting.

He closes his door and rolls on to his bed.

'What the *hell*, Mr Murray?' she starts when Banjo calls her back. He laughs in delight at her lovely voice, familiar and unchanged: the way it sounds in the café, the way it sounded at family dinner.

'You were competing somewhere?' She's so excited it radiates all the way through the phone and into his chest.

'Ya,' Banjo confirms. Then, because he needs to: 'Ye been busy?'

'Busy?' She sounds surprised. 'Oh, no – just having a bit of a Crohn's flare at the minute. I get migraines if I text too much.'

Oh.

'Oh,' Banjo murmurs, throat thick with sympathy and a strange, selfish relief. She's not avoiding him. 'That's shite. Is that why ye were off last weekend?'

'I promised Mum I'd go for lunch and I had some holidays to use anyways,' Alena says easily. 'So I just took it off.'

Banjo feels his face heat against his pillow. It was nothing to fucking do with him. He runs a finger over his duvet. 'Aw. That sounds nice.'

'I'll be back this weekend,' she assures him. 'But how was your competition? *Tell* me!' Alena drags her words out like Carlos and Jace would.

'Wus fine.' Banjo shrugs. 'Got second place.'

'*Second place!*' Alena cries. 'He's unstoppable! Raw talent that can't be contained! I'm telling Mum and Dad—'

Banjo keeps laughing, holding his phone as close as possible. Holding Alena as close as possible. He rolls on to his side and wraps an arm around himself, running his fingers down his side as he listens to her.

He wonders if Alena would've come to watch. If Paula and Henry would have, too. If they would have all rushed to hug him.

Maybe Banjo should actually mention these things to people. He gets in his own fucking way sometimes.

Three Years Ago

Ever since Marco stole Mr Black, Banjo and Finlay have created a new tradition. If one of them needs to lie on the floor, then they both do. Unspoken rule. It mainly relates to Banjo, because he's still going through withdrawal.

But one night Banjo falls asleep in the bathroom. Maybe Finlay wants to go to bed, or check up on him, or maybe he knocks and Banjo doesn't answer. But he makes his first and only mistake. He touches Banjo's shoulder.

Banjo uses everything he can to get away. He kicks, he scratches, he has skin underneath his nails until—

'Sorrysorrysorry,' Finlay chokes.

Banjo realises what the fuck he's doing and jolts backwards. Finlay runs out.

Banjo stays there for a solid hour until he can breathe. Eventually, he opens the door and goes back to their room.

Finlay is in bed, eyes closed. Banjo sits cross-legged on the floor by his head. He puts their faces right up close and watches Finlay.

Finlay's eyes open slowly. He was never asleep.

Banjo breaks first. 'Am no' scary, right?'

Finlay watches him in the darkness. 'No. Why?'

'Am no' like they addicts,' Banjo whispers, shuffling closer.

'What do you mean?'

'The ones that'll do anythin',' Banjo adds. 'The ones that frighten people.'

The frenzy, the rage, the crazed pit of agony in his stomach. It's not that. It's something else, but it's not that.

Finlay's eyes stay steady. 'You're not addicted to the painkillers, Banjo. You're dependent on them. Addiction is different.'

'Am an addict,' Banjo admits. 'I am.' Because he's seen them. He was raised by them. And he knows.

'Look,' Finlay begins, reasonable as ever. 'I did some

reading. You're definitely not. You're dependent because you've been taking them for a long time now. It's similar, and you can *become* addicted, but you're not. If you were, you'd want them all the time. You're just feeling the withdrawal. We'll wean you off them. You'll stop getting sick.'

Banjo hasn't told Finlay how long he was on painkillers before he came here, and that the reading he's done might be pointless. He lets Finlay have that fantasy.

Banjo swallows. 'Am sorry.'

'Don't be,' Finlay answers.

Banjo curls his fingers in his lap. 'I dinnae like being woke up,' he croaks. 'Makes me wannae claw ma skin off.'

Finlay's gaze is steady. 'Okay.'

'I shouldae told ye,' Banjo tries.

'I should've asked,' Finlay keeps on, but his gentleness is a knife gutting Banjo's insides.

'Naw, ye ...' Banjo shakes his head and squeezes his eyes shut. 'It's no yer fault. Sometimes I forget where I am.'

It's all he has to offer.

Finlay understands. He pulls his legs out of bed slowly, setting his feet level on the floor next to Banjo's knees. He leans over his thighs and holds his hands spread on his lap, facing upwards. Banjo looks at them. Nobody's ever just shown Banjo their hands before. Empty and open, fingers flat, as if approaching a horse.

Banjo lifts his own hands and hovers them above Finlay's. The heat off their skin radiates. Even from this distance Banjo can feel Finlay's warm body. It's basically the real thing. Touching but not touching.

Banjo makes himself look at Finlay's arm. The one he clawed. There are nail marks down his arm. Banjo moves his open palm and hovers it over the place. He hopes Finlay understands. *I won't do that again. See?*

Finlay hovers his hand over Banjo's. It looks silly but it makes them laugh. They're being stupid. But Finlay respects every distance Banjo keeps. *I won't do that again*, Finlay's hands say back.

Sometimes, Banjo just wants to fight so he can prove he's stronger. Because his whole life he's hated men. Hates their bad breath, their hard hands, their horrible voices, their fucking faces.

But Finlay's different. He's gentle. Banjo could win against Finlay, but he doesn't want to. Finlay's the kind of man Banjo wants to be.

Chapter Twenty

FINLAY

There's a dry field, cold stone porch steps, a high-rise council flat, the sour odour of plastic bins, burst pipes, and a fridge that's gone off. He's inside Glasgow, its smells, sounds, rushing creatures. Traffic lights and chip shops and loud pubs, cobbled pavements littered with wet rubbish. Banjo's there. Finlay sees his red hair in crowds, *do you mean cappuccino, regular or large*. His heart hurts with homesickness for nothing, the taste of boiled eggs, clumped-together noodles, rickety beds, ache in his joints, *can you do the six to eight the ten to six the eight to four?* A voice resonates across a room. It sounds like Banjo, and Finlay hopes it's Banjo. But a flock of birds pass over the window and it's gone.

Finlay jolts when he wakes.

When he checks his phone, the email headline is the first thing he sees:

Urgent – Academic Supervisor Meeting – Please Reply.

*

'So,' Grace begins.

Finlay clasps his hands so he can hide the trembling.

'Two extensions in two weeks for one essay. What's going on?' She presses her mouth sadly.

You won't stop emailing me, Finlay wants to respond, but of course he doesn't. 'I know, I've been really snowed under with my placement, and my other job —'

'Finlay, you really shouldn't be working right now,' Grace tells him.

Finlay squeezes his hands together so he doesn't explode. *Of course, really need to quit my obsession with work, should try to enjoy other things like sleep.*

'I need to work,' he tries.

'There're other ways—'

'I don't qualify for any other scholarships because I already have one; I don't qualify for a bursary because I don't have children, and I don't qualify for Universal Credit because you can't be attending university full-time, but even if I wasn't, I still wouldn't get it because you need to be out of work.'

Grace stares.

Finlay's heart hammers. Was that too much? Finlay can't really remember what a normal conversation sounds like. He's running on instant coffee and four hours' sleep. Despite the fact the construction work is finished, having what amounts to a full-time job alongside part-time work, plus throwing academic studies on top, has turned him into some kind of lifeless undead, capable only of basic motor functions. Finlay knows he's not seen the girls in a full week. That he allowed things to end with Akash. His life is work, eat, sleep, repeat. He would say rinse but sadly can't remember the last time he showered.

'Finlay,' Grace says, voice softer. 'I can ... appreciate all that. But I still need some evidence that you understand the learning outcomes. I was only going to say that there's other ways to *manage your time* – maybe talk to people on the course and see if there's a study group. You need to learn to ask for help, Finlay.'

Finlay grits his teeth. It sounds so easy.

'I spoke to your placement mentor, Rhonda,' Grace begins.

Finlay goes rigid. He keeps it off his face.

'She can do nothing but sing your praises. You're capable, Finlay, and you're smart. Don't throw it all away.'

Finlay swallows around a strange, hard pressure in his throat.

'I can give you till the end of the day for the assignment.' Grace sighs. 'Best I can do.'

Finlay hunts for the library. If he can find a computer, he'll find the sloppily written essay and maybe live to see another day at university. He can't go back to his flat without passing out. Everything is starting to look a little surreal and fuzzy from sleep deprivation, funny and frightening simultaneously.

If I don't get this submitted today I'm out, Finlay thinks, but that's hilarious, and his fingers are numb.

The West End in autumn is stunning. Everything tinged a little orange and pink, the air crisp with the wet mulch of dead leaves and dirt, the salt-smoke of frost and ice. The stone pavements have a thin sheet of white along their surface. The trees along the street sprout out from under the cobblestones and shed their leaves like shrugging off a thick coat, their bony skeletons bare.

It's not Glasgow's city centre: not the crowded line of curry houses, chip shops, and pubs along Sauchiehall Street. Not Merchant City with its stone pillars and archways, busy Buchanan Street with the carnival of cafés and retail stores, George Square's concrete monuments with traffic cones on their heads. There's no rushing current of life; rather a quieter stream. The West End is leafy suburbs and bohemian delis, antique stores and indie bookshops. It's sandstone houses and tiny community gardens.

Although nerves churn his stomach into mashed purée – his body desperately propelling him to panic – Finlay's mind can only float through the mapped route open on his phone, completely disconnected and on a flight to a faraway country.

Then he passes the window of a hip little coffee house and spots Akash reading.

Finlay halts right there.

Akash is so engrossed. Coffee half-full on the table, back bent over the book on his lap, ankle resting over one knee. The crusted rim of sugar and foam around his cup lip signifies the length of time he has been there. A few seconds pass and his eyes keep scanning. He looks so peaceful in his own company, totally lost to the world.

Finlay needs to go to the library. He needs to finish this essay. Everything hangs in the balance right now.

Yet the thought of leaving without speaking to Akash is unbearable. Finlay hasn't seen him in over two weeks. And every reason why he should deny himself the pleasure of Akash's company disappears.

Maybe it's lunacy. But before Finlay knows it, he's dipping inside, creeping up behind Akash and laying two hands on his shoulders.

'Blink twice if you're being held hostage.'

Akash spins around. His whole face comes alive with happiness. *'Finlay!'*

Finlay's powerless to that welcome: feels his own face sing with joy. He slides into the seat opposite.

'Fancy seeing you here.' Finlay leans both elbows on the table and links his hands.

'I know!' Akash laughs, and then pokes Finlay's chest. 'You never texted! I've been looking for you!'

Finlay's whole body flushes hot and cold. 'I—' he stutters, heat rising to his head.

He has no answer for Akash. No reason for avoiding him. At least not any that make sense out loud. *You terrify me a little. Your easy confidence, your ability to be alone, your complete acceptance of yourself, it's beautiful and terrifying.*

Akash smiles as if he can see through Finlay. As if he somehow has access to the deepest, most intimate parts of him. Finlay wants to shy away but at the same time wants to submit himself to it: this wonderfully raw, oversensitive feeling.

Akash lays his book down on its stomach. *Clinically Oriented Anatomy.*

Finlay nods to it so he can break eye contact. 'Any good?'

Akash runs a hand through the front of his hair, putting an elbow on the table. They're practically inches apart.

'It's for an assignment, but somebody wrote it to hurt me.'

Finlay laughs, now understanding Akash's focus. Akash watches him laugh; eyes creased with his smile, every detail of his face pleased. Finlay's stomach flutters wildly.

'I can't believe you picked medicine.' Finlay leans in again, helpless to the pull when Akash is so close. '*Traitor*.'

'We will remain mortal enemies until one prevails.' Akash narrows his eyes at Finlay.

'How will we judge the winner fairly?' Finlay lifts an eyebrow.

'A classic duel,' Akash says, and raises both hands as if gripping a sword. Finlay pretends to clash with it.

Akash laughs, abandoning the façade. Finlay laughs too, totally endeared to him. It's silly, and Finlay should feel embarrassed, but not with Akash. That's what's terrifying.

'Don't ask me why I picked medicine.' Akash exhales. 'Family of doctors. That's the short story.'

'So, not the vocational type?' Finlay asks.

Akash leans so far forward that he's pressed against the edge of the table. 'Don't tell anyone this, but.' He motions with four fingers for Finlay to lean in too.

Finlay's breath hitches. When Akash puts his face close to Finlay, his consciousness leaves him. Akash's lips part, his gentle breath rests on Finlay's nose, his clean smell clouds Finlay's senses.

Finlay has spent his whole life on the edge of human contact. In all that time he never fully realised what it meant to live alone, struck off, isolated from touch. But now, mere centimetres away from Akash, every particle in his body is desperate to bridge the gap.

There's a beat before Finlay realises Akash isn't speaking.

'What?' Finlay whispers.

Akash stares for a long pause. 'I'm horrifically squeamish.'

Finlay's laughter booms out of him. He'd almost be self-conscious if it didn't feel so good. Akash's whole body shakes when he joins in.

'I know the feeling,' Finlay manages when he's calmed. 'I'm—' He doesn't know how to say it. *Basically failing the course.* 'Struggling.' He exhales.

'What with? Placement?' Akash blinks gentle eyes. 'I've heard it can be intense.'

Finlay shakes his head. 'No, placement's fine. It's the assignments that are ... destroying my will to live.'

'What!' Akash's eyes widen. 'You should've said!'

Finlay frowns. 'Uh ...'

'I can help!' Akash explains. 'If it's anything clinical, my brain's bursting with it. Let me be of use!' He stretches both arms wide as though to demonstrate his own existence.

'Um,' Finlay tries again. The thought of Akash reading his horrendous essay makes quitting university actually appealing. But Akash looks so hopeful. And Finlay is exhausted. *You need to learn to ask for help.*

'... Okay.'

'Great!' Akash beams, blasting Finlay with it. Then he stands. 'First things first: coffee.'

Finlay watches Akash cross over and get served instantly because there's no queue. He takes a hold of the counter to push up on his tiptoes and see what's available. He's wearing washed-out blue jeans and a thick black sweater, a gold ring on his thumb. Finlay can see the edge of a pink T-shirt peeking out at his collar. Something hot and strange unfurls inside Finlay's chest. It feels like violent fondness.

Finlay wants to leave. This was a mistake. But as quickly as the feeling takes hold of him, Akash returns with two takeaway cups in hand. 'I got you a latte.'

'Oh.' Finlay takes it, dumbstruck, and instantly reaches for his wallet.

'No need. On me.' Akash pushes the coffee at Finlay's chest.

Akash is being kind. He doesn't understand the significance. But it's the flippancy of the act that pierces Finlay.

Finlay pulls out some coins and offers them to Akash.

Akash looks at Finlay, then huffs and takes them. His fingertips skim Finlay's open palm. It sends a small shock wave through him.

'Thank you.' Finlay clears his throat. He sips the bitter caffeine. It warms him after walking in the Scottish autumn air.

'To the library!' Akash declares with a finger, and it's so incredibly dorky Finlay has no choice but to laugh.

It turns out Akash is a seasoned visitor. They navigate through the IT area to a desk that's been booked. When Finlay opens his mouth, Akash gives a wry smile.

'Today's my revision day. You're in luck.' He powers the

computer up and stands back. 'All yours.' Akash waves to it and sits on the chair opposite, splaying his legs. His belt buckle glints, the muscles of his thighs evident.

'Finlay?' Akash prods.

Finlay sits quickly and busies himself with logging in. Akash tucks his hair behind his ears, and he's wearing earrings, square plaques with little floral designs on them.

Pull yourself together, Finlay thinks. He manages to find his essay after concentrated effort.

'Okay,' he warns, nodding to the screen. 'I am fully aware this is a mess.'

'Let's see.' Akash slides closer just as Finlay leans away. Akash reads over his shoulder, mouthing the words a little. His breath is on Finlay's throat. Finlay could weep.

'Okay. Okay.' Akash nods once he's finished. 'So – see this?' He points to the screen, stretching an arm around Finlay as though in an embrace.

'Mm?' Finlay rasps.

'You just need to explain your evidence. You've got a great case study, but just relate it back to the question. I can show you.' Akash smiles.

And he does.

They write for hours. The more they write, the more Finlay realises he does know this. He does have the mental energy, he does have the skills. He's just been avoiding it. Pushing it further and further away so he won't have to face the outcome of submitting something only to fail.

He was just trying to delay the inevitable of losing everything: university, friends, career, security. Now he realises how counterproductive that thinking was.

'And now you're finished,' Akash says as Finlay types the conclusion.

'Oh my lord, thank you,' Finlay babbles, euphoria rushing through him. He turns to Akash, about to throw himself across the distance – but stops himself, adjusts his glasses, and swallows. 'I owe you my life.' His voice goes quiet.

'Well, then, it was worth it.' Akash's voice is soft, almost tender.

Finlay glances away, a nervous quiver to his hands and his heart, as though something just transpired when all they did was look at one another. He focuses on emailing Grace with the essay, takes a breath, and presses send.

It doesn't matter that it hasn't been graded yet. A pressure flies away from him as his lungs finally open up. Finlay exhales all the way down to his toes.

'Do you want to come to mine?' Akash asks, completely at random. 'I'll make us something to eat: it'll be cheaper than the West End.'

'Oh, no, you don't have to.' Finlay shakes his head. He's already taken up so much of Akash's time.

'I want to!' Akash's hair shifts from behind his ears to frame his face when he looks at Finlay. 'I'm two minutes away. Seriously.' Akash tilts his head, ever responsive to Finlay.

His face is so expectant as he waits.

Finlay can leave at any point. He still has all the power. But more than that, he can't bear to let any small unhappiness mark itself upon Akash's face. Not just from the instinct to people-please. The thought of Akash being upset causes an ache in Finlay's chest.

Maybe that's an excuse, though. The truth is Finlay adores Akash's presence. He wants to bask in it for as long as he can. But he ignores that fact.

'Sure.' He smiles.

Three Years Ago

'How d'ye dae it?' Banjo asks on the toilet seat, face bloody and clothes ruined from his latest fight. He's been getting into more lately. He's still going through withdrawal, and Finlay knows that's his main reason for lashing out. He wishes Banjo would let Finlay tell the staff – let him ask for *proper* help, rather than just riding it out – but he also knows Banjo would only see that as a betrayal. He'd likely refuse their assistance in protest anyways.

'Do what?' Finlay murmurs as he picks tiny pieces of gravel and dirt from Banjo's chin. He never asks what happened. He never wants to know.

'Avoid fights,' Banjo clarifies.

Finlay goes silent for a bit. 'I don't really need to. When Marco took Mr Black ... that was my boundary. Fighting is my last response.' Not because of a moral high ground, obviously. But because Finlay's smaller and skinnier than most people his age.

'It's ma first,' Banjo admits, voice small, eyes downcast.

'Everybody's different,' Finlay tries.

Banjo laughs until he winces, doubling over. He'd been punched in the stomach, then. The confirmation always causes some kind of corresponding pain in Finlay.

'You need to learn to *pick* your fights,' Finlay says as he dabs some salve on to Banjo's jaw. Banjo won't let any of the staff do this. They all know that the only way to treat Banjo's wounds is through Finlay. 'Nobody bigger than you is worth it.'

There's quiet breathing.

'It's jus' worse fur me,' Banjo says.

'What's worse?'

Banjo goes quiet. 'Am so fucken *angry* aw the time,' he manages eventually. 'I feel as if it'll burn me up if I don' get it out. Am angry at nothing sometimes. Absolute *fuck* aw.'

Finlay holds out a hand for Banjo's T-shirt. Banjo grimaces as he pulls it off. Finlay sets to work on it at the sink.

'I feel that way too,' Finlay says eventually, rubbing the soap bar into the material as the hot water makes the blood run. Bitter metallic salt fills the air. His voice goes quiet. 'I feel so angry I almost want to take it out on everyone. I want them to hurt, because I've been hurt.'

There's a soft bump to Finlay's side.

Finlay looks down, confused.

Banjo is resting his head against Finlay's hip.

Finlay stays very still, as though a wild animal has unexpectedly given him their trust. Despite the fact Banjo lets Finlay clean him up like this, he never initiates touch.

Until now. The tap runs on. Finlay works on Banjo's T-shirt.

'I never get that way aboot you,' Banjo murmurs.

Finlay is going to do something. Touch his head. Reach out. But Banjo pulls away. Every muscle is tense, prepared to fight. Finlay keeps washing. Slowly, in his peripheral vision, Banjo relaxes.

Chapter Twenty-One

BANJO

Family dinner night at Alena's becomes a regular occurrence. Banjo doesn't even know how. All he knows is that when Alena returns to work at the weekend, she's bright smiles and *coming tonight?* After that, Banjo finds himself helping her parents set up the table and making them laugh over corny jokes. He sits close with Alena and rests their knees together. And it's as though he's always been there.

Jace is into science and physics: keeps her maths books neat and tidy, the numbers in little squares inside her jotters. Julie smells like cotton and her laughter is music. Carlos acts out his stories with his hands and is mostly one of the funniest people Banjo's ever met.

They're a family. Just that: a whole unit, a united thing.

Banjo doesn't know that much about them. He doesn't know where Julie works or what Jace's favourite animal is. But he doesn't need to. He already loves them.

That's all it takes. Give Banjo a little and he'll run the mile. Maybe they like him. Maybe they think he's Alena's mate that comes over now. But Banjo actually loves them, with his chest and his stomach and everything in between.

The café is doing Halloween. Morag decides to line the windows with cotton fluff. Banjo doesn't know what it suggests. Cobwebs. Or dust. Something spooky. They buy a couple of pumpkins and carve them out to sit at the window. Banjo's looks crap, to put it politely, but pumpkins are tougher than they seem. He near sprained his wrist trying to give it a smile. It turned into some demented grimace, but Banjo will claim until his dying day that was the whole idea.

'So what's the plan?' Morag asks. It's just them this chilly Saturday morning, November on the horizon and no customers in sight. Alena starts in an hour.

'Whuh?' Banjo looks up from rinsing the coffee filters.

'What's the plan?' Morag repeats. 'In life? What do you want to do? You finish high school next year, right?'

Banjo blinks, a little thrown. 'Uh. No' sure.' He swallows. 'Why, dae I need tae leave?'

Morag stops cleaning tables. 'Sorry?'

Banjo coughs. 'Will I need tae leave at some point?'

Morag just stares. 'No, of course not. What made you think that?'

'Jus' cause yer askin' whit I wannae dae.' Banjo's cheeks burn.

'Yeah, because I didn't think you'd want to do *this* forever.' Morag puts her cloth down. 'But you can if you want to. I might not always be here, but I'll make sure your job is.'

Banjo nods, throat tight with this new information. Forever is one way to put it. If Banjo had this forever, early morning shifts carving pumpkins and washing dishes with Alena, he'd never want anything else. That's the sad fact of the matter.

'So,' Banjo starts, 'see if I, like, move away or whut, I can still keep this job?'

He's been wondering for a while. Whether or not Morag would want to find somebody else if Banjo had to uproot town, school, and life again. It might be a bit inconvenient to sort out hours and everything. Plus it would be the worst thing to ever happen.

'Banjo, nobody's firing you.' Morag stares, hard and resolute. 'Sorry if I in any way suggested that.'

'Whut if I move tae Japan?' Banjo asks the basin. It's the most outlandish distance he can imagine. He's saying it really just to test her. He needs a limit.

'It would cost a fortune in transatlantic flights, but if you can get here every weekend I don't see a problem.'

Banjo smiles.

'Plus I think Alena would be pretty upset if you moved that far away,' Morag adds.

Banjo's glad his back is turned because he can feel his face erupt into flames. He hums, rough and throaty.

The rest of the morning passes quietly. Alena's a bit late, which is unusual. Banjo can't keep his head from lifting every time the door swings.

Then she's really late.

Banjo catches Morag in the back room.

'Is Alena off again?' He tries and fails to sound casual.

Morag blinks. 'She didn't tell you?'

Banjo stares.

'She's in hospital,' Morag says, as if it's the most obvious thing ever.

'Whut?' Banjo's holding a wet plate in two limp hands, feet glued to the floor.

'It's her Crohn's. She texted me last night.'

Banjo can't seem to say or do anything.

'It's fine,' Morag tries. 'She's had a flare-up, but they're treating her. I wouldn't worry about it. I know it sounds serious, but she'll be fine.'

She'll be fine. She'll be *fine*. What kind of fuckery is that? She's in *hospital*. The NHS don't fuck about. She's very clearly not *fine*.

'Where?' Banjo asks.

'EK Community. Not far from here.' Morag points. 'Can't miss it. Big building.'

Of course. Where they met.

Banjo thinks about throwing in the towel – throwing this bloody *plate* back into the sink, untying his apron, and sprinting away. But then he rethinks.

Would she want him there?

'Right,' Banjo says. His voice is flat.

He goes back to scrubbing like the regular Cinderella he is, but his head is somewhere else. He goes to pull his phone out to text Alena, *hey, you okay?* But she's not told him. He's not supposed to know.

She hasn't mentioned the fact she's in hospital, or that Saturday-night dinner is cancelled. Maybe she expects Morag to keep Banjo updated. Figures Banjo will hear it somewhere else.

The longer time wears on, the more the thought niggles at him: tightens his skin and crawls across his hands. His breathing comes out ragged before he just chucks the dish into the sink, half undoes the knot of his apron, declares it a lost cause, and runs out the back room.

'Sorry, Morag.' He gets his stuff underneath the counter, throwing on a jacket over his dirty work clothes. 'Got tae go.'

'Wh – Banjo, you've still got an hour left!' Morag splutters.

Banjo doesn't care. 'Fire me, then.'

Morag's still gaping like a fish. 'You know I could!' she shouts after him. 'I *can*, Banjo!'

When Banjo tries to unlock his bike, the chain is frozen stiff. Impatience squirms underneath his skin, making his fingers jerky and fucking *useless*. None of the dials will turn, they're all stuck, so Banjo stands there for a good *year* fiddling about with it.

'Awk, will ye jus' *fuck me*, then!' He shoves his bike so hard it clatters against the metal railing.

Banjo exhales in a sharp puff, scrubs a hand over his head, and starts running.

It's not as if there's any great hurry. But Morag's in the café all by herself. The sooner Banjo sees Alena is all right, the sooner he can get back. He grits his teeth against his muscles pulled tight after washing dishes and wearing his feet down to the bone.

It really is just across the road. Banjo's not been running long, so it only takes minutes before he sprints through the automatic doors.

Yeah. This is where he made a mistake. He's got absolutely *no clue* where Alena is. Clever plan. Storm a hospital expecting answers. Jesus, he's panting like he's in some critical state. Some of the nurses give him the side-eye. Banjo wipes his forehead and goes over to the main desk.

'Eh,' is how he starts.

The receptionist glances up.

'Do ye know, like, if,' Banjo fumbles, 'if someone had Crohn's – is it *Crohn's disease*, yeah?'

The woman blinks. 'Is what Crohn's, sorry?'

'Is that how it's said?' he asks.

It just seems to confuse her more.

'Are you visiting someone?'

'Where's Crohn's disease at?' He waves his hands to all the signs pointing in twenty different directions.

'Gastroenterology is Ward Eleven—' She looks as if she wants to say something else, but Banjo just nods, pumps some hand sanitiser, and bolts.

'You'll need to sign in!' she calls after him.

Ward Eleven is up two flights of stairs. Banjo's halfway through the first before he thinks about packing it in.

By the time he does get up, it's another walk down a corridor. He ducks into corners when nurses and doctors pass, terrified he'll get chucked out.

What if she's with her family?

What is she's sleeping?

What if she just doesn't want to see you?

He's made it this far, though.

The rooms have little windows. Banjo tries not to stare too creepily at the other patients. He doesn't know how he'd feel about some redhead apparition by his window.

Then he glances into a room with a girl reading a book and does a double take.

She's got a cannula in the crook of her elbow. Her hair is pulled up, and she's wearing a baggy jumper and pyjama bottoms. She looks comfortable.

But she also looks tired, dark circles underneath her eyes.

Banjo's feet stop.

He stands outside her door and breathes hard.

He'll have to do something before the nurses drag him away for stalkerish activity. Banjo knocks on the door.

Before nerves get the chance to clamp around his balls, he opens it.

Alena glances up. Her mouth drops. '*Banjo?*'

Banjo's been running for a solid ten minutes. His hair's a mess, stuck to his forehead, face – both smacked by the wind and cooked in a makeshift sauna all day – a lost cause altogether. His jacket's open, displaying his dirty apron and work shirt.

He grips the door handle. 'Hi.'

'What.' Alena is dumbstruck. 'How did you get here?'

'Jus' ran,' Banjo puffs.

Alena stares. 'You mean. You ran through this *whole hospital* looking for me?'

Banjo licks his dry lips. 'Yeah.' He exhales.

Alena is silent before she laughs. 'Why?'

Banjo twiddles his feet. 'Morag told me ye were here.' He clears his throat and glances off to the side.

'I just didn't want you to worry.' Alena's voice is light.

Banjo blinks. '*Worry?* Course I'd fucken worry! Ye didnae turn up tae work and it's dinner night!'

When Banjo doesn't want to be angry, he can never quite seem to keep his fists to himself. So the one time – the *one time* – he actually wants to be angry, he sounds like a wee boy about to burst into tears.

Alena's eyes widen. She scrambles for her phone. 'Shit.' Everything about her expression changes. 'I forgot it was Saturday, Banjo, I'm sorry—'

'But ye told *Morag*?' Banjo retorts. Jesus, why does he sound like a jealous boyfriend?

Alena doesn't look at him, picking at her frayed pyjama bottoms. 'I'm meant to get out tomorrow,' she eventually admits. 'I thought I'd see you and it would be fine. I always feel like an attention-seeker when I tell people I'm in hospital.' She smiles tightly.

'Ena, it's no' *seekin'* anythin',' Banjo replies, even though his throat feels thick. 'Course I'd come.'

Alena laughs a little and shakes her head.

'Even if it's *every day*, soon as Morag said—'

Banjo cuts off then. Hot blood rushes to his face. The sentence speaks for itself.

Alena smiles softly. 'If it makes any difference, I only told Morag because I'm obligated to. She's the only non-family member that knows.'

'Whut's this make me?' Banjo spreads his arms. 'Space alien?'

Alena laughs. It's a real laugh this time.

Banjo smiles. He crosses his arms over his chest and straightens up. 'Tell me when yer in here, *aight*.' He raises his brows.

Alena watches him for a moment. Her eyes are warm, like she's looking at him across the café, the dinner table, the kitchen sink. It makes Banjo's chest constrict.

'My parents are coming, so you don't have to stay,' Alena says all of a sudden.

Banjo blinks. 'Aw. Right.'

Alena squeezes her eyes shut. 'Wait, sorry, that sounded like I wanted you to go—'

'Ye.' Banjo pauses, foot turned on its side. 'No?'

'No! I just meant, don't feel like you *have* to stay, if you were just coming to check—'

'Ena,' Banjo cuts her off. 'I'll stay.'

Alena looks at him. 'Yeah.' She nods. 'Okay, good.'

Banjo nods back, and then takes the armchair by her bed. He looks at her IV drip: a little fluid bag hanging on the hook with a wire trailing into the crook of her elbow.

'Whut's this?' he asks. He almost wants to flick it but figures that would look stupid.

Alena smiles. '*Drugs*.'

Banjo grins at her voice. 'What kind?'

'These are steroids.' She tugs on it. 'They stop the inflammation.' She pats her stomach. 'In me bowels.'

'Right,' Banjo says. 'Why they inflamed?'

Alena lifts her shoulder. 'Nobody knows.'

Banjo swallows, embarrassed. 'Right.' His cheeks sting. 'Wus that, like, a stupit question—'

'No, no.' Alena reassures him. 'That's not what I meant. Crohn's is an autoimmune disease: your immune system attacks your bowel because it thinks something is wrong. But nobody knows *why* it happens. There are lots of drugs that help, though.' She beams as if it's all sorted. Banjo realises now that she does that almost as a reflex. As though it lightens the mood.

'No.' Banjo looks at her carefully. 'I mean, no' if yer in hospital.'

'Well,' she starts. 'I get immunosuppressants every eight weeks. I'd just finished an infusion when I met you. But they stop working after a while. Then you need steroids.' She rattles her drip stand.

'Why'd ye need the immune – *stuff*, if ye've got steroids?' Banjo's face scrunches up.

'Steroids aren't good for you. Temporary solution. Immunosuppressants, mm.' She tilts her head side to side. 'They're better. They work for a while. I've been on a couple:

196

Humira, Remicade. Sorry.' Alena laughs when she sees Banjo's face. 'This is nonsense to you.'

'Why'd they only work fur a bit?' he asks.

'Because you make antibodies for them,' she states. 'You become immune . . . to *immunosuppressants*.'

Banjo just sits back and tries to digest it all. 'Well, shit.'

Alena huffs a little laugh.

'I mean. *Shit*, Ena.' Banjo leans forward. 'There must be somethin' else.' He doesn't believe this is it. *This* is all she's got.

There's a softness to her eyes. 'They've been talking about surgery for a while. To take out the damaged parts of the bowel. But it's not a cure. Just something to do when all else fails.'

Banjo looks at her. He feels this sadness well up inside him.

'See, this is what I didn't want to happen.' Alena goes tight and humourless. 'I don't want you to feel sorry for me. Honestly, Banjo. I'm fine.'

'I dinnae feel *sorry* for ye,' Banjo replies. 'Am fucken *sad*. It's no' fair.'

Alena looks down at her knees, but when she looks up, she smiles gently. 'Thanks.'

Banjo tips his head in a gentlemanly manner. 'Welcome.'

Alena laughs again. That's three times now. Banjo's not counting or anything.

'Hiya! We – oh.' Julie blinks in the scene, standing at the doorway. Behind her Carlos has a duffel bag slung over his shoulder.

Banjo shoots to his feet, absurdly nervous despite the fact he's on first-name basis with them.

'Banjo's just—' Alena fumbles.

'Popped in fur a bit.' Banjo smiles. 'Am headed now.'

'You don't have to,' Julie tries.

'Naw.' Banjo waves her off. 'I've got work.' He looks at Alena with a smile.

Alena grins and holds her arms open. Banjo tries not to let his surprise show. They've never hugged.

The longer Banjo does nothing, the longer Alena waits.

After some hesitation, Banjo shuffles close and leans down.

He's wrapped in the circle of Alena's arms. She smells soft, clean, flowery, but her touch is gentle and warm. This sudden, crashing relief floods him, as though there's been this constant buzzing in his ear, so constant Banjo never noticed it as it grated his nerves and raked nails down his skin. But now it's gone. It feels as if every piece of him just fits right. He breathes and actually thinks he does it properly for the first time in his life.

When Alena's arms fall away, Banjo realises he needs to stop. It's over. He pats her back when he straightens, trying to play if off, hoping she didn't feel the slight way Banjo's arms tightened.

But Alena smiles at him. Banjo can't help smiling as he steps away.

Once he's at the door, though, Julie wraps him in a hug as well.

Banjo stiffens, frozen.

It's just as warm and gentle. Banjo really doesn't know what to do. People don't hug him. He wants to enjoy Julie's hug. Banjo thinks he wants to enjoy it so much he actually *doesn't*.

Julie releases him, then Carlos pats his shoulder.

Banjo leaves in a trance. That might be the most he's ever been touched.

Chapter Twenty-Two

FINLAY

When Akash takes Finlay to his place, Finlay soon discovers Akash was not talking about going to his student flat on one of the campus grounds. No.

Akash was talking about taking Finlay to his family's house in Hyndland, one of the fanciest neighbourhoods in Glasgow, with pristine red sandstone tenements, small communal gardens, perfectly trimmed hedges, huge front doors embellished with ornate carvings and stained-glass windows. This is not where Akash grew up.

The streets are clean and quiet, the roads littered with nothing but falling leaves and a string of expensive parked cars. Some of the houses have huge overgrown trees outside, towering above the rooftops, branches spreading wide.

It sinks in that Akash isn't some student city dweller: he's *local* to the West End.

Akash stops outside a high-rise with small stone steps fringed by an intricate black railing. It leads up to a beautiful wooden door encased within a stone archway that melts into the rest of the building, a potted bush at either side.

'This is us,' Akash begins, then adds, 'we moved when Mum got a job here.'

Finlay closes his mouth. He keeps his expression blank. Akash opens the front entrance easily, as though he's done it all his life. Finlay follows, but once inside he really starts to think he's dreaming.

There's a chandelier hanging from the ceiling, mahogany-panelled walls and stone-tiled flooring, a hallway that leads to a wooden staircase with banisters and a rug through the middle.

As they climb, Finlay glances up to see the most intricate artwork he's ever laid eyes on: stained-glass windows with aquatic patterns woven into their design.

Akash leads them along another hallway until they're standing outside a door.

'I don't know who's in,' Akash explains as he rattles his key in the lock. 'Not sure if you met them, actually I don't think they were *alive* when we knew each other, but I have two wee sisters, Binita and Kavya, and a wee brother, Ravi. They're ...' Akash holds the door closed. 'A lot.'

'Oh.' Finlay nods. He didn't think Akash's entire family would be home. His palms balloon with sweat, but he follows when Akash goes in.

'*HEY!*' Akash booms out. 'I'm back!'

There's the sound of slamming doors and scurrying feet. Then two young girls appear, hands clasped and smiles wide, eyes on Finlay.

They're very similar despite small differences: one wears her long dark hair in a ponytail with a bow, the other in two small plaits with pink hairclips in. They blink wide, innocent eyes, startlingly reminiscent of Akash.

'Hi!' Finlay waves a dorky hand. Both girls collapse into giggles, covering their mouths and turning into one another as if Finlay's a stand-up comedian.

'Finlay, meet Kavya and Binita.' Akash helpfully points, but the girls still giggle. Akash says something in a different language, voice fluent and light as a totally new accent emerges. He shoos them away, muttering to himself as the two girls run back into their room.

When he sees Finlay still standing there, he pauses. 'Coming?'

'I forgot you could speak another language!' Finlay beams. 'Is it Indian?'

That's a stupid question. That's not a language. Why did Finlay say that?

But Akash only smiles. 'It's Punjabi, and thanks. I was brought up with it.'

'That's amazing. I don't speak Polish.'

Akash sobers instantly. 'Oh. How come?'

Finlay shrugs. 'Never really learned.'

It's sort of the truth and sort of something else. Fleeting phrases and occasional words slipped through Finlay's grasp growing up. It would have taken dedicated effort to learn.

Sometimes Finlay hears it on the street and has to pause as the pain and love sweep through him. Then it makes sense. He never learned it because it was the centre of his trauma, the core of his abandonment.

'It's never too late to learn,' Akash says. 'If you want to.'

Finlay scratches his eyebrow. 'I don't really ... know anyone Polish. It would be pointless.'

Akash steps closer. 'Finlay, *you're* Polish.' He frowns. 'It's your language.'

Finlay swallows. He's never thought about it that way.

'Come on, we need food,' Akash resolves.

Finlay smiles fondly. Akash's Scottish accent thickens when he says that. The two facets of his personality and heritage sit side by side, content to coexist. Finlay can't help but wonder what that might be like.

Finlay follows Akash through a hallway. The room feels as spacious as a museum. Then Finlay spots something on the walls.

Photographs.

Akash standing straight and stiff in a school uniform, his three younger siblings all lined up. Akash grinning big over a birthday cake, every crooked tooth on display. A woman and man stand at either side, both beautiful and well-dressed.

Akash's siblings are there too: a boy thrusting a toy truck in the air, and two little girls at Akash's side – one trying to blow out the candles and the other one pulling her back by the arm. It's so in motion, a living snapshot of the perfect chaos in their lives.

One of Akash in his formal Indian dress, regal and stunning in deep hues of red, a sash wrapped around his shoulders, his hands on the tops of his little brother and sister's shoulders. His grin is so wide.

His parents took photos of everything. They've captured every second of Akash's life.

Finlay experiences this full-bodied sensation rise up inside him. He's never felt it before; it aches but in a lovely way, a beautiful way. It's then that he notices tiny notches along the wall, captioned by marker pen, underneath the pictures.

4ft – Binita
4ft 2in – Kavya
4ft 9in – Ravi
5ft – Akash

Finlay smiles at child-Akash. Somebody so far away from Finlay now, but recoverable through this small historical artefact. He wants to touch Akash's height. The tallest. The eldest. The first born. The one who shoulders all the expectations and sets the standard for the rest. Maybe child-Akash would feel it through all this time and distance.

'You coming?' Akash calls, totally unselfconscious. He waits at the end of the hall, watching Finlay.

Finlay jolts. He didn't notice he was reaching out. He rushes over to Akash, mortification blistering in his stomach at being caught. 'Sorry.'

Akash only smiles. 'Don't be! They're such old photos, I'm probably unrecognisable.'

His self-assuredness is somehow catching. It makes Finlay smile too.

'And, voila!' Akash opens a door, walks inside, and spreads his hands. 'This is me. You can put your stuff in here.'

Finlay glances around greedily, any insight into Akash's life utterly precious.

His room is tidy apart from a cluttered desk. There are piles of battered paperbacks, thick hardcovers lying open, textbooks of every colour, sticky notes crawling up the wall, posters with mind maps and diagrams of the human body climbing their way to the ceiling.

His bed is made. Directly across from it stands a huge bookcase crammed with all manner of novels. He's intelligent: so intelligent it fills his shelves and sprawls across his walls. There's a dresser at the other side of his bed. On top sit deodorant, sun cream, a bottle of water, a glass of water, and two mugs. Akash either loves hydration or forgets about his drinks. Finlay imagines Akash coming back with a cup of tea only to find the abandoned, half-finished one and trying to find space for them all.

That same fondness from the café happens again, that hot unfurling of happiness. Everything he discovers about Akash makes him want to keep discovering, reels him just that little bit closer, becomes a fishhook snagged in the soft underbelly of his gut ready to rip out.

'Want to eat?' Akash beams, setting his satchel down. He throws his jacket over his bed. Finlay does the same. Carefully.

Akash's kitchen is neat and compact. There's a little island counter in the middle with chairs tucked underneath, a bowl of fruit, and a fridge that holds a supermarket inside.

Akash rummages around, pulling things out and placing them on the counter. 'Now.' He picks up an onion. 'I always feel you can tell a lot about people by how they cook. Do you cook?'

'Um.' Finlay blinks, thrown. 'Not unless adding boiling water to tomato sauce counts.'

'Hm?' Akash's head cocks adorably.

'Ketchup packets, salt, little bit of sugar, water. Tomato soup,' Finlay explains with a gesture.

Akash's face lights. 'I've heard of that!'

Finlay's cheeks sting. Akash doesn't need to know this. He doesn't need to know Finlay is intimately aware of how long he can go without food or the fact he carries a snack with him so he can feel it: only eating it when he's in sight of other food. None of that is *cooking*.

'Come here.' Akash beckons him over. 'We'll make stir-fry.'

And so they make stir-fry.

Finlay washes and chops the vegetables while Akash prepares the noodles. He directs Finlay with a gentle touch or a soft word. Finlay forgets he's holding a sharp blade and standing beside an open flame. He forgets everything. Akash is a palm on Finlay's back, a chest brushing Finlay's shoulder, a hand over Finlay's wrist.

Finlay feels as though he might combust. He's literally about to go to the bathroom so he can calm himself down when a boy enters with a thick gaming headset around his neck.

This must be Ravi.

He peers in between them with no greeting. 'What's this?'

'Not for you.' Akash flicks his ear.

Ravi flicks Akash's arm, but he grumbles and pulls back. 'When's dinner?'

'Couple hours. Did you not get the leftovers in the fridge? They were for lunch.' Akash has to raise his voice as Ravi walks out.

Ravi only mumbles some confirmation.

'Done all your homework?' Akash calls after him.

'I started it! I'll finish it later.'

'Why don't you do it now so you can relax later?'

There's a drawn-out groan. 'I said I would and *I will*.'

Akash turns to Finlay with an exasperated look. 'Now you've met Ravi.'

Finlay knows he's smiling, but he can't hope to contain it. It's so lovely to watch Akash with his family.

'Oh, hello.' Akash looks past him.

Finlay turns around.

Kavya is at the doorway.

'When's Ma and Pa home?' she asks.

'It's on the board, see?' Akash points to the fridge, where there's a whiteboard with dates and times on it. 'Done your homework?'

'I don't understand it,' Kavya mumbles.

Akash purses his mouth, looking between Kavya and Finlay. 'You okay to keep an eye on this?' he asks Finlay.

'Oh – sure.' Finlay nods quick.

'Okay, bring it into the living room.' Akash directs Kavya out the kitchen. Finlay stirs the ingredients and listens to the noise of pages being flipped, shuffling on the couch.

'Algebra.' Akash sounds mildly appalled, and then he says something in another language. There's a quiet giggle.

'Okay, see this letter? That's called a *variable*. It doesn't have a fixed *value*, like a number does. So we need to find the value of the *letter* by using these *numbers* . . .'

You just need to explain your evidence. I can show you.

Finlay can feel affection spread everywhere, until he's suffused with it.

'Sorry, sorry.' Akash comes back a few minutes later, crowding over his shoulder. 'Hopefully no more interruptions.'

I like the interruptions, Finlay thinks. *I like being in the middle of your life. I would watch you brush your teeth.*

They both pick up where they left off. It's easy. Being with Akash is so easy.

After a few minutes, Akash pauses to lean his hip against the counter, stirring with the ladle. 'Hey.'

Finlay glances up. They're closer than he thought. He glances away. 'Hi.'

Akash's eyes crease with his smile. 'Can I tell you something?'

Finlay's heart is a frantic drum, but he nods casually. 'Course.'

'I like you.' Akash's voice deepens. 'I'm not sure if you've noticed.'

Finlay is very still. He doesn't absorb the words. He waits a beat. 'You like me how?' His voice is hardly audible. He barely moves his lips.

Akash smiles, small and private. 'I have a huge crush on you.'

Finlay does nothing for several seconds. He feels something slowly come to life in him. It lifts him above the ground and holds him there, completely weightless. It occurs to him that this is elation. It's neither pleasant nor painful: it's looking over a great, dark abyss as it slowly consumes him.

Finlay keeps his face composed. It's a superhuman task. 'Akash,' he murmurs evenly. 'I don't think ... this would be a good idea.'

The words burn his gullet to speak. But they're true. *I've never had something I didn't later destroy. I've never gained anyone I could later keep. And I'm terribly afraid. That feeling dictates me. I've learned to follow it to stay alive.*

'Oh. Absolutely.' Akash is trying to sound flippant, but he's a terrible actor. His voice is strained, clogged with emotion.

There's silence.

'Can we pretend I didn't say anything?' Akash asks softly.

Finlay nods.

'Good.' Akash nods too. 'Can you pass the soy sauce?'

Finlay picks it up. But when Akash tries to take it, Finlay holds on. Something forces his hand.

Akash gazes back at him, calm and serious. He isn't ashamed. He isn't denying it. He isn't backing off. *He isn't ashamed.*

'How ... do you like me?' Finlay can't stop the words. *A casual crush? A passing fancy? An offhand experiment?*

'I like everything about you.' Akash's voice is gentle. 'I want to be with you. And I know you feel the same way, otherwise I wouldn't have said.'

Finlay stares in shock. Somehow all his efforts were for

nothing. He gave everything away. 'You can't know that,' he tries: a last frontier.

Akash studies him. 'I can. Can't you see things when you look at me?'

Finlay's voice is barely audible. 'Like what?'

'Like what I'm feeling,' Akash replies.

Finlay wants to say no. Who can do that?

'I can feel how much you look at me,' Akash continues. 'You must be able to feel when I look at you.'

The food burbles gently. Finlay's skin hurts. He feels exposed. There's nothing else to say. Akash knows.

It takes several seconds before Finlay can speak. 'Why did you tell me this over cooking?' He wants a distraction.

'So you'd have something to do,' Akash responds easily, turning off the stove. He gets bowls and starts dishing out the stir-fry.

'So it felt less invasive. I didn't want to do it in public in case you got anxious around other people. But I also couldn't tell you the second we were alone, that would be way too intense. So I thought: we'll cook together.'

He sends Finlay a bashful smile as he collects the cooking utensils. But his hands tremble. He's nervous.

I've never had something I didn't later destroy.

The shame is rot and decaying death. Finlay feels it peel away from his soul as he watches Akash care about him, openly confess to it, own it with beauty.

'We can pretend I didn't say anything, if you want,' Akash continues, washing the dishes now.

Finlay steps close and touches Akash's shoulder with the pads of his fingertips.

Akash goes still. The water runs on.

He's so warm, emanating warmth. Finlay moves closer. He takes a hold of Akash's shoulders and gently presses his chest to Akash's back, pushing his nose into Akash's jumper. Akash's heartbeat echoes in Finlay's ears.

'I'm sorry,' he murmurs. 'I . . . I can't.'

It's nothing. It's not even an explanation. But Finlay doesn't have one.

Akash turns the water off gently. 'Finlay. Don't apologise.'

Finlay doesn't speak for a moment. Akash smells clean and cottony and familiar, like the combination of every good memory. Their bodies fit together. Akash is bony and soft at the same time, strong and small: his flat back to Finlay's flat chest, all boyish.

'Nothing changes. I still want you in my life,' Akash adds. He doesn't turn around. He's patient. 'As friends. As anything. So I rescind my declaration, all right? *Whoosh*. Gone.' He even makes the sound, fluttering a hand as though he's dispelled his own feelings.

Finlay laughs, throaty and sore.

'We're friends. All right?' Akash murmurs.

No. Finlay's just made the worst mistake of his life. He threw his hands out at the last second, but instead of stopping his fall it only made him hit the ground harder.

Three Years Ago

'Please, just take one.' Finlay holds out a sachet of paracetamol.

Banjo's in bed, damp with sweat, greasy hair, hot cheeks. Finlay doesn't take his temperature. He doesn't touch Banjo at all. He's learned his lesson.

Banjo shakes his head and curls into a smaller ball. It's been a few months since Banjo arrived at Finlay's door frame with a duffel bag and a grim face, but a week since Banjo decided to stop taking all painkillers. Cold turkey.

Finlay has no idea what the catalyst for this go-for-broke mission was, but there's no point guessing. The ways of Banjo are inexplicable – probably even to Banjo.

'Try *one*.' Finlay cracks a tablet out.

'No, Finlay.' Banjo's fingers close around his wrist. It's enough to make Finlay stop. Banjo never touches anyone. Finlay stares down at their joined hands, the way they both shake from the force of Banjo's tremors. 'It'll pass.'

'Banjo, come on, this works,' Finlay tries, crouching by his bed so they're level. 'I told you, we'll wean you off them.'

Banjo shakes his head, stubbornly adamant.

Finlay presses his thumb into his eye socket. He should get help. He's in so far over his head. But would Banjo ever trust him again?

'Please,' Banjo croaks. He looks at Finlay and Finlay knows then that Banjo needs him. Self-preservation leaves Finlay forever, the desire to crawl into his own bed, sleep and not care. All at once, an indescribable protectiveness comes over Finlay. Banjo is his kin.

'Sit up. Here,' Finlay instructs, passing Banjo a glass of water and holding the bottom when it trembles so much it bumps against Banjo's chin.

'Need 'aff 'em,' Banjo mutters as he lies down. Finlay pries the duvet from Banjo's tight fingers so he doesn't overheat.

Banjo's asleep in twenty minutes.

Finlay watches him all night. He realises they're two foreigners in this world. Two people who have nothing. They've travelled without ever knowing a place, they're men inside children's bodies, they're soldiers who have no awareness of war and yet understand its horrors. But they've found one another across the bloody barracks. Not even a lover could care the way Finlay does.

Chapter Twenty-Three

BANJO

Alena needs an operation.

'Fuck,' Banjo says instantly when he arrives in her hospital room and finds out.

Alena laughs. 'Don't worry!' She beams from where she's packing her things. 'I'm happy! This is good news. Plus I get to go home!'

What?

'Whut?' Banjo blinks. 'Yer going *home*?'

Alena grins. 'They don't have the specialists here. It'll be at Queen Elizabeth University Hospital, but they need to arrange it for a few weeks' time. So I can go home and wait!' She really is buzzing about this: happiness flushed in her cheeks.

'So ... this'll make ye better?' Banjo tries.

'Yes.' She nods. '*Much* better.'

Banjo does a little research. *Ileostomy.* That's the name of the operation. He scrolls through the images of inflamed, ulcered intestines online. She'll have a stoma: a little bit of intestine coming out her belly. To see the visible proof of her illness makes the idea of it worse. He finds himself rubbing his abdomen with a grimace.

It's as he's watching a video by one of these gastro specialists that the message comes in.

Hey :)

It's nearly *2 a.m.* She should be *asleep.*

Get to bed, he answers. *Full stop.*

:)))) is her answer.

Banjo smiles but doesn't reply.

:(((((Alena sends a couple of minutes later.

Banjo huffs and rolls on to his stomach.

What's up? he replies.

Working tomorrow? she asks.

Nope, Banjo writes, but realises that's a little blunt. He puts an *x*, but then realises that's romantic. *Nope :-)*, he edits.

was gonna ask if u wanted to go swimming?

Banjo looks at the message for a minute. Then he's hit with an onslaught:

just thinking about what I'll miss once I get the stoma!

I can still swim, but with a bag

totally ok if u don't want to

Banjo frowns at that. *Course I want to.*

Yay! Alena replies.

Banjo grins again. *Where?* he asks.

I can get mum to drop us off :D

Good plan, Banjo writes because his eyes are getting tired, and turns over in bed. He shuts his eyes, gets comfortable, drifts off.

Bolts upright.

'Fuck me, I cannae swim.'

This is how Banjo finds himself on a Saturday morning, backpack on one shoulder with a borrowed towel from Paula and Henry. He felt about four years old skulking up to them last night.

'Whut d'ye take to go swimming?' he asked.

'Alena?' Paula guessed with a smile.

Banjo nodded, a strange warmth caught in his throat, like the fact she knew was both embarrassing and nice. They dropped him off a couple of times at the hospital and noticed he'd been over there for dinner. They were paying attention.

If Banjo sits down and thinks about that, he starts getting indigestion, so he doesn't. Plus there's other fish.

Such as the fact he's going swimming. *Swimming.*

Of all his bad ideas, this is sure to be the best.

Julie answers on the first knock.

'Banjo!' She smiles. 'Alena's just getting ready.' She waves him through as if he needs a physical invitation like a vampire. Banjo smiles helplessly.

It's weird, but at the same time it's not. Julie asks Banjo about school, and running, and it's the way it's always been. Easy. Then Alena bursts into the room, rucksack on, wearing a faded T-shirt and jeans.

They all pile into the car. Banjo realises he's never been in Alena's car before. It smells like leather, seat belts, and clean fabric. Nice. Homely.

'So what's the plan?' Julie asks.

'To swim!' Alena replies with a fist pump, sending him a smile from the passenger seat.

'Fff – eck yeah!' Banjo almost swears. Julie and Alena laugh. It feels as though the whole car lifts with the sound.

Of course, then they get there. Banjo didn't know what to expect. Maybe just a building with swimming baths. Instead it looks like a bloody *water palace*.

There are slides coming out the building and snaking back into the wall. Some are half-open and Banjo sees people sliding down, fully giving up their lives for a minute of fun. Coming out of the building.

Out. Of the *building*.

Banjo gapes.

Alena jostles him with an elbow as they clamber out. 'Okay?'

Banjo closes his mouth and nods.

But one step through the entrance and Banjo's instantly hit with the smell of chlorine, salty sweat, and plastic. His feet falter. His heart does something very fucking similar to vomiting.

'Banjo?' Alena peers at him.

Banjo swallows and plasters on a grin. It's just *water*. It'll be fine.

'Here we go!' Alena gestures to the cubicles.

Oh. Right. Banjo needs to take his clothes off now. In the midst of being preoccupied by water, that somehow slipped his mind.

'Right,' Banjo states.

So now he's standing in a cubicle with a pair of Henry's old swimming trunks. Getting naked feels like a violation of the laws of nature.

Honest to Christ, Banjo strips off his T-shirt and feels as though he's peeling off his fucking *soul*. There's something about it – the strange place, being in a cramped cubicle, hearing voices and laughter all around him – that makes him feel pried open.

Banjo's on his tiptoes to avoid touching any of the damp, soggy tiles growing an undiscovered bacteria, but it still doesn't erase the *nakedness* of being naked in public.

And then he's not naked, and it's okay because the trunks fit (*thank fuck*). Banjo exhales as he glances down at himself. There's not much he can change in the space of a few seconds. It'll do.

'Banjo?' Alena's voice floats over. 'Ready?'

Banjo unlocks his cubicle, steps out, and focuses on walking the narrow path of un-wet floor.

'No' a fan, Ena.' His eyes are on his feet. 'They no' clean the floors?'

Banjo looks up.

Alena's staring at him.

Banjo blinks. He feels blood rush all the way to his head as if he's been tipped upside down.

Alena's wearing a bikini.

For some reason, something about *Alena* and *bikini* never registered in his brain. Never formed to create an image. Banjo doesn't know why. It's not as if Alena hasn't appeared in various ways inside his head, but never in a fucking bikini.

Even when she suggested swimming, Banjo's first thought was Alena in a swimsuit. But this.

An endless stretch of sun-soft olive skin. Alena's arms and legs and *waist* are all exposed, the small point of her belly button, the curve of her hip. He feels as if he's never *seen her* until this moment.

And then Banjo can't help it, doesn't even choose to do it, his eyes just keep moving—

Banjo looks at her boobs.

Fuck.

His eyes fly to meet hers, open mouth at the ready.

Alena's gaze is stuck somewhere at his navel.

'Oh,' she says. One word.

Oh.

Oh?

Banjo looks down, confused. Her gaze was trained on the line of his fuzz tapering down his belly button.

Banjo blinks.

'I—' Alena stutters. 'Sorry. You ready?' Shit, now *she's* blushing: ears red, face red, total embarrassment.

Banjo doesn't know what happened, what is happening, and how to proceed from this situation. 'Whut? It's fine?' he blusters.

Alena's probably just shocked by his ginger trail. Banjo doesn't like to think about it most days. If he were confronted with it in his face, he'd likely have the same reaction.

As they're walking to the pool Banjo bumps her shoulder.

She laughs and bumps back.

'I've gottae admit some'hin,' Banjo starts as they edge closer

219

and closer to the pool. Because she'll find out eventually soon as he starts splashing.

She stops instantly.

'I cannae actual swim,' he states.

Alena stands, unmoving, eyes wide. 'Are you joking?'

Banjo tries to swallow. It gets stuck somewhere in outer space. 'Uh. No.'

Alena blinks. Then she laughs, a warm sound. 'God, Banjo, only you!' She takes both his bare shoulders. 'Don't look so worried!'

Banjo's cheeks are hot, seeping down his throat. Her hands are on his skin, fingers wrapped around his bony shoulders. It's bliss. He crosses his arms over his chest and curls around himself to contain the feeling.

'Naw, I jus' never learned,' he croaks.

'Why didn't you *say*!' she cries. 'We could've done something else!'

Banjo swallows again with a little more success. 'Ye wannae dae it, though.'

Alena gives him a hard look. 'Banjo. Do you want to go somewhere else?'

Well. They're here *now*. Seems a bit pointless.

'Naw, I – I mean, I jus'—' Banjo waves a hand. It will sound ridiculous. It *is* ridiculous. 'Ye could. Teach. Me.' He coughs at his feet and burns hotter than a planet.

Then Alena smiles, squeezes his arms. 'I'd love to.'

Banjo breathes. 'Cool.'

When Banjo and Finlay were at St Andrews they went to the beach. It was summer, it was hot, and it was going to be great. It was a full hour's journey on the bus. They packed trunks, towels, lunch. They had it signed off and everything. Finlay was newly sixteen: he'd made a route, he'd planned the bus times. A whole day of freedom.

I'll teach you to swim! Finlay laughed. *Come on, it'll take two minutes.*

It didn't take two minutes. It took three hours, because every time Banjo got a little further in he had to stop.

I don' fucken wannae! Banjo's voice was reedy and thin. *Can we no' jus' stay here?*

Finlay changed. *Sure.* He made a show of lying in the shallow water, resting back on his elbows. *We'll stay here. It's nicer, anyways.*

They had their lunch on the beachfront, got ice cream, and splashed about with their feet. Banjo never went any deeper than his knees.

When Banjo climbs down the side of the pool, it's the exact same. Because anything that makes him feel out of control, that makes him feel *powerless*, just fucking terrifies him. Even after all this time.

Alena floats behind him.

'Ena,' Banjo says. That's all he says.

'You can stand here,' Alena replies. 'Look. Look at my feet.'

Banjo looks. Below the water, the lapping waves, he can see her feet touching the bottom. The water gets colder as he progresses. It engulfs his toes, his legs, his waist, until he's just left holding the bars of the ladder, white-knuckled and unable to let go.

Alena waits.

'Alena.' His voice actually wobbles this time.

Alena comes closer, her presence a warmth at his back. 'Hey. Watch this.'

And then she's gone. She ducks underwater for a moment, a blurry shape, then resurfaces.

Her hair is plastered to her head, soaking wet, but she just wipes it away with a huge, sparkling grin.

Banjo laughs.

Alena does it again. She holds her nose before she ducks back, only this time she's gone longer before she bursts free.

'See?' Alena holds out her arms after she resurfaces. 'Not a scratch.'

Banjo presses his forehead to the cool metal bars of the ladder. He breathes, in, out, and then he steps in.

There's a moment when he enters the water. A completely weightless moment, a complete nothingness. The whole world is struck off.

And there's a flash of scalding panic, a boiling bucket of *ohfucknofuck*.

Then his feet find the world again.

Alena's grin is waiting for him. 'You did it.'

Banjo's whole chest expands and unfolds out. 'Did it.'

Alena flicks him with water.

Banjo gapes, shocked, and does it back.

Alena flings a handful at him.

'Aay!' Banjo shouts. She ducks underwater again and hides from him.

Banjo follows her. He can't really see, because everything is murky. He resurfaces to the sound of laughter hitting his ears when water falls out.

'You look like a wet cat!' she shouts, both hands flattening Banjo's hair. Her touch is gentle, but it still makes Banjo's organs explode. He does the same. Then they're just standing in the shallow end of the pool scuffling like little kids, and Banjo's laughing in the water, in a *pool*. His nose stings, his skin is wet, and it feels good.

'Do you want to go further?' Alena asks.

Banjo looks at the people weightless and floating. He nods.

She swims out slowly. Banjo walks after her, but reaches out a helpless hand, grappling. She takes it. Banjo really wishes he could appreciate that a lot more than he does. As it stands he's too busy noticing how far the water rises, lapping at his chest, his neck, his chin, until he can't stand any more. His feet can't touch anything.

'Just float!' Alena nods in encouragement. 'We can just float. It's nice.'

We can stay here. Finlay's head tipped back, grin content, his whole upper half dry. As if an hour in a bus was worth it. As if the people having fun in the water didn't matter. So many things Finlay did for Banjo. A bitter ache twists sharp in his chest.

Banjo lifts off the ground.

Alena's grin is worth it. 'Look!' she cheers in victory, shakes their joined hands. She's so fucking *close*. 'You're swimming!'

Banjo knows he's probably crushing her fingers. 'Yeah,' is all he says. Because he's not. He's fucking immobile.

But then Alena releases him. Banjo's untethered. He bobs on

the water, but suddenly it's easy. He knows he's beaming: knows it probably looks maniac, wet-haired and wide-eyed, but Alena is too.

He's swimming. He barks a strange sound, which he'd be embarrassed about if Alena didn't give a little whoop. Then they're both whooping and flapping their arms like seagulls.

They swim all day. Alena touches him a hell of a lot more: jumps on his back and makes him carry her around, and then forces Banjo to get on her back. Alena being on his back is fine: it makes Banjo feel as if he's lost his mind, but that's all relatively normal. Being on Alena's back? The fuck does he do with his hands? His legs? *Anything?*

Eventually they find themselves at the edge of the pool, feet dipped in, hair dripping, hands splayed on the tiles behind them.

Babies are all flailing around like oversized fish, chubby fists and wrinkly arms trying to survive, but their parents celebrate every second of it. Banjo can't help focusing on this dad in particular. Just this regular nobody but for the total exaggerated excitement on his face. He lifts his little kid and squishes them with the wee armbands crushed to his hairy chest. The baby is none the wiser, won't even remember this moment, the look on their dad's face.

'I'll miss this,' Alena murmurs as she gazes out at the crowd.

Banjo frowns. 'Whut d'ye mean?'

Alena clears her throat, cheeks faintly glowing. 'Swimming. I can't do it for a while after the surgery, but even once I'm healed it'll be – weird. With a bag.'

Banjo tilts his head. 'How so?'

Alena casts a look at him. 'I … *poop* in the bag, Banjo.' She says this like it's news.

Banjo frowns. 'So? Everyone's in their fucken underwear here anyway, Ena.'

He's not expecting Alena to laugh. It's this big, beautiful laugh. And he joins in, same as he always does, high on the rush it gives him.

Alena calms down enough to inhale and say, 'Very true.'

Banjo swallows. He fixes her a look. 'So dinnae think like that. Ye hear?'

Alena swallows. She lifts a pinkie. Charmed, Banjo hooks them together and squeezes. That one little contact burns through his veins. He releases her quickly.

Alena has this soft expression on her face. 'Banjo.' Her voice is fond. 'Are you ever going to ask me out?'

The whole universe zeroes into this one second. It zooms until it's Banjo's heartbeat in both hands gripping the wet ledge of the pool, pulse in his throat, the backs of his ears, hot blood in his mouth.

Alena's eyes widen. 'Do you not—'

'*No!*' Banjo shouts, loud enough that some people glance at them. 'No, I never—'

Alena covers her face with a laugh, but it's so choked, so *embarrassed*. He's mucking this up, he's actually mucking it *all up*.

'Ena, wai— wai— wait.' Banjo is unsteady and frantic, but takes her wrist in a trembling grip and tugs it gently from her face. 'Ena, I thought it wus aw *me*.'

Alena's hands fall. 'All you what?' She's so close it almost feels as if they're touching, the heat of their skin pressed.

'I thought,' Banjo rasps, his tongue stuck, 'I thought it wus jus' me that wanted . . . more.' His face burns.

Alena leans closer. 'I've wanted this the whole time.'

Banjo stares. It can't be true. It's too good, too much. 'Why?'

Alena smiles, her pink lips shining damply. 'Because I like you.' Her eyes are warm. Sincere. Is this what light-headed means? Banjo didn't even think you could get dizzy while sitting down.

'How?' he chokes.

Alena shrugs with a laugh. 'Just do. You'll have to accept it, sorry.'

'Aw right,' he manages. His voice is strangled.

Alena leans back a bit. 'Good. Glad we cleared that up.' She beams the Alena Lekkas smile, full blast. And at this proximity as well. He near has heart failure.

Banjo swallows. His face an oven. Now or never. *Now or never. Pick up yer bloody balls.*

'So, like. Would ye. Will ye be – *like* tae be. Ma girlfriend?' Banjo mangles it to all hell. But he holds his ground.

'Very much.' Alena leans in to bump their shoulders.

Banjo nods sharp, once. It doesn't feel real. He probably passed out. Maybe he drowned in the pool. Because he's got a fucking girlfriend. And that girlfriend is *Alena*.

Three Years Ago

When Banjo finds out that Finlay is leaving because he's landed a foster placement, he doesn't talk to anyone. Least of all Finlay. He doesn't react. He helps Finlay pack in silence. St Andrews is only a stopping-off point for the disruptors and the delinquents – a means to an end to get people into the real homes. This is a good thing. Banjo can believe that this is a good thing.

They're stiff with one another. He wants to go to the bathroom and lie down, but there would be no point now.

Finlay says his goodbyes to the staff, nodding and chatting, so Banjo makes his escape.

He goes back into their room and crawls under his bed so he won't have to face it. It's what he used to do when he still stayed with his parents. When he just wanted to fucking disappear.

It takes five minutes. Finlay comes in and walks over slowly. He must be able to see Banjo's feet.

Finlay gets to his knees and squeezes into the cramped space. Banjo doesn't look at him. His eyes are squinted on the mattress above.

They've known each other less than a year. It hardly matters if Finlay leaves. It hardly matters if it feels as though Banjo's known Finlay his whole life. This was always going to happen.

'Half an hour away. *Half an hour*,' Finlay tries, voice gentle. It makes Banjo soft and he hates it. He twists his back to Finlay.

'Won't be the same,' he states.

'We'll make it the same,' Finlay promises. Banjo doesn't believe him. Every part of him aches to turn around because Finlay's *leaving*, but he can't make himself move.

After a beat, Finlay crawls out.

Banjo stays where he is. He doesn't know how long for. Something builds in his chest. It squirms and writhes until it just breaks free. Banjo scrambles up and rushes out the room—

'Banjo!' Douglas calls, because Banjo smacks into him in the corridor. 'Careful!'

'Where is he?' Banjo whips around. 'Where's Finlay?'

Douglas frowns. 'I think he's gone, pal.'

Banjo goes numb. He wants to hit himself, tear at his hair, slap his face, but he also wants to slap *Finlay*, fuck sake, couldn't he have waited another minute? Couldn't he have forced Banjo to turn around, hugged him from behind, done something?

Love me, just love me, even if it's hard and painful and I'm being shite, please just do it, Banjo thinks. He needs Finlay to be the one to do it.

He needs to run. He needs to run until he fucking collapses. Banjo storms outside, about to take off and do just that, until he sees someone.

Finlay is sitting on the concrete steps leading up to St Andrews. Waiting. He stands up when he sees Banjo.

Banjo looks past him and sees Lucy helping an older couple put Finlay's bags in a car, chatting away easily.

Banjo looks back at Finlay.

Finlay smiles. 'I thought you might come out.'

Banjo takes a few steps. He swallows. He doesn't know what to do.

Finlay looks as if he understands, and nods. Then he turns to go.

Before he can, Banjo grabs his wrist.

Finlay stops. 'What—'

Banjo yanks him in. Their foreheads knock together in a headbutt. But Finlay doesn't pull away when Banjo reaches with both hands and holds Finlay's head tight. He just does the same.

Banjo sleeps in Finlay's bed that night before it's stripped.

Chapter Twenty-Four

FINLAY

The day after Akash confesses his feelings, Finlay starts sleeping at Silver Lodge. He knows he's only working himself to the bone to avoid thinking about Akash, but there are too many spare beds to avoid the temptation. And then it's been a week and they're halfway through November. He might as well be a resident now.

Finlay also hasn't seen the girls since he started placement. Although they met for coffee after their first day, they're all too busy, skint, and exhausted to arrange another catch-up. They still text every few days in their group chat, and although coming out to them left him oddly fragile, it faded quickly. He misses them, but it's no longer terrifying to admit that. So Finlay has planned to meet them at Jun's placement in Queen Elizabeth University Hospital next week. They're all going to grab some dinner from there. It's closer to Derya but not to Finlay, yet Jun's placement is right in the heart of the city and there will be lots of places to eat. Plus Finlay wants to go this extra small mile for them.

Work at least provides some distraction from the terrible thing decomposing inside him: that thing being the memory of Akash's sweet warm smell and total acceptance of Finlay's rejection. *I want you in my life.*

After Akash said that, they sat down to eat the stir-fry, and Akash smiled the entire time, trying to demonstrate to Finlay that they were fine.

But Finlay has never felt further from fine.

At first he only goes an hour or two over his shifts. Then it becomes a nightly occurrence.

Rhonda blinks as she's leaving. 'I thought ye were meant to be away!'

'Ah!' Finlay laughs. He's in the living room learning to knit with some residents. He's got two needles and a mess of yarn, a cold cup of tea, and three old ladies trying to direct him every five seconds.

'No, Finlay, ye'll need tae undo that wan,' Rose instructs.

Finlay patiently does.

His shift pattern is meant to be strict nine-to-five. But they're short-staffed, and when the night shift crew slowly filter in nobody questions it, so Finlay just ... stays.

The night and day crew alternate between the five girls and himself, but it means that when he sees Beth in the morning she's gone by the afternoon and he's with Somaya that night.

It's not illegal. He's definitely not working the entire time. He watches detective shows on soft recliners and eats digestive biscuits by the packet. When everyone is in their bedrooms for the night, Silver Lodge falls into a sleepy silence and just the thought of the cycle back to his flat – now freezing since the weather changed – to catch a few hours before he needs to make his way back has Finlay nauseous.

But the dim yellow light, the carpeted hallways, the hum of the staffroom fridge, the whir and click of oxygen tanks and heart monitors, all make Finlay want to crawl into any available bed and stay forever. So he does.

Sleep is quick and painless, and there's no commute. Heaven.

The only trouble occurs when Finlay has to make his way to a cleaning shift. He tries to quietly sneak out at 5 a.m. only to sound all the alarms in the building.

Somaya flies towards him. 'Finlay! What are you doing?'

'Oh.' Finlay shifts his backpack higher on his shoulder. 'Sorry, I must've—'

That's as far as he gets.

'Silly.' She takes her ID card and presses it to the sensors. Instantly the beeping stops. 'We'll need to get you one of these.'

'Right.' Finlay smiles.

The next day, he has his own key card. Life is swell. Finlay can creep around a nursing home like a completely normal, well-adjusted individual.

His phone is silent.

Akash is probably waiting for Finlay to get in touch. Considering the fact Finlay shot him down, that would be an entirely reasonable way to behave.

I want you in my life. But Akash needs some proof Finlay wants that too.

Yet the thought of seeing Akash makes a giant cess pit of

misery and regret open up in his middle. Because this is what Finlay does: recognises his clingy need for somebody inside himself and rejects it, ignores it, runs from it. Because when he shows it, people disappear.

Finlay wakes up in the middle of the night to the sound of somebody in the bathroom across the hall. Soft feet, flushed plug. Disorientated, he lifts his head.

'Banjo?' His voice is rough. Then he remembers he's at Silver Lodge, and Banjo isn't here.

He doesn't fall back asleep for a long time.

Jeanie is the superstar of Silver Lodge. She's basically deaf but she's lovely, does her hair and makeup every day, smells like a meadow, and her room is always tidy. She's Finlay's favourite. She's everyone's favourite.

When Finlay comes into her room, she beckons him over and presses a wrapped mint into his hand.

'Thank you!' Finlay beams, utterly charmed. Then the mint touches his tongue. '*Whoa*, Jeanie!' Finlay's eyes water as he coughs. 'That'll singe the nostrils right off.'

Jeanie frowns. 'I've no' got any tonsils!'

Finlay laughs loud.

Most days they play crossword puzzles, or she chats to him about her family, or her career as a teacher, or where she's travelled and the things that she's done. Finlay's half in love with her. Admittedly, he's half in love with all of them.

Which is why when he comes in a week and a half after seeing

Akash to a sombre atmosphere and unsmiling faces, he knows something is wrong.

'Anne passed away last night,' Beth tells him quietly, her eyes tinged red. 'Stroke.'

Finlay knows it's terrible, but relief instantly courses through him. Not Jeanie, not Rose, not Edith. 'Oh,' he begins.

'She was alone,' Beth continues. 'She didn't use her buzzer or anything. She probably didn't know, but – she was alone.'

Finlay is silent.

'They've moved her, it's just her stuff—' Beth begins, and shakes her head quick. Anne was her patient. Finlay doesn't know how long for.

'Don't worry; I'll get it,' Finlay says. He considers placing a hand on her shoulder and changes his mind.

When he goes into Anne's room, everything is as it was. Her clothes, her toiletries, her books, all in the position she was used to. All in the place she kept them. Because she lived here. She still does. She's not gone. It's Finlay's job to remove her, to extract every small trace, but for now she still exists. Her smell, her presence, it all envelops Finlay.

He wonders who would be given this job if he passed away. Who would go into his flat and pack his things, donate his clothes and strip his bed. Life is something people have for a short time. Living means pushing that fact aside.

Maybe that's not true, though. Maybe he's in shock. Because when he's making tea in the staffroom, Finlay sees his shaking hand as it spoons in some sugar. He stares at it, confused.

He didn't know Anne. He met her a handful of times. She was a little prickly but otherwise nice; kept to herself, complained when the food was cold, and only really spoke to Beth, who reminded her of her granddaughter. But now she's dead. She died alone. In an empty room with nobody.

Finlay goes to the bathroom. He gets to his knees in front of the toilet, sure he'll be sick. But when he has his forehead against the cold porcelain, inhaling the citrus detergent, the feeling evaporates. Finlay gets to his feet, washes his hands, and continues working.

When the shift finishes, Finlay walks with his bike. It's raining, which makes holding his phone difficult.

It's been almost two weeks now. They haven't spoken once. But Finlay needs this. Maybe he can admit that, at the very least. He needs Akash.

'Hello?' Akash sounds different. Soft. Surprised.

Finlay ducks into an empty bus stop and sets his bike against it. The hailing rain batters the thin plastic roof. He covers one ear and presses his phone to the other. 'Hi. Sorry. Placement's been mad.'

'Don't worry about it.' Akash's voice is liquid heat, warming Finlay from inside. The soggy patches on his trousers are less miserable. 'How are you?'

'I miss you,' Finlay blurts. 'I want you in my life, too, Akash.'

There's a pause. Akash exhales. He sounds winded.

Finlay feels winded. He's winded himself. He had no intention of ever saying these words. But somehow they've spilled. Powerless. He's always been powerless here. Is there any point in fighting it?

Is there any difference – missing someone up close or missing them from far away?

'Are you all right?' Akash asks, because he'll always have the ability to understand Finlay.

Finlay runs a hand through his damp hair, hood blown off and rendered pointless. 'Lost a resident today. And – no.' He laughs, unstable. 'But ... maybe I've changed my mind.'

He waits. He doesn't breathe.

'Here's what I propose,' Akash begins. 'Don't change your mind.'

Everything Finlay did was to avoid this. This gut-wrenching pain.

'Oh.' He sounds punched.

'Because you'll never stop,' Akash explains. 'I think the problem is you see this as totally irreversible. It doesn't have to be that way. We can take things as slowly as you need.'

Finlay breathes. 'Okay.' He closes his eyes. 'You ... you still feel the same, though, right?'

'No,' Akash states. Finlay has a three-second cardiac arrest before: 'It's worse. Much worse. I'm being crushed by the insurmountable weight of my feelings. I seriously don't know how much longer I've got left.'

Finlay curls around his phone laughing. 'You're ridiculous. That was a serious question.'

'And a serious response!' Akash cries, wounded. 'I am *seriously* putting my affairs in order as we speak.'

'Stop.' Finlay's beam is big enough to split his face. 'I'm ...' He can't explain. He pauses.

'I know,' Akash murmurs, dark and serious.

Finlay knows Akash does. 'Do you know why I wanted to be a nurse?' he blurts.

'A stress-free life?' Akash guesses.

Finlay laughs. 'No. I wanted to be a nurse so I'd have proof that I'm a good person.'

Akash waits.

'I know that sounds really strange, but I just wanted to do something with my life that would give me evidence I'm good.'

'You are a good person, Finlay,' Akash tells him, like the fact is so obvious he's confused as to why it needs said.

'Thanks.' Finlay smiles, but he clears his throat.

It's hard to instantly believe something he's never been told. It's hard to think of himself as a good person when his mother left without a word and his father never met him. It's obvious he was the problem. And Finlay's made his peace with that. But he's also spent his life combatting any possible cause. He never gets angry, never gets sad. A model human being. And whenever any emotion is about to overwhelm him, Finlay empties himself of it.

'Finlay. You *are* a good person,' Akash repeats.

Finlay feels as though there's a fist gripping his windpipe. His eyes prickle. He presses fingers into his eyes under his glasses and gives a choked laugh. 'Well, I've never actually been told that before.'

'I'll tell you every day if I need to,' Akash states.

No questions. No pity.

Finlay swallows around the malformed lump in his oesophagus.

Akash gives so easily, so freely. Finlay knows if he opens himself to Akash, then he'll have to tell him. About Banjo. About his mother. About his life. But the mere thought of opening *himself* to all that physically hurts.

'Look, I can't promise this won't be a disaster.' Finlay is unravelling, a loose thread accidentally tugged until the whole infrastructure is destroyed. 'I'll probably have these freak-outs several more times and I genuinely—'

'Hey.' Akash stops him. 'Remember, *slowly*. Nothing needs to change. And who cares if you have freak-outs? We'll work through them. I have freak-outs too.'

Finlay swallows. 'Really? What about?'

'How cute you are.'

Finlay groans and falls against the bus stop. He literally swoons. '*Stop.*'

Akash giggles down the phone. The sound is so lovely that Finlay, for a brief moment, feels happy.

Chapter Twenty-Five

BANJO

Julie smiles when Alena and Banjo climb into the car after they're dressed and dried from swimming. 'How was it?'

'Good!' Alena smiles, and shoots a look at Banjo before her eyes dart away.

'You all right? You're a bit flushed.' Julie frowns.

Alena goes darker. 'I'm fine, Mum.'

'Have a good time?' The question is directed at Banjo now. It takes Banjo a solid four seconds before he realises. He'd spaced out thinking about Alena's mouth.

Alena turns around in the car. Banjo meets her gaze. A shock wave goes through his belly. Her eyes have connected to some internal part of him.

'Uh,' Banjo manages. 'Yuh, yeah.' He can *feel* his face scalding. How red is he at this point? It's probably radioactive.

The journey is excruciating.

Julie makes some idle chit-chat, but Banjo can barely form anything coherent. At one point Alena turns around to look at him and Banjo can't tear his eyes away.

He just holds her gaze, holds it, holds it, doesn't know how to let it go. He knows what his eyes are probably saying, broadcasting for anyone to see: *I want to kiss you, I want to kiss you, Iwanttokissyou.*

'You staying for dinner, Banjo?' Julie asks.

Banjo realises they've stopped.

'Mm. Yeah.' If he were dying, his voice would sound better.

Alena jumps out. Banjo follows. He doesn't know what's going to happen, what changes, what stays the same. He wants to find out, though. The desperate anticipation hurts better than anything Banjo's ever felt.

Carlos and Jace are in the living room. They make noises as soon as he comes in, but Alena stands at the stairs ready to sprint up.

'We'll be in my room!' Alena calls, eyes still on him. Banjo's not even got his *shoes off.* He's not about to waste any time doing that, though.

They must sound like a tornado storming up the stairs. Banjo can barely keep up, tripping and falling about the place, but then . . .

Alena rips open her bedroom door and says: 'Banjo.'

She says *Banjo* the way someone would say *finally.*

Banjo tumbles into Alena's bedroom, kicks the door shut with a foot, falls forward, and presses his mouth to hers.

It's a clumsy moment of contact, just the sliding of lips to parted lips, but as soon as it happens Banjo feels something take flight inside him. The world drops away beneath his feet, but there's no lurch. Only the bottomless nothing of floating.

They're kissing. Alena's mouth is hot-soft, warm moving against his. Arms rope around his shoulders, fingers comb into his hair, and then it feels as if they're *hugging* and *kissing* at the same time, which is far too much.

They're a little off balance and fumbling. Banjo ends up bashing his hip against her desk as they spin around. Alena ends up laughing against his mouth, *into* his mouth. He can feel the sound of it, the vibrations pressed to his teeth.

Banjo's never kissed laughter. He wants to do it with Alena all the time.

But he has no idea what to do with his hands, so he hovers them at her sides until she takes one and presses it to her back. Banjo takes that as his cue and slides a hand along her jaw, holding her face close. Alena keeps two hands gripped in Banjo's T-shirt.

It feels unreal good when she holds him: any part of him. It feels as if he'll live and die for this.

'Wis it any good?' Banjo whispers a little later, as they're washing dishes after a whole night of secret touches and smiles.

Alena is flushed pink, tousled hair, bright eyes. 'The kiss?' she whispers. Her grin splits wider. 'The best.'

Banjo doesn't try to contain his grin.

Both their hands are in the sink. Banjo finds one. He tugs her close enough that he can lean down and press his forehead to hers.

'Best,' he whispers into her face, and bumps their noses.

Paula takes Banjo into Glasgow the morning of Alena's operation at the end of November. Julie, Carlos, and Jace already took Alena in at 6 a.m. with all her stuff. He was going to get the bus, patch school for a day, but Paula offers and he'd rather fucking go with someone, truth be told.

Paula doesn't speak. She doesn't expect Banjo to speak, either. But still, he feels better for the company. He feels better because it's Paula, and she never expects anything from him.

The weather is dreary and drizzling. Then Banjo sees it.

His stomach drops to the floor.

The hospital is a tall, looming giant. The problem isn't that Alena is getting an operation here. The problem is that this is the same hospital where it happened. Where everything ended with Finlay. Of all the hospitals – of course it is. Why didn't Queen Elizabeth University Hospital ring a bell?

Banjo's never been back. He didn't even think he'd recognise it, but his body knows. He feels himself blanch and drain of all colour: swallows hard against the bile pressing into his throat. He crosses his arms and stuffs his shaking hands underneath his armpits.

He can't think about this now. He's not at St Andrews any more. He's not that person. He can do this. For Alena, at the very least.

Paula parks up at the entrance. 'Good luck,' she murmurs, same as she did on his first day at the café. Only this time she does pat his arm.

Banjo smiles, small. 'Thanks.' He nods. He waits for her to remove her hand. Then he forces himself to get out.

Banjo shakes as he walks to the ward. HDU. High-dependency

unit. It's the same route he walked to visit Finlay. The police with their crackling walkie-talkies, folded arms, vomit all down his front, snot and tears dried on his face. He can't relive this, but it's happening anyway: a leaden weight pulling him down, the oppressive silence pressing against him, the tension rising up like bile only worse.

And then Banjo sees her.

'Ayyyy!'

Alena's sitting up in a bed in a private room, two arms open, grin wide. There are wires everywhere. In her arms, up her nose, down her gown. She's chalk-grey and groggy, buzzing machines surrounding her.

Julie is having a cup of tea on the armchair, Carlos is standing with his arms crossed, and Jace is sitting on the bed, her legs in a basket. They all grin when Banjo appears at the doorway.

'Banjo!' Alena motions him over.

Banjo feels himself smile despite everything, crossing over to them all. He leans down and presses the lightest kiss to her head.

'Ah's ma boyfren',' she garbles to everyone.

Banjo's head becomes a roasted tomato. But then Julie laughs, Jace joins in, and Carlos clasps his shoulder. He's cocooned in their warm wee circle.

But Alena's exhausted. In the minute it takes them to chuckle, she's fallen asleep.

'It went well,' Julie murmurs to him, and Banjo breathes easier.

He sticks around for a little bit. They all make chat, but

when the opportunity to escape arrives, Banjo grabs it. He wants to be with Alena, but not here.

He exits quietly and doubts any of them will notice.

He's no use to her like this, anyway.

The walls, the lights, the beds, the curtains: everything ingrained in his memory and making his legs weak, mouth dry and sticky.

He staggers into the hallway. There are a few student nurses coming his way. Banjo lowers his head as they pass.

But something makes him glance up. A prickling along his nape. An awareness of eyes.

Banjo looks.

Finlay.

It's a bullet to the abdomen. Banjo rips his gaze away quick, an automatic instinct, but he staggers with the force.

No, he thinks. *It can't be.*

The group passes, and the moment is over, but Banjo looks behind him.

The two girls walk on, but the guy looks over his shoulder too.

Thin-wire glasses sit on his nose, ash-blond hair, a nursing uniform on, a lanyard around his neck. His eyes are Finlay's. He *is* Finlay.

He's here. Right here, in the exact same place it happened three years ago. He's all right. He's a nurse. He's exactly the same as before. He's nothing like before.

Banjo stops where he stands.

Finlay pauses at the corner.

Banjo opens his mouth.

'Finlay?' a voice calls, light and easy, as if Finlay's name doesn't hurt like swallowing blades.

Finlay looks away and disappears around the corner.

Banjo runs. He finds the disabled toilet and locks it quick. He drops to his knees. Nothing comes up. His mouth is open, panting, but nothing comes.

Three Years Ago

Finlay is back at St Andrews. He had a good few months at that foster placement, but now he's been dumped back in here for some reason. Whether by chance, or he specifically asked, Banjo has no idea. Why would Finlay ask to come back, though?

Everything feels fragile. The few months Finlay was away have created this gulf between them.

It feels like they're moving towards something, but the same way a landslide moves. Like everything they stand on is just crumbling beneath them.

They kept in touch. Banjo called a few times. He'd update Finlay on the goings-on just to hear his voice. But Finlay never swung by. And he never offered, so why should Banjo ask? He hates that he was left to ask. It's like a shard of glass snapped off inside him.

Either way, they're different and Banjo doesn't know how to fix it.

Maybe that's the reason he does what he does next. Maybe Banjo just fully loses his mind. He's got no idea what possesses him. He just wants some insight, something to go off, something to hold and say *look, get over yourself, get over your anger and your hurt and stop fucking destroying this.*

So when Finlay goes to brush his teeth for bed, Banjo checks his phone. It's charging on the nightstand. Locked. Obviously. Banjo types in Finlay's birthday.

He doesn't really know what he's looking for. He just wants to feel closer to Finlay, to bridge this terrible gap between them, to bridge the gap inside himself between how he feels and how he wants to feel. He thinks maybe if he finds evidence that Finlay's still the Finlay that Banjo knows, it'll pass.

But he doesn't get that.

He goes through text messages first. Finlay's never been one for replies, so there's barely anything. Just their own awkward exchanges, some stuff between Finlay and his worker. Banjo scrolls through Finlay's photos. Not much in there either. Clothes, books, scenery, screenshots. Nothing personal. Finlay is so private. Even to himself.

Banjo finds himself softening the longer he looks. The anger melts away. Then he clicks on the internet.

The sound of moans blast to life so sudden and sharp Banjo drops the phone.

He scrambles to pick it up and close the page. Then he just keeps closing all the other tabs:

Shirtless male models
Guys kissing
2 guys together

'Banjo.'

Banjo turns with Finlay's phone in hand.

Finlay stares at him. His face looks strange, like cracked ice before it shatters.

Banjo's stomach lurches up his throat. He wants to be sick. 'Whit the fuck?'

Finlay takes a half-step inside the room, his pyjamas hanging off his lanky frame. 'What?' His voice trembles.

'Whut's this?' Banjo knows he sounds small, little, but he can't change it. Somehow he knows that this is a bad reaction, it's not the way you're supposed to fucking react to this – but he feels lied to, he feels spit on and betrayed, like it was all a fucking *lie*.

'It's just kissing,' Finlay tries, the words shaky and warbling in his chest. 'It wasn't – it's nothing *bad*—'

Banjo chucks the phone on the floor.

Finlay looks at it but makes no move to pick it up.

'The *fuck*?' Banjo hisses, pain injected into his veins and flooding his whole nervous system. He's trapped in this corner of the bedroom, no way out. Because he's been made a fool by Finlay. *Finlay.*

'Yer *gay*?' There's this rising hysteria climbing up his throat and making it difficult to breathe. He wants to calm down, to hear Finlay out, but most of him wants to rip everything apart. Because Finlay kept this from Banjo the whole time.

'It's not a bad thing,' Finlay keeps saying, keeps twisting the blade further in, but his voice goes smaller and smaller.

Banjo is dumbstruck. Finlay doesn't understand. 'It's no' aboot that. I dinnae care aboot that. Ye *lied*.' The words come out wheezy. They wind him. 'When Marco an' aw that—' Banjo can't finish.

Here come the boyfriends!

Oh, look, it's the two queers.

Finlay knows exactly what Banjo means. Because Finlay always shut it down when it was just them. *We're not like that. They don't get it.*

But Banjo thought *Finlay* got it. Because Banjo always said, *It's fine if ye are. Am no', but it doesnae bother me.* And he wondered, sure; but that's the fucking reason he asked.

Yet Finlay always replied, *I'm not, either. I would tell you.* His eyes were clear and honest in the dark.

Banjo feels so used.

Finlay's whole face is chalk-white, paler than his hair, just ghastly pale. 'I didn't—' He reaches out.

Banjo flinches away from him.

Finlay goes stiff. His eyes fill with water. He looks blurry, though. Banjo realises his own have done the same.

Because of course. Nobody stays. Banjo alone isn't enough; there's always another motive. There's always something else. Finlay never cared the way Banjo cared. He just wanted something else. He wanted – something fucking else. That's obviously why he lied. Banjo asked and Finlay lied right to his face.

The betrayal burns Banjo's entire body. He feels so betrayed that nothing, not even Finlay taking a pair of scissors to his spine, could hurt worse. Every single moment is reshaped and redefined in Banjo's eyes. Every smile, every word, every touch. All of it is ugly now. None of it pure.

He was stupid. So childish and naïve, so fucking *stupid*. As if boys stay up late at night laughing, press their foreheads together, lie at opposite sides of a door. It was everything to Banjo and now it's all rotten, putrid shit. Finlay was lying to him; it was all just some *lie*.

'Stay away fae me,' Banjo states. His mouth feels full of salt, bitter and aching inside his jaw. His teeth are a cage trying to hold it in. His throat tightens to the point of pain. It rushes all the way up his face, prickles across his cheeks and stings the inside of his nose.

Finlay's eyes just stream tears silently, wide open and fixed on Banjo. 'Banjo, I'm still me.'

'*No!*' Banjo makes a shrill scream, and then it won't stop, it's all just pouring out: 'Ye lied, ye fucken *lied*, aw this time yer a fuckin' *liar*, Finlay—' Banjo needs to move, to get Finlay to move, so he shoves Finlay backwards with two hands on his shoulders. Finlay's so bony, so breakable and small, and he doesn't even fight back.

'Ye never – *ever* gave a single *shite*—' Banjo's hands curl from flat palms into fists, and he feels the punch before he even makes it: feels it connect with Finlay's sharp ribs and knock the air out. It's not even a hard punch, but Finlay isn't expecting it. That's the worst part. He's not expecting it.

Neither is Banjo.

Finlay stumbles away. He bends double to make himself small, arm wrapped around his middle. Frightened. Frightened of Banjo.

Something strange happens to Banjo. He goes deaf. This loud,

loud ringing takes over every available noise. It swallows him, swarms him from every angle.

This is why nobody has ever cared about him. Who the fuck could?

They stare at one another. They're both empty. They can't believe what's just happened. They've both stabbed each other in the throat, and now they're watching one another bleed out, gurgling around the blade.

What have I just done? The thought comes down on Banjo like a bolt of thunder. The fury evaporates, his mind clears, and Banjo thinks, *What the fuck have I just done?*

This wild, strangled desire grabs hold of him. The desire to laugh really loud and make it a joke. The desire to pretend he didn't see anything. The desire to rush forwards and cling to Finlay's pyjama top. The desire to burst into tears. To take the knife out. *Just take the knife out.*

Finlay breaks eye contact first. He collects his phone off the floor and stares at it.

He doesn't make any noise, just gets into bed as if every muscle hurts. He turns his back and does nothing.

Banjo does nothing too.

This is it.

They'll forget one another. They'll move on and live different lives, meet different people. Banjo can see it in front of him. He doesn't want it. He'll never want it. He wants Finlay. He wants their beds across from one another, their breaths lulling each other to sleep.

Finlay once said they were family. They could fall out, but they'd always be that. It's not true, though. It was a nice idea. But it's not true.

Banjo goes into the bathroom and lies down on the floor. He waits for hours, but nobody comes.

They don't speak. They don't look at one another. The staff know something is wrong. Nobody asks. Finlay is listless and sullen, doesn't eat, doesn't get out of bed. Banjo avoids their room and runs until he tastes blood.

The shame came to Banjo less than an hour after their fight. It trickled in like a thick, heavy substance, as though he'd swallowed wet cement and it was hardening inside him, turning him to stone like some folk creature.

It's not a bad thing. Those words are an open wound in Banjo's chest. Of course it's not a bad thing. There's nothing fucking bad about being gay. That's not the problem. The problem is that Finlay lied. Kept it a secret, stored it away, made their whole relationship have this other twisted side to it – one where Finlay was lying in wait, laying down a foundation, to take what he wanted from Banjo and go.

But the more Banjo sits with it, the more he realises the truth. That didn't happen. Finlay didn't lie. He was just afraid. For good fucking reason, it seems.

Why didn't Banjo stop and listen? He always thinks the worst, most fucking vile things of people.

Banjo wants to erase it. Even while it was happening, some part of him wanted to erase it. But clarity comes like a new morning and wakes Banjo up to the way he reacted.

He was awful. He was disgusting. He needs to apologise. He knows he does. Every day he thinks about it. Every second that passes. For a week. And every night, they climb into bed and turn their backs. Every night Banjo cries himself to sleep while he listens to Finlay cry himself to sleep.

When Finlay goes for a shower, Banjo spots something on his bed. It's tucked under his pillow, just visible. Co-codamol. A familiar itch arrives. Banjo scratches his arms. But he knows that won't cut it.

In a flash, he grabs the box and opens it. Banjo blinks. He takes the sachets out. He goes through each of them. All empty.

This heavy mass presses down on every one of Banjo's organs.

Banjo creeps over to the bathroom. The shower's running.

'Finlay?' He keeps his voice monotone. The shape of Finlay's name in his mouth is strange. As though he hasn't said it in years.

There's no response.

Banjo knocks hard now. 'Finlay, come oan!'

Still nothing.

Finlay would respond. That's what's taken so long for Banjo to pluck up the courage to talk to him; because whoever breaks first has to accept what the other person says.

'Fuck sake, Finlay, Ah need in!' He's pounding on the door non-stop now.

Silence. Running water.

'Finlay, please.' Banjo twists the door handle this way and that, but it's jammed. He kicks it with a flat foot once, twice, and then it explodes.

Part of him is expecting to find Finlay in the shower.

But he's not.

He's on the floor. He's grey. His whole body is grey. His hands, his face.

He's unconscious.

Banjo is very still.

'Finlay,' he tries.

Nothing.

Banjo rushes to Finlay on the floor and sits him up quick. Finlay is a dead weight, flopping uselessly. No. Banjo slaps his face. *NO*. He gets Finlay's mouth open and shoves his fingers inside. He wriggles them around Finlay's throat, touching all the sides until Finlay's throat spasms. Banjo keeps forcing it, keeps pushing them down and pressing on his tongue until hot acidic vomit spills all over his wrist.

But Finlay's still out of it, his eyes fluttering wildly, not conscious in the least despite being sick. This should have worked. He saw his maw and da do this to each other. *It needs to work.*

'Finlay, come on, come on, come on,' Banjo babbles. 'Please no, no this, no, no no, please—'

'What's goin' on?' One of the other boys is at the door – maybe Sonny or Calum, Banjo's not paying attention.

'Leave us the fuck alone!' he shouts, trying to shield Finlay from him.

'What the fuck?' Marco chimes in; his familiar voice like pins and needles. 'Is he dead?'

253

'*Leave!*' Banjo's voice is shrill. A little boy's voice. He presses wet, sick-covered fingers to Finlay's throat, feeling for a pulse. He tries the other side, lies Finlay down and puts his ear to Finlay's chest.

'Is he not breathing?' Calum appears.

'We should get someone,' Sonny adds.

'Please, God, Hail Mary, Mother of God—' Banjo puts hands over Finlay's chest and starts pumping. His arms are too weak, too limp. He knows he needs to shove his hands down hard enough to break ribs but his body won't co-operate. He can't hurt Finlay. Banjo's not even breathing properly; it's gasping out, it's so high-pitched and weird, he might be moaning he doesn't even know—

'Banjo, *Banjo*.' Douglas touches his arm, trying to be gentle but insistent, yet Banjo won't move until two people in green uniforms crowd around him.

'Banjo, can you tell me if your friend has taken anything?' the woman asks as she takes over pumping Finlay's chest, wearing a bulky high-vis jacket with a walkie-talkie and a backpack strapped on.

'Whuh—' Banjo whips his head around. 'Uh, painkillers, I think—'

'Do you know how much?'

When Banjo shakes his head, they give Finlay that naloxone nasal spray stuff and shuffle him on to a stretcher. Banjo watches in a state of shock. Finlay's head lolls. He's been unconscious for too long now. It's been too long.

The paramedic shines a light in Finlay's eyes, then she starts pumping his chest. Her arms are straight and solid, her breathing calm, but Finlay's not doing anything. Nothing.

This noise erupts from Banjo. It's this horrible, ugly whine. He wraps both hands around his throat to stop it, too mortified to allow it, but then something else happens.

A rattling wheeze. Another one.

Finlay starts breathing.

'We need to get him to hospital,' the paramedic states.

Banjo follows everyone blindly, out into the freezing night and to the ambulance with just his threadbare T-shirt and shorts on.

Banjo throws a desperate look to Douglas after he climbs in behind the paramedics lifting Finlay. Douglas sighs but jerks his head to the seat beside him. Banjo scrambles in. Douglas pulls a jacket around his shoulders when he sits.

'My name's Alison.' The paramedic smiles as they're all falling about on the tiny back seats with flimsy belts across their thighs. Banjo doesn't look at her. He doesn't look at Douglas. He can't look at anyone but Finlay. Finlay's got tubes in his arm and up his nose. The other paramedic straps stickers to his chest, connecting him to a machine. Banjo watches as the steady pulse of Finlay's heart appears on the monitor. His own feels ready to burst out his throat.

Banjo tries to follow Finlay into Queen Elizabeth University Hospital before he's stopped.

'Am I able to take a quick statement from you, Banjo?' Alison, the paramedic, asks. A police officer joins her. Douglas stands at his side, a hand on his back.

'We know this must be scary, but it's better to do this while it's still fresh.'

Banjo stares at them. He can't really understand English right now. He frowns, and then grins. 'I jus' started sayin' Hail Mary.' Banjo barks a laugh, but then he can't stop. He laughs so hard he's actually gasping with it, standing in front of the police and the paramedics fucking *laughing*.

'Okay,' Alison states. 'We'll get you checked over, but can you tell us how you found him first?'

Banjo tells them. It's not enough: they want details, times, *where did the painkillers come from?*

From me, Banjo knows. *All this came from me.*

He sits on a paper sheet over a bed while a nurse checks his eyes and inside his ears, even though there's nothing wrong with him. Douglas goes to get some water.

'Is Finlay in trouble?' Banjo asks Alison quietly, watching the police officers talk in the hallway.

'No,' Alison says simply.

After a while he's allowed to wash the vomit off and go visit. Banjo storms with Douglas to where Finlay is and almost drops dead.

Finlay's awake, pale and groggy, holding his arm up for a blood pressure check. There are four nurses around him. Douglas rushes in quick to Finlay's side. Finlay blinks up at him, and then he spots Banjo. Their eyes meet. Finlay turns and looks at the wall. His face is blank.

Right. They're still over. Banjo doesn't have an apology big enough for this.

He leaves. He wanders the long corridors without a clue where he's going. He does that for a little while until he just sinks to the ground and cries. People need to pass so Banjo presses his back to the wall and brings his knees up. Thank God nobody asks what the problem is, content to let him lose whatever the fuck he's lost.

Chapter Twenty-Six

FINLAY

Finlay recognises the hallways as soon as he enters Queen Elizabeth University Hospital. Then it comes to him, like the resurfacing of a past life, *Oh yes, I've been here before.* This is where it all happened.

He's always quite impressed with his ability to block. Until he's actually standing in the middle of an old memory and it's violently brought forth, he has no recollection of a single detail of it.

Finlay can't even remember what age he was when he made an attempt on his life. When he was rushed here.

But it was also a few days in his pyjamas, eating jelly and watching cartoons, a check-up every half hour until he was sent away with some leaflets. There were counselling sessions with a middle-aged lady for six weeks where he drew diagrams and wrote some mindfulness goals. None of it as earth-shattering or formative as one might expect.

Yet Finlay feels a perverse nostalgia for that time. Navigating the wards right now, where elderly ladies in gowns chat with their porters, it brings with it a sense of calm and safety.

When Finlay finds the girls, they hug him instantly, but Finlay hugs them back. He surprises himself with the strength of his own grip.

'I missed you!' Finlay moves from embracing Jun to Derya. 'I am so sorry it's been so long. Placement is so chaotic.'

Jun waves a hand. 'Please, I barely remember my family's names,' she assures him. 'I just need to finish up and then I'll get you down there?'

Finlay and Derya start walking.

'I am so excited for food; I've literally been daydreaming about it,' Derya says, but Finlay can't hear.

There's a boy passing them in the hall. Finlay sees the hair first. A shock of messy orange. It stabs him with a known pain. Finlay might've glanced away three years ago, but now he's made a space for it inside himself: rearranged the furniture to give it room.

Only the boy is wearing a school uniform. His nose is a little crooked. He looks up.

The pain transforms.

It's Banjo.

He hasn't changed. His eyes meet Finlay's. Horror. That's the only thing Finlay can see.

Banjo looks down instantly. That gesture says everything it needs to say. But Finlay can't do the same. It feels too miraculous. Banjo is here – he's safe, alive, *okay*.

They're passing one another. Finlay's heart is being squeezed in an agonising chokehold.

Banjo looks back.

Finlay's feet pause. He waits.

Banjo looks right at Finlay. He does nothing.

The chokehold tightens past the point of crushing. Finlay turns away and leaves Banjo where he stands.

Banjo's face appears every time Finlay blinks. His expression. His eyes. His horror. The way he stopped.

Finlay doesn't touch his messages for a week. He doesn't contact anybody. Not Akash. Not Jun or Derya. Nobody. He can't see them and be normal. He can't let himself crumble if they ask him what's wrong.

He ended up abandoning the girls once they got out of Queen Elizabeth University Hospital, claiming he suddenly felt sick and couldn't eat – which wasn't a lie, and was probably made more convincing because he looked it. They were so sweet, and asked him to text once he got back to the flat.

Finlay didn't. He ignores their messages along with Akash's, and only uses his phone for its alarm. There's nothing they can do for him, and it's easier to be by himself.

Time is something Finlay now experiences inside his body. He has to drag it along with himself: force his jaw up and down to chew food, put one foot in front of the other to walk. At the same time he feels detached from his body, experiencing hunger as if he's looking at it from across the room. If Akash saw him like this, he'd run for the hills.

His cleaning shifts pass quietly. The physical labour is nice. It makes Finlay feel useful. His Silver Lodge shifts are difficult.

Finlay never realised how much he must have smiled throughout the day. The effort of pulling his face into one is exhausting.

The residents don't notice all that much, too busy demanding things. Finlay complies without a word. An extra pillow, more meds, the remote control.

The staff notice plenty.

'Yer quiet today, Finlay,' Rhonda murmurs as he's making some tea in the staffroom.

Finlay glances over. She's rummaging through the fridge.

'Headache,' he thinks up on the spot. The least infectious problem of all time.

Rhonda hums in sympathy.

'You want some tea?' he asks.

'Yes, please.' Rhonda smiles. 'No milk, six sugars, thank you.'

'Sorry, did I hear you say *six* sugars?' Finlay raises an eyebrow.

'You did,' Rhonda confirms.

'Rhonda, you're a wonder,' Finlay tells her, and she laughs loud.

Finlay feels one corner of his mouth twitch. It's all he can manage.

He likes Silver Lodge. He likes the yellow-and-blue carpet and the small, cosy rooms. Even the fact the corridors always smell like fish pie is comforting. It's a hospital but it's also a home. It has a living room. It has recliners. Finlay thinks that if he had grown up with these corridors, with these paintings, with these people, he would've been content.

He sees a full banana in the food bin when he's throwing out his twice-used teabags. It has a small black patch along its spine, but it's unpeeled, untouched. Finlay tries to ignore it. A few hours pass and he hasn't stopped thinking about it.

He goes back to fish it out with rubber gloves on. He washes it, peels it open. It's ripe.

Finlay eats it quickly by the sink and watches outside the window as two people exchange parking tickets. The woman waves the man goodbye as he drives off. Maybe they know one another through their visits here. What a strange way to connect to someone; tangentially tied through this shared experience of a loved one living in a care home. But it's a little beautiful, too.

After a week and a half of ignoring everyone, Finlay gets a message from Derya that was probably drafted over several hours.

Hey Finlay, just wanted to let you know if you need us at all for anything we are here. Placement can be tough. Take your time. Love you.

He's read it so many times now he could perform it onstage. He reads it aloud in his frozen room while bundled inside his duvet and two jumpers, but still he can't understand it.

Finlay cut all contact. He assumed they would shrug and move on. He's not even seen them since the hospital.

Love you.

How could they possibly love him? They've known him for three months. He stares at that tiny two-word last sentence. Is it just a closing line, a send-off the same way *x* is? But wouldn't they just use an *x*?

He ignores it the same as the other unread texts on his phone.

Throughout December, Christmas explodes at Silver Lodge. Fairy lights and tinsel and tiny dancing Santas. It's a strange time to feel so melancholy when everyone around him is actively trying to put themselves in a better mood. The festive spirit, the Christmas cheer, everybody wants it. Finlay just feels numb from the inside, a hollow, carved-out thing.

Yet as the weather turns bitter, Finlay gets closer to the residents.

Patrick has softened up after the wound-dressing incident and cracks jokes about the meals ('Caviar and liver again?') and planning an escape ('It'll be oan the news!').

Alice is a little different because of her dementia. Finlay adopts the habit of introducing himself every day. Sometimes he's her high school teacher and sometimes she turns around and tuts: 'I know who ye *are*, Finlay.'

Rhonda was right. In his own way, Finlay loves them. He worries about them, and laughs with them.

Jeanie notices the second he steps into her room. 'Wit's the matter wae you?'

He blinks where he's making her bed. 'Nothing.'

'Come oan.' She nods to the armchair opposite her.

Finlay complies, exhaling a slow breath as he sinks into the leather. She waits, perfectly plucked eyebrows raised.

'I'm fine,' he murmurs.

Jeanie somehow pulls it out from between his teeth.

'I saw somebody I haven't for years.' Finlay gives a half shrug, swallowing. It gets caught in his throat, a square lump. 'We didn't ... end on the best terms.' That makes it sound as if he and Banjo were in a relationship. But there's no other way to put it.

'Aw, I see,' Jeanie murmurs.

'Yeah,' Finlay huffs.

It's more than that, though. *I can't bring myself to contact the people I love.* How does he say that? His body, so different to his mind, longs for Akash's arms around him, his gentle voice in his ear. But Finlay's mind keeps him in a cage. Every time he goes to reach out to Akash, Jun, Derya – he can only see Banjo and the horror on his face, and is rendered immobile.

Jeanie reaches over and clasps his hand. Her touch is soft, even with her thin, wrinkled hands. A wave of fondness crashes over Finlay. He wonders what it would be like if he was visiting her. If Jeanie was his grandmother, if he'd grown up on her strong mints and gruff affection.

Finlay clears his throat and stands up.

'Thanks, Jeanie.' He smiles. 'Really.'

'Anytime.' She smiles back.

Finlay takes himself to the library on Saturday so he can focus on the final assignment due for the end of the year that he's been neglecting. Neglect being Finlay's one and only skill. He avoids all the social areas. Even still, his chest aches for the sight of sleek black hair, a soft jumper, a sloped nose. If he could just *see* Akash, not interact, not touch, he knows the ache would leave. He knows this is why he's pulled to all the places Akash might be.

Akash has reached out every day – voicemails Finlay doesn't listen to, messages Finlay can't bring himself to open. But he'll give up eventually.

Finlay takes a break when his eyes blur words together and his temples throb. He leaves the study area to find the kiosk-café on the ground floor. Finlay's convinced they add petrol to their coffee, but their prices are decent.

He joins the queue before he spots them.

Jun and Derya are at a table in the group area, cramped around their laptops. They see him at the same time. Their faces light up: bursting with happiness, relief, *love*.

Finlay acts before thought: spins around and bolts.

Later that night, he pictures their faces. So happy to see him, although he's ignored them and their concern.

Would Akash feel the same? No. He can't afford to think about Akash at all. He made a vow to himself three years ago. He'd never need anyone again.

The holidays are fast approaching, but instead of being excited, Finlay's just numb. He's spent Christmas alone before. But for some reason this one feels different. The prospect of his cold flat and a takeaway for one isn't the huge celebration it previously might have been.

'Finlay, are ye coming fur our Christmas night out?' Rhonda

asks when she finds him holed up in the staffroom with his instant noodles.

'Please come!' Beth beams, clapping her hands, right on Rhonda's coattails. 'Everyone will be there!'

'Ah—' Finlay shakes his head, overwhelmed. 'Sorry, I'm busy throughout December—'

'Oh, we have ours in January,' Somaya chimes in with a smile behind them, because somehow they're coming into the staffroom at once. 'So it doesn't clash with anything.'

'Ah,' Finlay tries, nodding into his plastic container. 'I'll see.' He stands up and dumps his empty noodle pot. They can't all take their break right now. Somebody needs to be on duty.

'Just let me know by the end of the week so I can book it.' Rhonda smiles at him as he makes it to the door.

Finlay nods again before he leaves.

It's probably a formality. How many student nurses have come and gone? How many have been invited to the Christmas night out? They'd probably have more fun without an outsider to the team.

This doesn't need to be dragged out longer than necessary. He'll leave and they'll forget his name, no longer a colleague and never a friend.

It doesn't occur to him that they might have arrived in the staffroom at the same time because they were looking for him.

Chapter Twenty-Seven

BANJO

No matter how much time passes, Banjo can't see his parents as bad parents. As bad people. It's a psychological thing. Comfort is in the familiar, even though Banjo's never known anything that could be described as comforting. He's wired all wrong.

What's familiar is his parents passed out on the floor, the landlord shouting through the wall, chest infections for a month, doctor's office for hours, bruises on his arms, fist through the wall, footsteps searching for him, crammed under his bed, needles on the table, sour smoke burning his eyes, ice cream as an apology, kicked in the side, ice pack held to his head, big hands he wants and hates at the same time, screaming matches, fingers in his ears, sitting on a knee waiting for it to hurt, scared of them, hating being scared of them, forgiving them, hating to forgive them, painkillers.

Banjo would tell himself it was his fault. He was always wrong, he was never how he should be.

Life was like this game nobody taught him the rules to. He wanted to play, to join in, but whenever it came to his turn he didn't know what fucking move to make. He tried different things, hoping for a new outcome, but it never worked. He kept losing and nobody explained why.

Co-codamol was the only thing Banjo did right. They gave it to him and it shut him up and that's all that mattered. It stopped the tears after being punished, the complaints about being hungry; knocked him out so nobody had to deal with him. Everyone was happier.

Nobody even noticed until Banjo started falling asleep in class. Spaced out, mind blank, some child zombie. Social work got a call and that was that. He wasn't addicted, no, but he was on his way. And the withdrawal turned him into some demon. Raiding the cupboards of foster homes, scanning the supermarket shelves, shoving them into pockets, feeling worse than mouldy shite.

Banjo remembers when the headaches came. The sweats. The shakes. He'd curl into a ball and think *you're strong, you are strong.* By that time he knew what it was, and what to do to stop it. He felt weak. Something inside him had gone wrong, or maybe it was always there. It was a gene. A thing he was fated to become.

Were they bad people or did they do bad things? Is there even a difference? When Banjo was ten he was pulled out of class and told by a stranger he wasn't going home. He screamed. When Banjo was ten he was told his parents were going to prison. All he knew about prison then was that it was some awful place for awful people.

It took Banjo a long time before he understood that the parents he loved and the parents that went to prison were the same. For so long, they were separate.

He knows they're the same now. For the things he'll always hate them for, there are still a million other things he loves them for. An apple in his backpack. A hand stroked through his hair. He can't take that love out of him: hold it in his palms and pick it apart. His love is tinged with bitter shame, but his bitterness is tinged with this rotted type of terrible affection.

Banjo doesn't think he'll ever have kids. The anger at his parents sits restless and ready, pent-up pain waiting to shape something out of him. Waiting to turn him bad.

When Banjo makes it back to Paula and Henry after he's seen Alena, after seeing *Finlay*, he's well past curfew. He ended up just getting the bus and paid with some money from the café. But it's going dark, and he's missed dinner. They've called him a hundred times. He wouldn't have put it past them to have phoned the police.

He tries to come in quietly, but soon as he opens the door they're waiting.

'I told you I'd come get you from Glasgow. Where have you been?' Paula begins, arms crossed. Banjo really isn't in the mood.

'Nowhere,' he states, voice flat.

'Because we've asked you to *text* us and let us know,' Paula carries on. 'We'll come pick you up wherever you—'

'Nowhere, I've been nowhere, fucken *nowhere*!' Banjo shouts.

'Don't raise your voice—' Henry starts behind her.

'Fuck *off*!' Banjo cries, thundering upstairs and slamming the door so hard it vibrates on its hinges. He paces the room. There's this desperate urge to hurt, to really fucking *hurt*, to tear his hair and claw his skin and rip everything that's inside him out – his lungs and his stomach and his heart. He wants to tear it from his chest and fling it out the fucking window.

He doesn't come down all night. Not even to eat. He jogs on the spot until he's panting and his blood is hot and his clothes are plastered to his skin.

He doesn't check his phone. Jogs up and down on the spot for an hour, two hours, three hours, non-stop constant jogging. After three, though, Banjo's legs give out.

He crumples to the floor with a thud.

There's the sound of scurrying footsteps. Footsteps come to find him.

'Banjo?' Paula calls outside his door. Terror floods his brain like a white-hot chemical, like an animal instinct overriding any humanity he's got left, because she's going to punish him now.

Banjo squeezes himself under the bed and curls into a ball. 'Sorry, am sorry, am sorry, am sorry!'

The floorboards creak. She waits for a minute. Then she goes back to bed.

The fear takes a long time to evaporate. Banjo almost forgot how sharp it tastes. He presses his back to the cool wall.

After a while he falls asleep. He dreams twice.

The first dream is about mud-caked boots and the smell of beer right next to his head. Banjo lies still and makes no noise until he remembers he's with Paula and Henry. The second dream is about a warm body next to him underneath the bed, breathing slow and even, here to keep him company.

Banjo wakes himself up by reaching for him.

Somehow, that one is worse.

Chapter Twenty-Eight

FINLAY

Two and a half weeks after seeing Banjo is Finlay's breaking point. He's floating along fine, numb to everything, but then cracks begin to show.

He cycles to his cleaning shift at 5.20 a.m., dark and early. It might be his lack of sleep, of human contact, of proper nutrition, or a combination of all three, but he's snappy and irritable. He's angry at the wind, the cars on the road, the people on the street, the slippery pavement, the handlebars of his bike.

When he arrives and starts unlocking everything, the blaring alarm raises the hairs on the nape of his neck. He grits his teeth as he punches in the code.

The problems begin when he pulls the hoover out. Someone's put the nozzle on backwards, or something inside is stuck, because when he starts hoovering it doesn't work. It's not picking up anything, drags wrongly against the carpet, and makes a high-pitched whistle.

'Piece of *shite*,' Finlay hisses, bending to take it apart. It won't budge. Won't twist, turn, move, hoover, come apart, come together – he can't even get the vacuum bag out to check if it's full.

Someone has completely and utterly *fucked* his hoover.

'Fuck!' Finlay kicks it.

It feels so good that he does it again. Then again, slamming his foot down because he wants it to break, *he wants it to break*, Finlay picks it up and throws it to the ground.

The lid comes off. The vacuum bag bursts. Dust and dirt erupt in the air like a cloud.

Finlay stays there for a long time until he actually looks at what he's done.

'Shit.' His voice is shaky.

He locks the building and cycles to the nearest Sainsbury's.

Finlay scans the options until he finds the cheapest one. It's this or eating dinner tonight – but Finlay would have no excuse for leaving dust all over a school he was meant to clean. He definitely can't afford to get fired. He balances the box across his handlebars, cycles back, unboxes it, and hoovers up his own mess.

Finlay takes the broken one to his flat. He has no idea what to do with it. He's got an hour before Silver Lodge. He'll need to put this in with his rubbish to get collected, but it's too big for a bin bag. He'll no doubt get in trouble if he just leaves it outside. Finlay sits on his bed and pulls the broken nozzle out of the box. He looks down at it and starts crying.

It comes as a total surprise, the strength of it. Finlay can't help but choke out laughter as he sobs, gently cradling the hoover in his lap. But he can't outrun this one, he can't force it down. The crying shakes his body and holds him hostage, as if to tell him *I will be had, I will be done.*

Finlay feels the cold on his swollen face as he cycles to Silver Lodge, tastes his coffee he makes in the break room through the salty tears. The crying makes something come loose inside him.

'You okay?' Beth asks him in a quiet moment, and Finlay can nod now.

It's his last week here. He wants to end his time at Silver Lodge well. He wants to give it a proper goodbye, at least to himself. He wants to come away having learned something – learned more about his ability to do things, to give medication at a specific time, to bathe and dress patients, to check wounds, do blood pressure, oxygen levels, stoma outputs, catheters.

The long winter has set in now; only a week until Christmas. Sparse, grey daylight colours Glasgow, but it's almost entirely dark by the time Finlay steps outside with a yawn at 5 p.m. He shudders in the cold and goes to unchain his bike. His fingers are numb. The handles are stiff ice.

It's hard to be careful during a twenty-minute cycle in complete darkness on icy roads after working twelve hours. All he wants is to find a bed and collapse. He would've slept at Silver Lodge but he's off tomorrow.

He starts cycling, legs aching, back aching, everything aching. His body is so exhausted he genuinely has to think about each action before he does it: imagines setting his feet on the pedals and pushing down one before the other.

It occurs to Finlay he should walk with his bike. He shouldn't risk icy roads and rush-hour traffic on zero sleep or food.

But he does.

When Finlay turns down a road, he doesn't look and is immediately blinded by the boom of a horn. His bike wobbles out of control, the tyre sliding, and his heart lurches up his throat; he anticipates the weight of heavy impact so viscerally his skin hurts.

But nothing happens.

The car passes around him with a prolonged, furious honk.

Finlay gets to the pavement and staggers off his bike. He retches behind a lamppost. It takes a while for the tremors to fade, for the rushing blood at the backs of his ears to ebb.

This is so dramatic, Finlay thinks. He wasn't even injured. Finlay forces himself to get a grip and starts walking. But his knees are weak, barely able to support him.

There's somewhere closer. Is he delirious? Finlay tries to ignore the thought, but it presses in with more urgency. *So close. So tempting. So warm.* His legs feel as though they've gained enormous weight, his fingers can barely grip his handles, his eyelids are magnets being pulled together.

Finlay stands outside Akash's mansion and rests his bike on the metal fence. Akash's message history finally opens on his phone. Finlay's throat constricts. He stares at the last and final text: *I'll leave you alone.*

Finlay ignored Akash for three weeks.

But if he asks for Akash's couch, Akash will give it. *You're about to pass out*, Finlay tells himself, but he knows the real reason. It's buried under his denial.

He needs to see Akash. He's splitting apart at the seams just to look at Akash's face. Finlay can pretend all he wants but it's pointless.

Finlay presses *call*. It rings on for a long time. The knot of anxiety in his stomach becomes an abyss that slowly consumes him.

The line clicks.

Finlay holds his breath.

Akash breathes softly. He says nothing.

'I'm outside,' Finlay croaks.

Akash sighs. The line cuts off.

Finlay stares at his phone. Their text history floods his screen. Faced with the evidence of Akash's worry, stress, heartache, it slams into Finlay. He did this. He destroyed them. He knew he would.

Finlay stands there for a long time. His tears are warm, caressing his face.

The double doors open. Akash stands wrapped in a baggy jumper and soft sweatpants, arms crossed. He's haloed by the warm glow of the porch light. Finlay realises this is the first time he's ever seen Akash in comfy clothes.

He's expressionless, but when Finlay looks at him, Akash rushes over in his fuzzy sliders.

'Are you all right?' Akash asks, even though he keeps his distance. He balls his hands at his sides.

Finlay shakes his head. He wants to speak, but nothing is enough.

Akash is silent too. He opens his mouth, closing it after a beat. He looks at Finlay. The question is written all over his face. *Why?* His face is so stripped bare, his longing palpable to Finlay because it's Finlay's longing too.

Finlay's windpipe spasms with pain. He has no answer. Tears drip off his chin. Akash's arm twitches at his side in an aborted motion.

'Come inside,' Akash instructs, his voice curt. 'It's freezing.'

Finlay follows. Akash holds a finger to his lips before he opens the door.

'Hi,' he calls when he steps in, monotone. He's so different.

'What were you doing?' a woman asks. His mother. She sounds young, stern, loving.

'Parcel.' Akash starts walking towards his room. Finlay barely manages to keep up.

'Better not be more books!' A man joins now; deeply accented, loving as well.

'God forbid!' Akash replies before he ushers Finlay into his room and closes the door.

Finlay looks around the place he's missed for the best part of a month. The details are so different. The bed is unmade, cluttered with clothes and textbooks. Akash's laptop is open on his desk, alongside a mug of coffee and a glass of water. There are more diagrams stretching the whole length of the wall now.

He must be neck-deep in studying.

'I'm sorry—' Finlay was going to finish *for disturbing*, but Akash waves him off and reclaims his study chair. He points to the bed across from him, not meeting Finlay's gaze.

Finlay sits down and instantly wants to be unconscious. Akash waits, probably for the rehearsed speech, but Finlay can barely hold his eyes open.

'I'm sorry,' he murmurs.

Akash still says nothing.

'Can I lie down?' Finlay risks. He might do it anyway.

'If you want,' Akash states. There's a hardness in his tone. It might just be his neutral voice. Finlay probably never noticed how soft Akash became around him.

Finlay lies down. He's still wearing his jacket, but kicks his shoes off. And it feels like sinking backwards into Akash's arms: his masculine smell, his warm embrace. Finlay's eyes sting as he closes them.

They both do nothing for a while. Finlay floats in bliss, trying to memorise this.

'I heard I was the first person you ever spoke to in primary,' Akash whispers, probably because of his parents, but it still lends a gentleness to him.

Finlay opens his eyes and looks at Akash.

Akash has his legs propped up on the desk, staring at the ceiling. He looks so at ease. He spends every day and night here. It makes Finlay feel indescribably close to him.

'I remember it, too,' Akash continues. 'I was – maybe eleven? And upset because someone told me my lunch smelled. Typical. But it was a thousand other things. The way the teachers couldn't pronounce my name. The fact I couldn't come to Mass. Mass was a fucking day out.'

Finlay smiles.

'Anyway. I took my lunch outside because I was crying. Someone sat beside me. You.' He smiles at his ceiling. 'I don't know if you knew why I was crying or you were already outside. I was so homesick to my stomach for India, for my home in Mumbai, that I didn't even care. But then you said, "It goes away." I remember thinking your voice was the nicest thing I'd ever heard. And then we were friends. We were so close, Finlay. But after I spent the summer in India, which I did every year, I came back for our last year in primary and you were gone. No note. Nothing. Nobody ever told me why. They just told me I was the only person you really spoke to.'

Finlay studies Akash, trying to commit him to memory, the bow of his upper lip, the curve of his jaw tilted upwards. This is the reason he came.

Then Akash looks at him. 'I'm not going anywhere, Finlay,' he says, dark eyes intent. 'But I need things, too.'

Finlay stares back. 'Yes.'

I'll never be able to give you them. I'm fundamentally incapable. You'll find someone who can without even asking. You'll find someone who just knows how.

Akash swallows, nodding. He looks across the room. Even then Finlay can see the wretched misery that twists his features. *He's trying to hide it*, Finlay realises, until he actually understands. No. Looking at Finlay is what causes the pain.

Finlay closes his eyes so he doesn't have to see it. 'I sometimes have this dream,' he murmurs. 'I'm at the airport, and the plane is leaving, and everyone I care about is on it.' He sees it so clearly. 'They didn't check to see if I was there. I'm trying to get on it, but I won't make it in time. I don't know where they're going. And I know why I'm not on it then. They didn't want me.' He breathes through it for a moment, and then adds: 'I watched a movie when I was younger where this person was trying to reach someone getting a flight and missed them. It just stuck with me. I think it's because I don't know what I did to make my mother leave, so I don't know what I should never repeat. If there's always the risk that someone might get on a plane and leave, it just feels safer to be alone.'

He's never said that to anybody. Anyone in the whole world. Maybe he's delirious. Maybe he's not been near Akash in so long, he's forgotten how much Akash pulls the truth from him.

Akash is quiet. 'I didn't know that,' he croaks eventually.

Of course not. Finlay was put in foster care with strangers: taken out of St Mary's and placed into another primary school.

'Yeah,' Finlay explains. 'She left. My mother. When I was eleven. The summer you went back to India. I don't know where she went. I looked for a while. But I didn't tell anyone; I just waited for her to come back. Then social services found out because the rent hadn't been paid and some of the neighbours were worried.'

Akash says nothing. Maybe it's exhaustion, delirium, or Akash's presence, but the words force themselves free where they've always been repressed.

'A month,' Finlay says as though in reply. 'I was alone for a month. I keep – sometimes I wonder if she came back. Probably not.' Finlay has no idea why he says that. It exists in the quietest, smallest part of him: the boy-child inside him.

A month. That time is a blur of hunger and loneliness to Finlay: the same day over and over. He barely remembers it, or made himself forget.

There's silence. They breathe together.

'Finlay . . .' Akash's voice is hoarse.

Finlay shakes his head. 'Sorry.' He chuckles roughly. There's a beat. 'I think the only way I'd ever feel truly safe is if I could absorb people. If I could just swallow them and keep them inside me or something.'

It's the truth. Grotesque, unrealistic, Finlay wants nothing more than to swallow Akash, Derya, Jun, Rhonda, all of them, and keep them inside his stomach forever. Never able to leave.

'I never knew my dad,' Finlay confesses. 'But it's easier that way. It's easier than my mother leaving. Because she knew me. She decided to leave after she got to know me.'

It was always just them. But Mum worked odd jobs to stay afloat, and by the time Finlay was eight he could fix himself dinner and take himself to bed easily. Of course Mum did the chores around the house, washed his clothes and put food in the fridge, bought him a coat in the winter, but none of that really made it feel as though she was there. Maybe it was always just him. That's a better way to word it. He only ever imagined her hand through his hair and a love he so needed.

Sometimes Finlay thinks it would have been easier if he had a reason. Some insight into his Mum – was she estranged from her family and that's why they never visited Poland or why he never had grandparents? Was she struggling mentally and couldn't cope with raising him? But never understanding why has become part of the grief.

Akash is quiet for a beat. 'But what if I was there at the airport?' he whispers.

Finlay opens his eyes to meet Akash's, red-rimmed and sore. His legs are hugged to his chest, chin resting on his knees.

Finlay frowns.

'What if we were getting a plane together?' Akash asks.

'I'd get lost.' Finlay knows with surety.

'I've got your hand.' Akash raises his own and squeezes the air. 'I'm not letting it go.'

Finlay stares. 'I don't know where we're going.'

'I'll show you,' Akash replies.

Finlay tries to picture it. The willingness to trust. Where does he find it?

'I don't want to leave.' Finlay's voice cracks.

'We can't stay here.' Akash keeps his gaze.

His black hair is tucked behind his ears. It reveals more of his features than Finlay's used to. His eyebrows, nose, and cheekbones all unobscured by his falling curtains. He really is beautiful, and coupled with his baggy clothes and thin glasses, oddly vulnerable in a new way.

Finlay feels it stirring inside him, that old instinct to love somebody, to allow himself to love somebody, but he shirks away from it, because:

'The thing is,' Finlay whispers. 'Everyone I care about just leaves me.'

There's embarrassment there. Beneath the soul-crushing loss there's also the half-mortified *there must be something wrong with me*. But some part of Finlay recognises disgust. Not for himself, no. For Akash.

He's disgusted by Akash's easy ability to love, how easily Akash puts feelings into words and on display. Akash was spoiled. Finlay resents it, wishes Akash was hurt just a little, shared a little of his pain, so they could know each other through it.

Finlay realises he's resented everybody who hasn't experienced his very specific pain. He was owed a mother, owed maternal love, and the world denied him it. He came into being ready to be loved, ready to be normal, and was met with nothing.

Hating himself can only be directed outwards: it has no home inside him. He aims it at everyone in his life as if it gives him control.

'Then why are you here?' Akash responds.

Finlay is silent. It's a simple question, but it feels like a stab wound.

Akash says nothing else, just waits. Arms around his knees, he looks childlike in the pose.

Finlay has nothing inside his mouth. He's totally void.

'Until you can answer that, Finlay, you should go.' Akash stands up. He stares at a point on Finlay's shoulder. But he's strong now, his aura totally changed.

Finlay pushes himself up off Akash's bed and stands.

Only he doesn't.

The world slants on its axis. The floor flies upwards. But before it hits him, strong, solid arms are there.

He doesn't know what happens after that. Time becomes weird. Dark spots and multicoloured whorls appear and disappear. He's not in his body. He's too much in his body. It hurts. It's nothing.

When Finlay floats to awareness, he hears the soft beeping of machines. The heartbeat of Silver Lodge. He sighs softly. But then he inhales. *Akash*. His smell is clean and earthy, not a forest but something equally natural. Finlay's mind has somehow managed to conjure up the sensation of Akash's nearness. Heartbreak is making him lose his mind.

But then Finlay frowns. Blinks fuzzily. He's in bed, but not one of Silver Lodge's. He's on a soft, expensive mattress permeated with a specific male-sweat scent.

Finlay's eyes open. It's morning, the gentle glow seeping through curtains, everything warm and lit. The noise-memory of heart monitors and oxygen tanks fades away. It wasn't real. He's in Akash's room, wearing the clothes he wore to work yesterday.

The door opens.

Finlay bolts upright, heart in his throat.

Akash steps in quietly, holding a mug. He pauses when he sees Finlay. Their eyes connect. It's like meeting for the first time.

Akash passes the mug to Finlay. Their fingers brush.

Water.

'You passed out,' Akash explains as he sits at the edge of the bed. His hair is flat on one side, tufted on the other. 'I left you here after I realised you were sleep deprived. Just took the couch when everybody went to bed. They're gone now. House to ourselves.'

Finlay drinks to avoid speaking.

'Okay?' Akash asks, and Finlay realises his cold voice has gone soft again. Akash's dark eyes are focused on him.

'Yeah,' Finlay manages after an age.

'You're an idiot,' Akash informs him. 'You should have told me you were exhausted. I think you're anaemic.' Akash runs a hand through his hair, slightly harassed.

Makes sense. Finlay's diet consists of instant noodles and black tea. He also dreams about sleep while he's asleep. He's very much an idiot.

'I'm sorry,' Finlay says finally. 'Sorry I came. Sorry I stole your bed.'

Sorry.

Akash's body radiates warmth from his distance. Always so warm. They stare at one another. Finlay looks away first.

'I think you were right,' Akash says softly. 'I don't think . . . this would be a good idea.'

Finlay doesn't reply. He knows it's true. They both do. But to hear the words is a new kind of hurt. The pain of being known and found wanting. Akash's ability to understand him felt wonderful at first. Now Finlay wishes he could erase everything Akash knows; feels repulsed by how vulnerable he allowed himself to become.

'I . . .' Akash looks down. His eyes are glassy. He does nothing for a moment, but when he blinks the tears spill. Finlay is in so much pain it feels as if he's swallowed fire.

'I am falling for you, Finlay.' Akash is barely audible. Then he croaks a little laugh. 'We've barely started, I know, but I am and I just ... wanted you to know.'

Finlay knows Akash is telling the truth. He understands. All his life, Finlay thought romance would be something punishingly passionate: yanked in for a frantic kiss, thrown against the wall. But Akash's love is not a punishing force. Everything about him is cleansing. His laughter, his cooking, his care, his touch, all feel like stepping into a strip of sunlight. Nothing about him brutalises.

Akash looks at him silently. 'But I don't think you're ready for that,' he says, pained. 'So maybe we should just stop here.'

It's true. Finlay's love is not like Akash's. It's a nebulous vapour: it surrounds, but when reached for it disappears.

'Okay,' Finlay murmurs. He sets Akash's mug on the bedside table and stands.

Akash stares at the floor, an empty look on his face. Finlay steps close and cradles Akash's jaw: touching gently, the way Akash taught him.

Akash meets his gaze.

'I'm not ready. But I do feel the same,' Finlay tells him. The words set him free, even now that everything is over.

He leaves after that.

Chapter Twenty-Nine

BANJO

When Banjo goes back to school, a few days after everything happened at Queen Elizabeth University Hospital, after abandoning Alena and her family and smashing his life to pieces once again, he's so angry he wants to burn it to the fucking ground. And then halfway through class Banjo realises what he really wants. He wants the thrill of a fist coming his way, the taste of metal in his mouth, the pain of a bruise beginning in his side.

He wants a fight.

Banjo finds it at athletics. They're all outside, doing their stupid stretches, faffing about and slapping each other's arses. He's so excited his whole body hums. He's ready. *He's ready.*

One good punch. If somebody gives him one good punch, it'll knock the anger right out of him. Anger only lasts until Banjo remembers what it leads to. He's always hollow and empty after a fight, tired in his fucking soul, but in some ways it's like needing a fix. Something to balance him out, reset him to baseline.

Kyle glances up when Banjo comes over. '*Whoa*, late night?' He laughs.

There it is.

'Still beat ye half-asleep.' Banjo grins, even though his upper lip curls with a nasty edge to it. 'Facts I already did.'

Kyle frowns. 'What?'

'Yer so fucken *slow* it's pathetic.' Banjo laughs a hard laugh, tips his whole head back. Some of the guys have stopped stretching to watch. The fight crackles in the air, fizzes and pops like static.

'Banjo, what the fuck?' Devlin hisses.

Kyle just stares at him.

'I let ye win yer wee medal.' Banjo waggles his fingers in Kyle's face. 'Didnae want yer maw tae be too disappointed.' He shoves the wound into salt.

There's some soft snickers. Devlin stares.

Kyle's eyes are wild. His whole posture changes. 'Stop talking shite. You lost.'

'Beat ye every day at practice and somehow pull a hamstring oot ae nowhere?' Banjo grins. Kyle transforms because he realises it.

It's all over Banjo's face. It's all over everyone's face. Banjo let Kyle win.

'Why?' Kyle comes right up to him. *'Why?'*

'Cause yer the saddest sack ae shite, it's unreal.' Banjo forces his grin to stay in place.

The laughter dries up now. Kyle's cheeks are bleeding red from the embarrassment, and punch, *just punch*, what the fuck? It took nothing for Kyle to beat him to a pulp before and now he wants a conversation? Fuck this.

When Kyle scoffs, turning to pick up his water bottle, Banjo can't miss the opportunity. He sticks a foot out to trip Kyle, not really expecting much: mainly expecting a bit of a wobble.

Kyle lurches and sprawls face first into the dirt.

The guys all rush to help. Banjo's clearly crossed a line. There's no laughing now. Good.

Kyle jumps to his feet and rushes at Banjo.

Banjo's ready. Soon as Kyle's hands connect with his chest, shoving him backwards, Banjo beams. Kyle looks confused, or scared. Too late.

Banjo throws his head forward so it smashes into Kyle's nose. The first contact bursts open inside him like a cracked nest of bees. After that, he's a raging swarming blur of limbs and teeth, kicking and spitting, willing for pain, gagging for it.

Banjo doesn't get it, though.

They're only getting started when there are hands on him: grappling at his sweaty skin, yanking at any bit of his PE kit, his shorts, his shirt, his arms, his hair.

A whistle pierces the air.

Banjo slaps hands over his ears. Every grip on him disappears. But the missed chance of a beating *hurts*.

'Fuck sake!' Banjo screams so hard his voice cracks.

Anderson doesn't stop. The ear-splitting whistle continues. She keeps her eyes on him and keeps *blowing*.

Banjo can't bear it. He charges at her.

He gets one foot forward when he's tackled.

Banjo's blindsided. He falls to the ground. There's a knee to the centre of his back. Kyle shouts: 'Hold him! *Hold him!*'

Banjo thrashes, mouth in the grass. Then the whole team pile on. Terror threatens to choke him. Banjo really starts to panic when hands wrap around his ankles and wrists. His screams turn high-pitched, his thrashing takes on this new hysterical edge.

Kyle kicks him in the side.

Banjo goes still, his whole body prepared for the next one.

'*Ask* if you're that desperate, you psychotic bastard.' Kyle bends to spit in Banjo's face.

'Right, everyone, athletics is cancelled,' Anderson calls. 'Banjo, that's it. You're out.'

Everyone leaves for the lockers. They mutter amongst themselves as they pass him. Devlin shakes his head.

Kyle doesn't even look backwards. His saliva cools on Banjo's cheek.

Banjo doesn't tell Kyle that it doesn't work when he asks for it. It needs to be real. He doesn't do anything. He just lies there in the cold and the dirt as the emptiness begins to eclipse every other feeling inside him. It lifts him up outside his body and floats him along into the clouds.

Banjo has unread messages from Alena. He ignores them; can't make himself type anything to her when heavy shame sits in his stomach. Most of him is crying out for her, but he won't let himself have the reward when he doesn't deserve it.

He has another dream that night. He dreams about Finlay. It feels so real, so right there in the moment. They're out in the back garden of St Andrews. They're lying on the grass, arms close the way they used to be. Not quite touching, just close. And Banjo's neck is strained because he's twisted as he watches Finlay run his mouth. Finlay's hands are moving, always moving, gesturing around as he pulls faces and performs the words.

It feels as if it's happening. Banjo really feels the wet tears on his face, feels them soak his neck and inside his ears because he keeps saying, 'I cannae hear ye, I cannae hear ye,' over and over *and over*.

Finlay keeps on speaking, totally silent, because he can't hear Banjo either.

Banjo wakes with a jolt. His face is hot. There's a rotten taste in the back of his mouth. He stares at a dirty spot on the ceiling.

He creeps out to the back garden and sits on the stone slab of cement by the door.

Time ticks away into 5 a.m., 6 a.m. Something has come awake inside him and won't rest. Banjo wraps two arms around his knobbly knees and rests his chin on the fuzzed hair at the top.

He looks out into the garden, the long, dry grass whistling as the wind passes through. In that moment Banjo feels totally wired to everything. The trees, the ground, the earth, everything. The cold stone on his bare feet makes Banjo feel as if he's really in this world.

And he's so tired. He wants to stay here. He wants this house, this life, these people around him. He wants to be good. He's tired of angry, tired of sad. He wants to be something else. He's ready to be something else.

He doesn't go to school the next morning. He allows Paula to drop him off in silence, but then he walks through, signs himself in, and

291

walks right back out the other door. He grabs his bike from the rack and starts cycling.

It takes a long time to get to Queen Elizabeth University Hospital. He follows his instinct mainly, which is stupid, and it's freezing as all hell. December really is bleak.

But he needs to see her. If he sees her, everything will be all right. All the bad, all the pain, it'll all melt away.

She's been moved from HDU, but she still has her own room. She texted him the ward number. He never responded. He's not seen her in nearly a week. He stands outside her room, stomach tying itself around his lungs.

She's reading in bed, fewer tubes all around her, an IV gently puffing away. She glances up and puts her book down instantly: worry all over her face.

Banjo looks at the wall, every muscle braced for impact. He was so desperate to see her, but now he wishes he hadn't come.

'What happened?' Alena asks, because she knows. Her voice, so lovely, so loved, does something to Banjo. He doesn't want to break. He can't break.

'It's no use, Ena,' Banjo tries. He sounds awful.

'What's not?' she whispers.

'Me.' His voice shakes. 'Am no use.' He doesn't look at her.

Alena says nothing. If she touches him he's done for.

'Come on,' Alena murmurs. 'Sit down.'

Banjo blinks. He looks at her socked feet. They've got penguins on them. 'I—' He shakes his head.

She pats the space. Banjo sits helplessly.

His eyes hurt so much it feels as if they'll burn up inside his head. He holds a sob back behind his teeth. But when Alena touches his face, he can't stop it. Her gentle touch sets it free. He never wanted a fight. He wanted this.

They lie on her small hospital bed and trace each other's faces in silence. Banjo runs a fingertip down her delicately crooked nose, the gentle bow of her lip, her soft fuzzy eyebrows, all the things he's memorised during long quiet shifts, all the things he's dreamt about when they're apart. Alena touches his jawbone, the rim of his nostrils, the shell of his cold ears. Her touch is light, but Banjo feels it inside every part of him.

She doesn't speak. She doesn't ask. The words well up in the silence, though: float to the surface of his empty ocean.

'Ma parents . . . they used tae chuck me oot when Ah wus bad,' he whispers as quiet as he can. 'Ah'd sleep on the porch till they let me in. Actually caught, eh, bronchitis once. Lungs still hurt in the cold. Ma maw used tae smack me aboot, nuthin' terrible, but ma da . . . he wis different. Ah really felt A'd done wrang when it wis him. He wis so angry.' Banjo frowns at Alena's ear, avoiding her gaze. 'And he'd say stuff like, *It's fur yer own good. It'll teach ye.* It got in ma head maybe Ah need tae be punished.' He swallows. 'Sometimes Ah sit oan the porch when . . .' He pauses.

Alena is still tracing his face, her fingers steady and unwavering.

'Am in foster care the now. Ah live wae a couple. They're nice,' Banjo confesses, barely audible. 'But . . . sometimes Ah wannae be punished. Sometimes Ah make people punish me so Ah feel better. It makes sense in ma head, but it's fucked, Ena.'

Alena's hand slots against his face, and her thumb brushes his cheek. Banjo realises it's because he's crying.

'A couple years ago, Ah did somethin',' Banjo whispers, blinking away bleariness. 'Ah hurt somedae Ah really fucken cared aboot.' His breath hitches. His mouth trembles around the words; around the thing he's never been able to say, but it's clawed itself up his throat now. 'A've never . . . said sorry. Ah want to. Ah 'hink Ah need to. Ah don't wannae be ma parents.'

Alena strokes a thumb over his cheekbone. His eyes flutter at the contact.

'Never,' Alena whispers.

'Ye don' get it.' He shakes his head, whispering. 'It's in me.' Banjo taps his stomach. 'Ah cannae get it out.'

Alena sits up on the bed. Banjo looks at her, confused. She crosses her legs into a basket and pats the spot beside her. Banjo straightens and crosses his legs, too. Their knees connect.

She holds out her hand. 'Let me read your palm.'

Banjo swallows, but he places them in both of hers. Alena studies one carefully, angles it this way and that.

Banjo smiles gently.

She holds up a finger, concentrating. His smile widens.

Alena runs a fingertip along one of the lines in the middle. It sends a bolt up Banjo's spine. He swallows.

'Do you know what this is?' she asks, touching the deep indent.

Banjo shakes his head.

'That's the heart line. Look, yours is really deep.' She keeps running that fingertip back and forth. 'That means you feel deeply. You have a lot of empathy.'

Banjo can't swallow.

'This is your life line.' Alena touches the one below that looks like a gash sliced across his palm. 'See? It's really long, which means you'll have a wonderful life. You'll be happy, and loved.'

Banjo sucks in a harsh breath. She's prying him open, undoing his sewn edges.

She says nothing, recognising his brink. Slow as possible, Banjo takes Alena's hand. He turns it palm up. She doesn't refuse. Her palm is small, smooth, an array of criss-crossing lines inside.

He glances up. Her eyes are on him.

'Perfect,' he informs her.

Alena's fingertips twitch. Banjo's leg goes into a cramp. She leans a little closer, tilts her head. He senses that she wants to kiss him. Kiss his mouth that's spat the foulest shite, that's provoked a punch, that's grinned during a fight.

He turns his face away. 'Ena.'

Alena pauses.

He shakes his head. 'Am no good. Ah mean it.'

'Maybe we're good for one another,' she murmurs.

Banjo shakes his head. He stares down at his open palm. The only way it knows how to reach anyone is through violence. It's not capable of a soft touch.

'How?' Banjo whispers.

Alena leans forward so that their foreheads are brought

together. They're not kissing, but it feels the same. Her breath touching his breath.

'Because I know you,' she says.

You don't know me, Banjo could say. But it would be a lie now.

'I'm telling you. We're a good thing,' Alena whispers.

Banjo wants to believe it. More than anything in the world, he wishes he could believe it.

When Banjo makes it back to school, he's only missed first period. He sneaks into maths until Mr Mitchell calls him over.

'Banjo, you're not marked down for attendance—'

'Sorry, sir, missed ma first period, sore stomach.' Banjo grimaces, rubbing his abdomen for dramatic effect. The sweat he's built up from cycling probably helps his case.

Mr Mitchell waves him off with a hand.

Only trouble is, Banjo has maths with Kyle. And Kyle's seat at the front is empty.

Banjo racks his brains and tries to think whether he hurt Kyle to such a point he couldn't come in. He realises: yeah. He headbutted him so hard he got vertigo halfway through the fucking act.

Shit. *Fuck*.

All the guys from athletics give him the side-eye when he passes them in the halls. Devlin doesn't speak to him at all. He's back to square zero.

He's in fourth-period biology before lunch when Headmistress comes in.

'Banjo, a word.' She crooks her finger at him. Banjo keeps his head down as he collects his stuff. There's a cacophony of whispers like it's the National Orchestra.

'So.' Headmistress folds her hands on the desk. Anderson sits in the chair beside her. Banjo picks the skin of his thumb and doesn't look at anyone.

'There was an incident involving Kyle Simmons yesterday, who's off sick. Can you explain?'

Banjo is silent.

'I know this year has been tough, Banjo.' Headmistress's voice is low. Banjo hates when they try to talk about it. Try to coax him like a stray cat into acknowledging the fact he's in care. Every road leads to it. As if he needs a fucking reminder.

'But it's not an excuse any more. If you don't give us an explanation, I won't have a choice.'

Banjo keeps his head low.

'You were doing great there,' Headmistress tries. 'Second place at the athletics competition. Homework handed in on time. What happened?'

Banjo is silent.

'Okay. I've decided that another suspension will do,' Headmistress says. 'But if there's anything else, Banjo, I'll have to expel you. No more chances. You only get three on record. This is your last shot.'

Banjo just nods.

'Right, you can go.'

Banjo doesn't move.

Everybody waits.

'Whut's ... his address?' he manages. Kyle told him for the party and now Banjo can't fucking remember.

Headmistress blinks. 'Sorry?'

'Kyle.' His voice is croaky. 'Where's he live?'

'I can't give out information like that, Banjo.'

Banjo picks up his stuff and leaves. He's halfway down the hall when there's a hand on his shoulder.

He jerks around, muscles tense.

Anderson's eyes are wide. She steps back. He hates it. He hates her a little bit, too.

She sighs when he says nothing. 'Will you sort this out if I tell you his address?' she asks.

Banjo looks at his shoes.

He nods. Anderson doesn't touch him again.

Banjo bikes it over while Headmistress probably calls Paula and Henry about the suspension. He'll deal with it later. It's absolutely Icelandic temperatures, winter well past arrived, but eventually he finds Kyle's house. Banjo rests his bike against the side and knocks on the door.

His heart has an attack when he realises Kyle's parents will probably open up, because how does he explain, Christ in Hell—

Kyle opens the door.

He takes one look at Banjo and clenches his jaw. He keeps a hold of the door handle. 'Come to finish the job?'

He looks terrible. His nose is all crooked and swollen, a purple bruise crawling over his cheekbone from his left eye. Banjo doesn't drop dead or anything, but he does feel sick. The lasting impact of a fight always takes a few hours to show itself. Banjo never knows how hard he hit until then. He hates being faced with it.

'*Well?*' Kyle prompts.

'Ah ...' Banjo begins, rough, but his throat closes over before he can finish. Not that he even had a fucking plan. He looks at the ground.

'Why me?' Kyle asks.

There's a beat.

'Nobody else wid fight back,' Banjo tells the dirt.

'That's what you wanted?' Kyle grins this mangled sneer. 'A fight?'

Banjo kicks some gravel. 'I wanted someone tae hit me.' Out loud, the reality sounds stupid. Why the fuck would anyone want that?

'Nah, come on.' Kyle steps out and closes the door. 'You wanted to hit someone.'

Banjo shakes his head quick. 'I swear—'

'Banjo, you *wanted* to hit someone. Fucking admit it.'

Banjo just keeps shaking his head, but he says nothing because he's got nothing. Fucking nothing.

Kyle storms inside and slams the door behind him.

Banjo scrubs his head and kicks the stone porch. '*Shit!*'

He steps up to knock again. When he does – he stops. Kyle's shadow is still there, visible from his hallway.

'I got fucked up,' Banjo tries. 'I – *fuck*. Am *sorry*. Ye never even said sorry tae me!'

'I didn't enjoy it. I could see it on your face, Banjo. *You enjoyed it!*'

'I didnae!' Banjo cries, slapping his head, trying to punch it into himself, because he didn't, he wouldn't, he'd never, *he never.*

Kyle rips open the door. 'Shut the fuck up.'

Banjo goes silent, hair gripped in both hands.

Kyle huffs and sits down on his front porch step, despite the fact it must feel like a block of ice on his arse. He's only in joggies and a T-shirt.

Banjo isn't much better. He's still wearing his school uniform, cheap nylon and polyester. After a second, Banjo joins him.

Kyle blows out a breath and rests his head against his door.

'It wasnae true,' Banjo throws. 'I didnae beat ye. At the race.'

Banjo's not a bad liar or anything, but the words fall flat on their face, totally useless.

Kyle breathes slowly. 'You know, running was basically the one thing I had over everybody,' he murmurs. 'The one thing.'

Banjo puts his elbows on his knees and his head in his hands. 'It's the only 'hing I've got, as well.'

'I hated you 'cause you took it from me. Took Alena, too.' Kyle huffs a laugh. 'I noticed. At the café. You're both obvious as fuck.'

Banjo had no clue. All the way back then.

'What did I take from you?' Kyle asks. 'What the *fuck* did I do to you?'

'Ye dinnae *get it*.' Banjo presses the heels of his hands into his eyes. 'It's no aboot that, it's no aboot anythin'—'

'Calm the fuck down.' Kyle reaches for him.

Banjo sees the hand coming. He throws himself back so hard he slips off the porch step. Banjo cowers, arms over his head. Christ sake, either he wants to be hit or he doesn't want to be hit, which one is it? He doesn't *fucking know what he wants.*

'Banjo, *Jesus*—' Kyle leans over him.

Banjo scrambles back and rushes to his bike.

'Banjo!' Kyle shouts.

Banjo jumps on his bike and bolts. He cycles as if his life depends on it, adrenaline and fear charging his legs. He's bleeding but he doesn't know where, his chest is tight and heavy, his palms stinging from the concrete.

He has this split second where he thinks about running away. Going someplace where he knows nobody; where nobody knows him.

But his body rejects the idea. It decides for him. It turns off the main road and heads somewhere else.

Banjo goes to Alena's house. He sends Paula a message to avoid another fallout. *Talk later. Visiting Alena.* It's technically true. Plus the thought of Paula and Henry worrying just makes his stomach hurt now.

Banjo hasn't seen Alena's parents since the hospital. He wants to give an explanation, but also wants their warm, welcoming comfort.

'Banjo.' Julie squeezes his shoulder and steps aside in open invitation when he arrives.

Everyone's already sat at the table digging into their heaps of food.

'Banjo!' Carlos booms. Banjo wants to shrink away from them all, even though he's the one that's shown up unannounced.

'Hi.' He waves when he's three feet away from them, because he's an idiot.

'Come, come.' Carlos beckons. Jace nods with her mouth stuffed.

Banjo takes his usual seat. It feels weird to notice that.

'Have you been over?' Julie asks when she hands him a plate. 'To see her?'

'Oh – yuh.' Banjo nods and doesn't touch any of the food. 'This morning. Sorry I never managed before. Jus' been busy.'

It's weak. They all know it.

'Not to worry.' Carlos smiles. 'Nevertheless,' he begins, eyebrow cocked. Banjo falls a bit in love with him for using the word *nevertheless*. Alena gets everything from them. 'Try and let us know, next time, before you go disappearing. You're part of the team. We were worried when you left last week.'

Banjo's too stunned by *you're part of the team* to even understand the rest, but then he does. They were worried? At the hospital? They should have been thinking about their daughter.

'Sorry,' he croaks. 'Jus' got a bit ... overwhelmed.' It's not true. He doesn't want them to think he can't handle Alena's illness. But it's all he has. 'Won't happen again.' He wants those words to matter. To be a promise.

Carlos beams wide. 'Glad to hear it. Welcome to the family.'

He says it as though it means nothing. It's probably just a metaphor, a joke.

But Banjo's gut swoops as if he's been dropped from a great height. He tries not to react, but has to look away so they don't notice.

Nobody pays him any mind, already eating and chatting.

Those words won't leave his head. He chews numbly, barely tasting the food. *Part of the family.*

We're a team. Finlay's eyes shine in the darkness of their room. *Me and you.*

The food tastes like ash in his mouth. He picks it apart.

Then he lifts his juice.

The glass falls right through his fingers. It goes everywhere. The table, the floor, his lap, everywhere.

'Shit!' He jumps up from the table, heartbeat in his mouth. 'Sorry, sorry, am sorry—'

'It's all right!' Carlos holds his hands spread.

'I'll go get a towel,' Julie says gently, not the least bit angry. Nobody is angry. Jace moves her things. They all just decide to solve the issue.

Banjo freezes stiff. He's waiting for the rug to be yanked from under him.

'It'll dry in,' Jace tells him, because she can clearly sense his panic.

Julie comes back in with a towel and starts wiping the table. Banjo wants to take the towel away from her. He wants to help, to *do something*, but he needs to keep as still as possible.

'Can't be helped.' Carlos pats his back.

Banjo flinches so badly he jerks.

Carlos stares at him. Something new comes across his face. Banjo doesn't want it. He doesn't want them to look at him like this.

'I'll—' Banjo holds out a hand for the towel. 'Please.'

Julie gives him it. Banjo scrubs the table, wipes down the chair and floor, then charges into the kitchen.

He's rinsing the towel when Julie comes in.

'You don't need to do that, Banjo.' She tuts fondly, her warm smell surrounding him.

Banjo goes still as she takes the towel from his hands. She wrings it out and sets it aside. Then she puts a hand on his shoulder.

'You're a lovely boy,' she murmurs. 'I'm glad Alena's got you.'

Banjo's throat goes tight. He's so tense he could pull a muscle.

'I never said thank you for coming to see her,' Julie continues. 'It meant a lot to her. And I know this is tough. You don't want to see her in pain. But she needs you there.'

Banjo feels as if someone's just chucked a handful of grit into his eyes. He squints as he nods, unable to speak.

Julie squeezes his shoulder, a gentle touch.

'I'd better head,' he croaks, bends away from her hand and rushes out the door.

When Banjo makes it back to Paula and Henry, they've left food out for him. Banjo scoffs it down quick, ravenous because he left Alena's in a mortified rush. He hears them in the living room, chatting quietly over the hum of TV. Banjo hears his own name. The door is open. A whisper. *Is that him?*

He steps inside quietly. He's basically tiptoeing.

Paula and Henry glance up instantly. Paula exhales when she sees him. She gives a sad sort of half-smile. No anger. No fuss. She's just glad to see him.

She would have been called. They must know he's been suspended.

'Thanks,' Banjo croaks. 'Fur the food.'

He waits for the speech.

'It's there whenever you want,' Paula says.

It feels like she's talking about more than food. The open door. No need to apologise.

'See, the suspension—' Banjo starts, words bubbling up with no real thought.

'We'll talk about it tomorrow,' Henry promises. His deep voice holds Banjo in place, but somehow there's no anger, no threat. Banjo can tell Henry means it gently. He means, *There's time to listen, time to discuss.*

'We spoke to your athletics coach,' Paula adds. 'There's a lot of people at that school rooting for you.'

Banjo can only nod.

'Thanks for letting us know where you were, son,' Henry adds quietly.

It's just a phrase. *Son.* People just chuck these words about.

But it rips the last of Banjo open. There's no fighting now. Banjo realises he resisted them the most. With Alena, Morag, Julie, Carlos, Jace, it was easy.

But Paula and Henry waited patiently. And they gained it in the end. His love. Whatever the fuck it's worth.

When Banjo has a shower, he replays the whole day in his head like a lullaby to calm himself down. Alena's fingertips gentle along his jaw. Julie's hand on his shoulder. Carlos's pat on the back. So many points of contact, Banjo feels loved all over.

He stares at his hand, palm open, and curls his fingers. His knuckles are misshapen, knobbly things, rough and cracked, restructured by pain. The water runs on. He makes a fist again. His hand is used to this. It knows how to form one by instinct.

Banjo thinks about Alena's fingertip running along the inside of his palm, tracing the lines there. She did it so carefully, as if Banjo was a fragile thing. As if his hand might break. She's never seen that same hand break things.

A lovely boy. He's a lovely boy. Lovely as in loveable. As in good.

Banjo wants to be good. He knows now what he really wants. He wants to talk to Finlay.

Three Years Ago

Finlay settles into bed, his glasses two moons in the dark because he keeps them on when he wants to talk. It's only been a month since they met, but Banjo feels as though he's known Finlay his whole life.

So Banjo shifts on to his side, his cheek against the pillow, and waits.

'Did I ever tell you about when I first came to St Andrews?' Finlay whispers like it's a secret.

Banjo shakes his head, shuffles a little closer to the edge.

'Well, I've moved around a lot with my mum; I've never really been in the city centre until now, and honestly when I first came I felt like I was surrounded by *pirates*—'

Banjo laughs so sudden he has to cover his mouth.

'Seriously!' Finlay's grinning, cheeks bunched, 'Everyone was all, *aye matey*—'

The absolute *worst* Glaswegian accent Banjo's ever heard comes out Finlay's mouth, and Banjo arches off the bed with his laughter. Sometimes when he laughs with Finlay, it feels like it's shaking something out of him; really cracking him up and into a new shape.

Finlay nearly falls off the bed. He presses a hand to the chest of drawers to support himself when he almost goes overboard. Their laughter melts into the air between them. Banjo reaches up and puts his hand on the drawer, too. He touches his hand to the wood touching Finlay. They reach one another that way.

Chapter Thirty

FINLAY

When Finlay arrives for his last shift at Silver Lodge, he really doesn't expect any kind of fanfare. It's a quiet, cold morning, dry with a sharp chill in the air. When Finlay nods at Charlotte, however, she leaps up and rushes away from him. Finlay is very confused until he heads to the staffroom to set his things down.

And finds everybody there.

'Uh, hi, guys.' He frowns as they all try to hide what's on the staffroom table.

'Charlotte!' Beth tuts, obscuring the desk with her hands. 'I thought you said you'd give us a warning!'

'It's not my fault he's early,' she replies, shooting Finlay a raised brow that makes him feel guilty for punctuality.

'Finlay, ignore them.' Rhonda smiles wide. 'We all chipped in for a wee something to say bye.'

'Can't believe it's your last day,' Somaya adds. 'It's gone so fast.'

'You're always welcome back, you know that.' Leanne grins. 'We'd offer you a job if it were up to us.'

'Hope you like it!' Beth cuts in. 'I picked the chocolates.'

Finlay remains in shock as they stand aside to reveal a small *Good Luck* card and a box of sweets. He huffs, too overcome to really react.

'Aw, guys. Thanks,' he croaks, and holds his arms open for the closest available hug. Instead they all pile in, and it becomes a team effort where they're all holding on to one another and laughing.

Then there are the residents.

'That you away then?' Patrick asks as soon as Finlay steps into his room.

'Yup.' Finlay nods as he divides Patrick's tablets.

'Uck, well.' Patrick waves a hand. 'On tae bigger 'hings.'

'Patrick, don't get sentimental with me,' Finlay warns. 'You really won't like the consequences.'

Patrick laughs, and it instantly makes him so much younger.

Alice thinks he's just leaving for the Christmas holidays, so just says, 'Have a nice time. Suppose I'll see you in the New Year.' It's a good day for her, Finlay can tell. Her eyes are brighter.

'I'll see you.' Finlay smiles.

'Not another one gone,' Edith grumbles quietly. 'Can't you stay?'

'Afraid not,' Finlay sighs, and he means it. If he had the chance he'd stay in a heartbeat. But he needs to do another placement, join another team, meet new patients, reattach himself all over again.

'Send us a postcard, will you,' she asks as he lifts her from her bed on to her wheelchair, arm around his neck for support.

'Absolutely,' he promises, putting her down carefully.

Finlay pokes his head into Jeanie's room. He finds her at her armchair by the window.

'Finlay, darlin', sit wae me,' she calls without glancing up.

Finlay smiles and takes the seat opposite.

'Think ye'll miss this view?' she asks him as she nods to her window. Silver Lodge's car park is spread out, and beyond that the main road. Finlay takes it all in. He watches a bird settle on the large oak tree planted in their front garden, and after a second another one leaves.

'I'll miss everything,' he answers honestly.

Jeanie laughs. 'Yer a wee bit strange. Not many people enjoy this.'

Finlay smiles at her. 'You're probably right.'

Before he leaves she stops him with a touch to the arm. 'Take care.'

Finlay closes his hand over her touch, his thin rubber gloves allowing for a little warmth. 'And you.'

He washed dirty bedsheets, emptied catheters, changed stomas, handled medical and human waste. He was exhausted, could never find a vein, did dressings terribly. And even still, he'll miss it all.

Once he leaves, after many hugs and promises to keep in touch, Finlay discovers it snowed during his shift. There's a soft sheet, crunching as he walks, smelling clean and fresh.

Finlay pulls out his phone to check the time. He could nip in somewhere for a celebratory takeaway and bring it back to his flat.

Only he stops in his tracks.

He has a missed call.

Three minutes ago.

From Banjo.

Finlay used to periodically block and unblock Banjo's number. He used to imagine looking at his phone one day and seeing Banjo there, finding him changed, finding them both changed.

Now there's a missed call from him.

Finlay stares. The hope threatens to consume him. He presses *call*.

It takes Finlay a solid second to put his phone to his ear. He stands in numb silence.

The line connects.

Banjo breathes. Finlay feels as though he grew up to that breathing. He can't speak.

'Hello,' Banjo says, so formal.

Finlay could cry and laugh. That voice is a rush of pain and love in one sound.

'Hello,' Finlay responds.

And this time Banjo laughs. It's croaky and rough. Finlay doesn't do anything. The moment feels oddly surreal. He's worried he'll shatter it by accepting it as reality.

'How, um. Eh – actually, sorry tae just call,' Banjo stutters. His nerves are palpable. Finlay would guess Banjo's pacing, but Banjo has this terrible quality of planting his feet in any bad situation, ready for a fight, so Finlay can't really imagine him doing that. Then again, maybe he's different now.

'Okay,' Finlay murmurs. He feels like he's floating.

'How are ye?' Banjo asks.

'Good,' Finlay says. 'How are you?'

'Good,' Banjo sounds shaky. He's so scared. By contrast Finlay sounds monotone, robotic.

'Ye a nurse now?' Banjo asks.

'Student,' Finlay confirms.

'Brilliant.'

'Are you still at school?' Finlay asks.

'Yeah. I do athletics. Piss poor at everythin' else. But I work in a wee café too. EK Barista.'

'Brilliant.' Finlay only realises he's echoed Banjo afterwards.

'Can – can come down an' see it, sometime,' Banjo mutters.

Finlay's heart soars. 'Yeah. Yeah.' He barely believes this is happening.

'Finlay.' Banjo's voice goes quiet. '. . . Am sorry.'

Finlay doesn't move. The thing he was sure would never happen has happened, and not even in a very momentous way. Banjo's just said it. The unreality of it all sinks straight through without being absorbed.

He still can't even believe Banjo called. Even if Banjo were swearing down the phone right now, it would still be unbelievable. Three years have passed. An unspoken agreement.

At St Andrews, whenever Banjo was annoyed he'd go sullen and stiff. It took a long time for Finlay to recognise that the silent version of Banjo was hurt, not angry. Banjo could be every emotion in the span of a sentence, but when he was hurt he carried it around and held it close. It took a lot of prying his fingers apart to make him let it go. They understood each other in that way. When Finlay was hurt he would throw sand over it, bury it, avoid it. Banjo knew every which way to dig. *What is it what it is what is it?* In explaining the hurt, sometimes Finlay felt it pass from inside him.

Maybe they can do that for one another now.

'I'm sorry, too.' He exhales.

'Whit the fuck are ye sorry fur?' Banjo's voice cracks in the middle. It sounds thin and small.

Finlay doesn't understand. He blinks. 'For what happened.'

'But it wis me.' Banjo's voice trembles. 'It wus aw *me*.' There's a ragged inhale, exhale. Crying.

He remembers the look on Banjo's face when he held Finlay's phone. The numb, vacant look. His eyes were full of water but that face was immobile. Now, Finlay hears him actually feel it. He can actually *hear* the pain in Banjo's voice.

'It wasn't all you,' Finlay states. It's the truth. Finlay was too scared to come out. He should have, but he was terrified of its destructive power so he avoided it. He was a coward. Or maybe he was just fifteen.

'But ye ...' Banjo tries. Finlay can hear Banjo's throat close over, hear how difficult the words are to push out. 'Ye almost ...'

'That wasn't your fault,' Finlay says. He's wanted to say this for a long time now.

'Come oan, Finlay,' Banjo rasps. 'Ye couldnae even look at me when Ah came tae see ye. At – at the hospital.'

Finlay starts to shake. 'I . . .' He swallows a few times. 'I was ashamed,' he manages to force out.

'*Why?*'

'Because.' Finlay's crying now, too, but silently. 'It's the worst I've ever felt. I can't believe I did it. I still don't even know why.'

'Because of me,' Banjo confirms with a shuddering breath.

Finlay shakes his head, his own breath hitching. 'No. No, Banjo. It's not your fault.'

'Finlay, fuck *sake*, quit it!' Banjo shouts. 'Ah know Ah wus fucken awful, the shite Ah said wus so bad, and Ah didnae care if ye fancied me or whutever, who the fuck would care, Ah jus' thought that's the only reason ye hung aboot wae me—'

'What?' Finlay blurts, surprised. 'I – I didn't fancy you.'

There's a short inhale. 'Ye didnae?'

'No.' Finlay shakes his head.

Banjo coughs a strange laugh. 'No' that am aw that. That's no' whut Ah mean.'

Finlay's laughter rattles from his chest. 'I know. I just – Banjo, it was never like that.'

Banjo swallows. 'Ah jus' thought if ye'd lied aboot it, it was aw a lie or somethin'.'

'No,' Finlay states, sharp pain stirring in his chest. 'That's not true.'

'Ah know,' Banjo whispers. 'And it doesnae even make sense. Ye dinnae fucken owe me an explanation. Fuck if Ah even care whut ye are – it's a scale an' that, yer sexuality.'

Finlay is stunned. 'Are you saying . . . *you're* on a scale?'

'Yeah,' Banjo states, like a challenge and a promise at the same time.

Finlay smiles. 'Did you read that somewhere?'

Banjo's laugh is warmer this time. 'Yeah.' He swallows, takes a moment. 'Finlay, Ah wus so wrong. Maybe Ah didnae know any better, but it doesnae fucken matter. Ah wish A'd never done it—'

'I should've explained,' Finlay cuts in. 'I just froze—'

'But am so sorry,' Banjo gasps. 'It was so bad, Finlay. Ah never shouldae reacted like that. Ah wish A'd been fucken understandin'. Ye must'ae been so scared. Ah wus the worst ye could be. Ah regretted every'hin Ah said the second it came oot, Ah just didnae know how to stop mysel, Ah didnae know how to say sorry, but am so, *so* sorry.' His breath hitches with sobs in between the words.

Finlay closes his eyes. He has to swallow a few times. Banjo's voice after all this time, saying everything Finlay needs to move past this, is almost overwhelming. So much time has passed. It became such a certainty this would never happen. If Finlay speaks, he'll sob.

When he's composed, he tells Banjo: 'They told me you basically saved my life.'

Banjo goes quiet.

Finlay remembers flashing lights, vomiting for so long his lungs hurt, not being able to feel his hands for hours. The terror and the nausea and the regret. All of it buried underneath the soul-crushing embarrassment of having to explain to everyone why he'd made an attempt on his life. Talking to the police with his head lowered, cheeks stinging, fiddling with the pulse monitor on his finger. Being signed up to the mental health services and the weekly counselling sessions. He wanted nothing more than to disappear. To blink out of existence, no warning or fanfare. Then a cool breeze blew in his hospital window that night. Finlay walked over, pressed his cheek to the glass, felt his heart thrum. And he was so glad it hadn't worked.

'I felt so guilty you saw me like that,' Finlay admits, hoarse and croaky because this is the first time he's ever spoken about it. 'But I was humiliated, too, and angry, and hurt. Then after a while, all those feelings just . . . went away. I only missed you. I knew you cut ties and I wanted to respect that. But all this time, Banjo, I've just missed you. That's all.'

Banjo is silent on the other end. He's silent for so long, Finlay is sure the conversation is over. He wouldn't even mind. He knows he's said everything he wanted to.

Then Banjo says: 'Ah didnae 'hink ye wanted me to get in touch.' His voice is deep. 'Ah thought ye wanted me oot yer life. But Ah missed ye so fucken much, Ah thought it'd kill me.'

Three years on from that night and it feels as though they've come to one another minutes afterwards. All that time. All of it wasted. They could have been a part of one another's lives. Then again, maybe they were, in a way.

'We fucked it,' Banjo decides.

Finlay chokes a sound, not a laugh, but an intense explosion of relief. It settles over him the knowledge that he's talking to Banjo, *Banjo*, and it almost feels the way it used to.

Only something fundamental is different.

'Banjo,' Finlay begins, because it's time. 'I . . .' He swallows. 'I'm gay. I'm sorry I never said it when you asked. I know this might sound weird, I don't mean romantically, but I think it's because you were my first love.'

Finlay scoops the words out from the deepest cavity inside him. He knows he has to say them in order to go on. He has to tell the first person he's ever loved that he can love, so he knows how to say it.

He can't even explain the love. He loves Banjo in a way he has never loved anything and never will. It's a necessary love, a love to teach him how to love. It's not romantic, no, but also not paternal or platonic. To restrict it to any one category reduces it entirely. And maybe Banjo won't understand, but Finlay does. He finally understands it within himself.

Banjo exhales. 'You're ma first, too, Finlay.'

Finlay is totally still. 'What do you mean?'

'Yer ma first love,' Banjo states, resolute.

Finlay's mouth is dry. He hoped for Banjo's acceptance, not for Banjo to join him. But Finlay remembers when he lay on the floor, Banjo followed. He holds his palm spread in front of him as snow floats down. He pictures Banjo's hand hovering over it. They have always touched. He never noticed until now.

'I'm glad,' Finlay murmurs. 'I . . . I'd love to take you up on your offer to see your café—'

'Absolutely.' Banjo almost jumps down his throat. 'Am openin' next week, Christmas Eve, if yer aboot.'

'I'll be there,' Finlay promises.

The day after his last placement shift, Finlay scans the bouquets carefully arranged in a small flower shop nestled between a café and a retail store, chewing his thumbnail and scrolling a *flower language* website online.

Once decided, he watches the cashier wrap them up delicately.

'Um,' Finlay starts. 'Are these good apology flowers? Or do they say something else? I'm trying to find these, but I don't see them.' He shows her his screen with the list of flowers that mean *regret*.

She smiles at him. 'These are perfect.'

Finlay nods, cheeks scalding. That was probably a stupid thing to ask. Flowers are flowers.

He develops a cramp while walking down the student halls. It starts in his side and travels into the middle. He needs to loosen his grip on the bouquets: the stems are being crushed. But as he lifts his hand to knock, there's nothing else to hold on to.

Thankfully Derya opens the door. She stares, mouth open.

'Hi,' Finlay croaks. He holds them out. 'I'm sorry.'

She reaches for them slowly.

'Um – actually, these are yours.' Finlay detangles the two bouquets, offering her one. 'They're the same, unless, I mean, one flower is smaller or something.' He attempts a humorous tone. His ears feel burnt.

Derya takes them gently. And then she wraps Finlay in a hug.

'I was *so worried*.' She squeezes him hard.

Finlay is rigid until he melts in her embrace, one arm wrapping around her waist and holding her close.

'Sorry,' Finlay murmurs.

'Are you all right?' she asks. The immediacy of the question causes him a strange pain.

'Yeah,' Finlay answers, even though he doesn't feel halfway there. Yet he realises he can't remain a blameless victim his whole life: a child of circumstance and chance, a creature that things just happen to. It's made him his own self-fulfilling prophecy: so desperate to find any betrayal that he creates it.

Jun's reaction is a little different.

'Where the *hell* have you been?' she shouts.

Then she lunges at Finlay and crushes her flowers between them. Jun squeezes him so tight, it's as though she re-forms him into something whole. Finlay squeezes her back.

The flowers are a little crooked and bent when she sends a photo of them in a coffee mug, but they'll survive.

Please meet me at Kelvingrove if you're free, Finlay sends Akash. Then adds: *Museum*.

Okay, Akash responds. One word. Then: *give me an hour*.

Akash is wearing a long woollen coat and his jumper-and-linen-trousers combo, hands in pockets, hair fluttering in the wind.

'Hey,' Finlay murmurs.

'Hi.' Akash rubs his throat as he looks at Finlay. 'Coming?' He always makes the first move.

Finlay's never been inside Kelvingrove Museum. His eyes widen at the scale of it. They walk through a set of wooden doors and into the immaculate tiled flooring of the centre hall where a grand organ sits, chandeliers lining the way towards it. Finlay's neck bends as he admires the stonework.

'Hey,' Akash whispers at his side. 'What are you doing?'

'Sorry, I've just never been inside,' Finlay explains, embarrassed.

'*Never?*'

Finlay glances at Akash. Akash gazes at him, the glow of the daylight cast across his thick black hair.

'No,' Finlay murmurs.

'Why did you ask me to come then?' Akash asks, shoulders stiff up at his ears.

'I wanted to talk to you,' Finlay begins softly. 'But not somewhere we had to sit or eat, and you felt like you had nowhere to run. And not somewhere really private where it might be too intense. So I thought: a museum. We can look at the paintings. Less pressure.'

Akash's eyes slant as he smiles, head tilting sideways. 'Well played.'

Finlay thought he'd never see that smile again. He feels struck by it.

'I read an article,' Finlay confesses softly, an awkward pressure in his throat, 'recommending good date ideas.'

There's a heavy pause.

'Well.' Akash spins with his hands still in his pockets, elbows sticking out, gangly and unsure. 'Come on then.'

Finlay follows through a stone archway and into another hall. Then his mouth parts as floating heads in the middle of the room come into view, each one tied to the ceiling, each face displaying a different emotion.

Akash laughs. 'Your awe is the best part.'

Finlay smiles.

Akash ducks his head, cheeks blazing. They can't help being like this, even after everything.

They walk around the marble statues beneath the floating heads: a woman with talons and wings clutching her naked breast, face grim. Finlay stares for a moment, the incredible attention to detail in her clawed hands. *The Harpy Celaeno.*

'Don't keep me in suspense, Nowak,' Akash murmurs close to his ear.

Finlay turns around.

Their chests are close together, their faces inches apart. Finlay goes light-headed. They stand there for a beat. Akash's dark gaze has such a focus. Finlay feels exposed but he offers himself up to the scrutiny; desperate to be close and powerless to hide it.

'Okay,' he murmurs. 'There's ... a few things I want to say.'

Akash is quiet. Kelvingrove isn't busy at this time of day, the occasional passer-by here and there.

'When I was in foster care, I didn't really ... know anyone. I had no friends. I had nobody,' Finlay begins. He inhales a long breath, steadies himself. 'But when I was fifteen, I had to share a room with someone.' He swallows thickly. 'I met a lot of people in care, but I ... I got this feeling when I met Banjo. I wanted to make sure he was all right. I got the feeling he wanted to do the same. So we decided we'd look out for one another.'

Akash is quiet as they wander around the empty gallery of the Scottish Colourists.

'We were closer than anyone,' Finlay says. 'We were family. But then Banjo found out I was gay, and I think we were just too young to know how to ... navigate it without it blowing everything up. At the time, I felt so alone. So I did something ... stupid. I hurt myself.'

Akash slows. Finlay turns to look at him. Akash studies Finlay carefully. Then he seems to understand. He swallows thickly, looking ill.

'I didn't want—' Finlay's throat closes, but this is the point he always arrives at, and he's never able to move past it. He needs to move past it. 'I didn't want to die.' Finlay hears the words for the first time. He sucks in a breath and continues: 'I just wanted to stop feeling so alone.'

Because that's the real reason. The truth Finlay has always known.

Akash looks at the paintings. He nods. His jaw is tense, his eyes wet and glistening. But he's silent, compelling Finlay to continue.

'I bumped into him a few weeks ago,' Finlay states. 'It was ... too much. I needed some time to process. And I didn't go about it

322

the best way. I think I just retreated into how I used to deal with being overwhelmed. But I don't want to do that any more.'

Finlay focuses on a painting of a fruit bowl. 'Because I've fallen in love with you, Akash Singh,' he murmurs, his hands wrapped around his biceps to feel like he's holding on to something. 'I tried not to, but I doubt there's a person alive who wouldn't love you, if given the chance. And I know I'm not ready for a relationship. But I can be. It'll take a lot of effort on my part, but there's nobody else I want to make the effort for.'

Finlay glances over to find Akash's head bowed.

'So, now you know everything,' he says.

Akash looks at him, tears on his cheeks. The gallery is empty.

Finlay steps close. He takes Akash's face in both hands and strokes his thumbs over it. Akash stares at him.

Finlay leans in and angles their faces, so close their breath mingles, the tips of their noses brush. They're the closest two people have ever been while still being able to see one another.

But Finlay waits, just to be sure. When Akash gives the barest nod, Finlay kisses him.

Their mouths meet. They stay in the moment of contact, just touching. Finlay's mouth is gentle, soft, the lightest pressure. Bare skin on bare skin. He feels the way Akash is trembling.

Finlay pulls back. 'Akash,' he murmurs.

Because he understands now. The minute he was born, the second his lungs breathed, he wanted this tender love. He wanted someone to come along and adore him, and he wanted to adore them in return. He wanted Akash's gentle nature, his warm presence directing him around the kitchen, hands on top of his shoulders to avoid a fright.

They go back to Finlay's flat. Because they both haven't slept in weeks, they take off their shoes and crawl on to his rickety, lumpy student bed. Akash goes behind Finlay; wraps arms around Finlay's chest and presses himself to Finlay's back.

'Falling asleep already?' A hot voice brushes his ear.

Finlay jerks up. 'No.'

Akash's laughter shakes them both. Finlay turns around in Akash's arms and rolls on top. Akash shuffles until one arm is supporting Finlay's back, his other moving to Finlay's face, running his fingertip along his cheeks and chin. Finlay shivers. He does the same to Akash's full lips, now obsessed. Akash's mouth parts beneath his fingertip. His gaze flits up to Finlay's.

'Do your parents know?' Finlay asks, because the question welled up and he allowed it free.

Akash swallows. 'They will. When I'm ready. If that's okay?'

Finlay nods. 'They're your parents.'

Akash meets his gaze. There's something new on his face. Akash looks at him and Finlay feels as though he is being looked into.

'Do you want to talk about your mum?' Akash asks.

Finlay blinks. He forgets that Akash might actually remember her. A person in the periphery of Finlay's life but never the focus.

What can he say? He's almost lived more years without her now than he ever lived with her. When he's an adult, with a full-time job and his own place, with people he loves to populate his existence, he'll think back on that time with a detached sort of sympathy. Both for her and for himself. He's reaching for that day.

'When I'm ready,' Finlay echoes with a smile. He will be. He knows it.

Akash returns it, fingering the blond strands at the front of Finlay's forehead. 'Can I stay here tonight?'

'Of course,' Finlay says without hesitation.

Akash nips into Finlay's bathroom and Finlay collapses on to his bed, sure he's about to burst.

When Akash comes back out, he's in Finlay's borrowed joggers and T-shirt. All his pristine edges are gentled. He's wearing Finlay's things, smiling a private smile for Finlay: possessed by Finlay in every way. This strangled, feverish sanctity that can only be described as *devotion* overwhelms Finlay, this divine worship that says *we can never be apart, never*, even while distant rationality now realises much of his life will be spent outside of Akash's arms, forever chasing to be back in them.

But Finlay thinks he can live with that. A small price to pay.

'What happened with Banjo?' Akash asks softly when he climbs back in. 'You never said.'

Finlay glows inside that Akash remembered. But he swallows as he tries to answer. 'Well, actually, we talked a few days go. I'm going to see him next week.' His heart lurches at the thought, but he smiles shakily. 'I . . . I'd love for you both to meet. Maybe not right now, but at some point.'

We can cook stir-fry together. I can invite you into my life the way you invited me.

Akash smiles his signature-sunlight smile. 'I'd love that as well.'

Finlay remembers his first cleaning shift when he sat down to watch the sunrise. He remembers the warmth touching him through the windowpane and illuminating the wall. *MY FAMILY IS . . .*

At the time Finlay didn't feel as though he had an answer. He'd never been face-to-face with the question before. Now he realises it's more than parents. He pictures how carefully he'd draw everyone: Akash, Jun, Derya, Banjo. *My family is . . . who I allow it to be.*

Chapter Thirty-One

BANJO

Alena's recovery is slow. She's sitting up, and then manages her legs over the bed, until she walks, bent double and gripping her IV, the three steps to her bedside chair.

Everyone claps once she sits down. Even the other patients. Even the fucking *consultant*, and that's a trick.

She's desperate to get out before Christmas. She's been in for a few weeks, but she's pushing herself to heal now, and Banjo doesn't know how to tell her to slow down.

He buys a teddy. It's not that expensive. Not that big, either. Just a soft plushie from the hospital shop.

He arrives with it held over his face, using one of its arms to wave.

Alena gapes as if he's given her the moon.

'I love him!' She holds out her hands. Her hair is brushed down, face bare. She's wearing a long jumper and sweatpants.

Banjo comes close and presses the teddy's snout to her cheek.

She laughs, hugs it, then pulls back to stare it in the face.

'We'll call him Murray,' she decides, after a good hard look at the teddy.

Banjo sits down gently on the bed, using a finger to stroke some hair behind her ear.

'I like it,' he tells her. Alena looks at him with this fond face.

Banjo touches her nose with the tip of a finger. Then he swallows. 'Alena. Ye know how I told ye I . . . wanted tae say sorry tae somebody?'

Alena sobers instantly, her brown eyes open on his face. She hasn't asked any questions since Banjo said this. But Banjo needs to tell her anyway.

'Well, I did,' Banjo states. Because he wants her to know he did. 'His name's Finlay. See, we basically grew up together in care. But when he tried tae come out, ye know, I didnae . . .' Banjo grimaces, a bad taste in his mouth. 'Listen tae him.' He stares hard at Alena's bent knee, her patchwork pyjamas. 'I wus, eh, fourteen. And aw the ideas of whut it wus, in ma head, were aw wrong. I know that. So I called him. Couple days ago. We're seein' each other Christmas Eve.'

Alena's face unfolds in a smile. 'I'm really proud of you.'

Banjo exhales slowly.

The stress of keeping that inside, of containing it squeezing it shutting it down, all just releases with that breath. Something he never thought he'd tell anyone. And now he's done it by choice. He's owned it because he needs to. Because he needs to own it to know he's changed.

Alena taps his knee, fingertips light. 'I was actually going to ask if you wanted to come to mine for Christmas Eve.'

A rock forms in Banjo's throat. It's the best thing he's ever been offered. But . . . 'Dae yer parents know am in care?' The unspoken:

Won't they wonder where the fuck my family are?

Alena shakes her head. 'I haven't said. That's your choice.'

'I – I lied tae them.' Banjo brushes fingertips over Alena's knee now.

'It doesn't matter.' Alena speaks with total certainty. 'They'll understand.'

Banjo meets her gaze. 'Okay.'

Alena gets out in time for Christmas. First thing she wants to do is see everyone at the café. They go over before it properly opens, even though it's stupid early and Banjo is scrubbing sleep out of his eyes.

Morag embraces her and squeezes tight. 'I can't believe they don't allow visitors in HDU!'

'We've been so worried!' Lizzy chimes in.

Banjo has to stop himself from interfering: from jolting forward and saying, 'Careful, fucking *careful*.'

But he shares a look with Alena, because he knows for a fact that they *do* allow visitors in HDU. Alena just smiles over Morag's shoulder, and Banjo can understand. She didn't want the fuss.

Alena eventually caved one night. Banjo sat on her hospital bed while she revealed the little red blob that was her intestine, just above her waistband. It felt more vulnerable than Alena being *naked*. Banjo just stared – at a total loss – before he blurted, 'Cool.'

Alena laughed. Just like the first time they met.

While Alena chats with Morag and Lizzy, Banjo snaps a picture on his phone; tries to sneak it quick for the memories.

Morag notices, though, and insists Banjo be in one. She forces Banjo and Alena to stand with their arms around one another.

Banjo drops a kiss to Alena's head.

Morag makes the noise of a strangled duck.

The chaos has everyone asking how long they've been together, when it happened, *how* it happened – and Banjo's no prude, but *really?*

Morag's so astounded that Alena keeps stopping mid-sentence to laugh. Banjo manages to snap pictures of that, too.

He looks through them that night.

He grins at the ones of Lizzy and Morag with all their thumbs up, trying to be gentle as they tilt close to her. Alena in the middle, a safe distance between everyone, a little blurry because Banjo was shouting over his phone for everyone to cool it. In the morning he goes to get them printed at Boots.

Banjo sits in art class during lunch, last day of school before Christmas break, because he's imploded all his friendships with everyone at this school.

He's stripping his sad cheese string when the door to the art class swings wide.

Dev walks right up to him and glowers. 'The hell is that?' He nods at Banjo's hands.

Banjo's barely had the chance to blink. *Paula buys them 'cause she thinks am seven and I don't want them to lie in the fridge.* But that's no argument.

He's managed to avoid Devlin for a while. Devlin's also started hanging about with the athletics lads again, and doesn't seem to want to talk to him. Banjo almost feels like beating up Kyle was *cheating* on Devlin, which makes no sense.

So Banjo just shrugs and strips his cheese string in silence.

'Look,' Dev huffs. 'Come talk to Anderson, explain that you apologised—'

Banjo frowns. 'How d'ye know I've apologised?'

Dev frowns back. 'Kyle told everyone.'

Banjo is silent, stumped.

'Everyone at athletics, at least,' Dev carries on. 'Think he wants you back. Seriously. It's pretty boring without you randomly attacking people.'

Banjo can't help but chuckle there, but then he falls silent. He wants to give Dev an explanation. He can admit that they were friends. And Banjo pressed destruct.

'Ma da used tae hit me,' he blurts. He keeps his eyes on his knees. 'Ma maw as well, but ma da wus . . . yeah.'

A year passes before Devlin speaks. 'Shite excuse.'

Banjo snorts, more because it's genuinely funny than anything.

'Mine died,' Devlin continues. 'My dad.'

Banjo nods and scratches a hole into the wooden desk.

'Did your parents ever apologise?' Devlin asks.

Banjo is so blinded by the question that he looks up. Dev meets his gaze head-on.

The thought has never even entered his head. Did they say sorry? Did he push it so far down he can't even reach it? No, that's not true. They never apologised. It was always an explanation:

don't do this and I won't get angry, why were you standing there anyway?

'No,' Banjo states.

Dev shrugs. 'So you're already better than them.'

That statement is a spear through Banjo. His throat feels impaled. Devlin sees it.

For the longest time in Banjo's life, Finlay was the only one who knew him this way. They were always that person to one another. That person who knew the things nobody else did. The ugly things nobody actually wants to know, the terrible horrible parts of life nobody can even respond to. Banjo knows all those parts about Finlay, too.

And now he has a whole crowd. Devlin standing here trying to get him to come back to athletics. Kyle fucking Simmons putting in a good word with the team even though he tried to get Banjo booted off before. Morag and Lizzy. Paula and Henry. Carlos, Julie, Jace. *Alena.* And Finlay.

'Talk to Anderson,' Dev states. 'The team wants you to.'

The same team that tried to kick him out. Banjo swallows. He's still unable to talk.

'Sort it out before you come back to the track.' Dev points a finger at him. 'Everything.' He taps his head, then he's gone.

Banjo sits there for a long second. He smiles slowly. Then he goes and does as he's told.

*

Banjo's opening up the café this morning, even though it's Christmas Eve and who the fuck wants to roll out of bed and open up today of all days? *Him*, that's who.

Mainly to pay off everyone's presents. Mainly because he told Finlay he would be here. And mainly to take his mind off that fucking fact.

He hasn't slept, and can't eat. He won't even so much as look at coffee. Finlay said he'd be here for lunch, so Banjo has some time.

He's seeing Alena after his shift; going over straight after work to meet her grandparents and all that. He's got his best stuff laid out over at Paula and Henry's – new shirt courtesy of them, too. He also has no idea what her parents would like, so just bought wine. Pretty failsafe, right? Wine at Christmas? Or is that something else? Wine any day of the week, fuck it.

It's freezing as all hell, and his breath turns to smoke, but Banjo just rubs his hands and gets to work.

He pulls out the photos he got printed of Morag, Lizzy, Alena, and him and sticks them all above the Wall of Employees. He stands on a chair to do it because he's absolutely no height. He places the one of Alena in the middle, stands back and stares up at his handiwork.

THE TEAM is written in block capitals.

After that's done, Banjo jumps down and starts unwrapping the foils on the cakes to put them on display. His hands are shaking, his pulse hasn't slowed in about three days, but he just clenches his jaw and gets on with it.

This will be good, he tells himself. His body won't be convinced, though. Banjo figures he'll have to endure it.

The door opens.

Banjo scrambles to straighten up. He's not even flipped the sign out front.

'Uh, sorry, we're no—' He lifts his head.

Finlay's stood at the entrance. He's early. He came early.

Everything stops. Even his own heart. And it's so silly, because it's just Finlay. It's just the Finlay Banjo's known for what feels like his whole life.

Yet all the details Banjo missed at the hospital are here in full view now. His hair is a little longer. He looks taller. It's tiny things. But all of a sudden, it just looks like a different person wearing Finlay's face. He's wider, somehow. He's been eating better. His nose is pink, and there's a scarf wrapped around his chin, and his eyes are bright as he smiles.

He's Finlay, but then he's not. Because Finlay was this thin-faced skinny little kid, and now he's a grown man.

There are so many things Banjo wants to say. He wants to tell Finlay he thinks about him all the time. He wants to jump across the counter and bounce up and down. He wants to hear everything Finlay's been doing and everywhere he's been.

Banjo hasn't said a word since Finlay came in. He doesn't know how to break the silence. He just wants Finlay to talk, to say something, to show that he's actually *back*.

Finlay takes a step, smile soft. 'Hi.'

'Hi,' Banjo returns in seconds. Too quick.

'Sorry I'm a bit early.' Finlay takes a few more steps inside. 'I saw you inside so I thought ...' He waves a hand at the tall glass windows. When he turns, his eyes fall on the Wall of Employees.

He steps up to it instantly. Embarrassment catches in the base of Banjo's throat.

Finlay surveys the pictures. His shoulders go loose. 'This you?' he asks, points to the one at the top.

Banjo nods. 'Yeh, I – ma girlfriend. Me an' ma girlfriend.'

Finlay turns to Banjo, smile wider. 'Oh. Lovely.'

Hearing his voice now, in person and not just in one ear, Banjo feels as though he's being transported all the way to St Andrews: back to a time and place he started to believe there were things to live for.

Finlay stands, and Banjo stands, and nothing happens. He needs to move. He realises there's a physical barrier separating them. There's no way to cross it. The distance is too great; there are countries upon countries between them.

'Banjo,' Finlay starts. 'I'm so sorry—'

'Finlay, *am* the one who ruined it,' Banjo babbles, the words welling up and flooding. 'I wish I'd never said—'

'I wish I—' Finlay carries on.

'Finlay, *I* wish—'

Finlay shakes his head wildly, tries to speak so fast he ends up blurting, 'Buwah—'

He stops with a frown. Banjo feels laughter burst free from him. Finlay laughs too. Then they're both laughing, and Banjo forgot how good it felt to laugh with Finlay.

It makes Banjo unstick his feet and walk out from behind the counter. He needs to take the first step. Fuck, Finlay came all the way to East Kilbride just to see Banjo's crummy little café. He needs to do *something*.

Finlay blinks, surprised.

There's no graceful way to do it. No subtle way to leap the distance.

Banjo walks up and throws his arms around Finlay.

He's never hugged anyone like this. Never just lunged at somebody full force.

Finlay is solid. It's kind of awkward: Banjo clinging on and Finlay unresponsive like this. Finlay's actually a little shorter than Banjo, surprisingly. Banjo never noticed before. He could almost laugh because Finlay's a full *year* older. Never did eat his fucking greens.

Finlay pats Banjo's back, unsure. 'Thanks.'

'Finlay, come oan.' Banjo squeezes Finlay tighter.

Maybe Finlay just needed the confirmation. Because then Banjo's being crushed in Finlay's arms.

He hugs Banjo hard, all bony shoulders and elbows, weird skeleton fingers digging into Banjo's back, chin hard and pointy on Banjo's shoulder. His jacket really is puffy, and he's cold from outside, but he's *Finlay*.

It's so strange that they've never done this before. Banjo realises he could've always hugged Finlay. It was always there.

And they don't speak. This is the first hug they've ever shared. Words aren't exactly big enough. Finlay laughs. Even through all the layers, Banjo feels it. And it makes him do the same. When they pull away, Banjo holds Finlay's head to his own, and Finlay knows what it means. He does it back, just like he did the first time.

When Banjo hears Finlay's going to be alone in his tiny student flat in Glasgow for Christmas Eve, he makes a snap decision.

Finlay is going to stay with him at Paula and Henry's tonight.

'Honestly, I'm kind of looking forward—' Finlay tries.

'Yer no dain it and that's final.'

So Finlay needs to go back and pick up his things, but they arrange to meet later.

Morag arrives shortly afterwards with a Santa hat on, doing a twirl through the door. Banjo laughs even though it's hardly that funny. Lizzy greets him with a one-armed hug. The shift passes in a blur. Banjo's cheek muscles ache as much as his feet.

When Finlay returns, his bag is fit to burst. 'Are you sure it's okay?' He worries at his lip.

Banjo just shows him Paula's message: *of course you can have family stay over!*

Finlay's pretty awkward at first. He's all stooped shoulders and *I won't be staying long*, but Paula hugs him on sight, and then Henry near swallows Finlay in his arms.

They look at Banjo, waiting, as though they want to do the same. Banjo just ducks away.

'Got tae get ready!' he hollers halfway up the stairs.

Not that he isn't used to their affection or whatever. He eats with them every night now, helps with the shopping, and shows them how to cook something other than oven pizza. Banjo's no chef: he just copies the soup recipes from the café. But it makes dinners a bit more of a team effort.

Despite that, they're still scared to touch him. Alena and her family just do it without asking. But Paula and Henry want some kind of permission, and Banjo doesn't know how to give it. They'll get there eventually.

The four of them pile into the car. Henry and Paula are dropping Banjo and Finlay off at Alena's on their way to see their son, but they want to meet Alena first.

Alena opens the door in a fluffy jumper and reindeer antlers. She's so cute it's painful, and Banjo's feeling randomly confident, so he kisses her full on the mouth.

She squeezes his middle tight, and then turns to the people he's brought with him.

'Hi!' Alena beams. She hugs Paula and Henry first, who start embarrassing Banjo right in front of him.

'We've heard so much about you, it feels as though we've met already!' Paula laughs as they embrace.

Banjo sorely regrets going into the details, showing them her picture, and generally being an absolute sap. Still, the beam Alena gives him makes up for it.

'*Really?*' Alena's face glows as she waggles her brows.

Banjo knows he's glowing too, so he shrugs. He can't wipe the smile, though.

Alena steps back. 'And you must be Finlay!' She holds her arms open to Finlay, scuffing his feet behind everyone.

'Oh!' Finlay laughs. He dips into her hug, pink as a berry. It's as though Finlay didn't expect Banjo to have told Alena about him.

That very second, Julie and Carlos appear at the door.

'Hello, hello!' Carlos booms, and everyone starts introducing themselves.

'It's so lovely to meet you.' Paula steps forward instantly.

'Absolutely! Thanks for stopping by!' Julie embraces Paula on the spot.

Henry and Carlos shake hands.

'Thanks for looking after him,' Henry murmurs, just close enough for Banjo to hear it.

'It's our pleasure.' Carlos claps Banjo on the shoulder, allowing him in on the moment. 'You've got a great kid here.'

Banjo goes beetroot, because there's nothing else he can do. It almost feels like too much, just the edge of overstimulating, as though he wants to turn away. He catches Finlay's eye, because Finlay is watching him with a gentle look as though he understands: he can see it, he can feel it. It makes Banjo's throat go weird.

'Finlay, is it?' Julie asks, noticing.

Finlay shrinks inwards at the unexpected attention. 'Um, yes – thanks so much for having me.'

'You're more than welcome.' Julie smiles as she hugs him.

'The more the merrier!' Carlos proclaims, patting Finlay's back.

Finlay looks at Banjo in complete bewilderment, his head now a tomato. Banjo can only smile helplessly, like *get used to it*.

'We'd best be off.' Paula checks her watch, her smile slipping. 'We're actually visiting our son and his family, we just thought we'd pop by to say a hello.'

'Of course.' Julie waves at them. 'Don't let us keep you. Have a wonderful Christmas!'

'Swing by anytime!' Carlos adds.

'We will.' Paula smiles at them all. 'Merry Christmas.'

No confusion. No hesitation. There's not even any curiosity. They just accept it.

Banjo asked Alena to tell Julie and Carlos he's in foster care. He didn't want any lingering lies. He knows the topic of his parents might come up again one day, and he wants to be honest when it does.

But Banjo thought Julie and Carlos might be stiff and unsure around him. And instead, there's nothing to worry about.

Banjo jumps forward before Paula and Henry can disappear.

Paula blinks, surprised. She stops.

Banjo lunges before he can overthink it. He wraps arms around her shoulders and hangs on. Paula's arms come around his middle, but her touch is gentle. Then she pulls away so Henry can take Banjo into his chest. Banjo closes his eyes and grips him.

When he manages to untangle himself, Henry clasps the space between Banjo's neck and shoulder while Paula touches his face. And it feels so good. It doesn't feel weird, or fucked, or wrong. It just feels right.

When Banjo jogs back to the house, Alena and Finlay are waiting for him. Julie and Carlos are inside.

'Okay?' Alena laces their fingers together. Finlay places a hand on his shoulder.

Banjo nods at them. He puts a hand on Finlay's back and gives Alena's hand a squeeze. He almost wants to squeeze them *together*, squeeze the absolute life out of them, and barely resists.

'Am brilliant.' He grins.

The whole table is lined with bowls of bread and cheese, butter and salt, spoons and knives, tissue-paper crowns and candles. Finlay sits on the couch with Alena's grandparents and chats while Jace hunts for board games and Banjo mashes potatoes.

They play charades. Finlay and Banjo team up only to discover Banjo's horrendous at miming and Finlay's even worse at guessing. *A horse! A shoe! A blanket!* Banjo's got such a stitch from laughing that he can barely do the gestures.

That overstimulated feeling comes on sometimes. And other times Banjo thinks, *Is this even real?* It's like a fantasy he would have played in his own head. Corny and unbelievable and totally out of reach. But somehow it's here and he's in it.

Finlay's phone keeps blowing up – there's two different girls sending pictures with their families, and more messages flooding the screen. 'Just friends,' Finlay explains with a smile. When he goes to take a picture in return Banjo presses in, shoving their cheeks together and pulling a face.

It's a little blurry, the angle underneath their chins, but Finlay looks pleased as punch in the photo. Banjo does too.

Eventually Finlay gets a call from his boyfriend. Akash holds up a straight-fingered palm for a virtual handshake. Banjo copies, laughing. Akash chatters a mile a minute; Banjo can tell he's frazzled by nerves, and that *Banjo's* the cause. It makes Banjo's chest feel full. Maybe this is how Finlay felt when he realised Banjo told Alena about him.

Finlay nips into the kitchen to talk to Akash more privately. Banjo leaves him to it, smiling, but when he returns from the bathroom he overhears Finlay's soft voice saying, 'I'll see you tomorrow.'

'Make sure that you do, please!' Akash's tinny reply comes.

Banjo's whole body feels warm listening to them.

Devlin texts, *Merry Christmas ya filthy animal*, which is a bit weird. Banjo sends the middle finger back.

He thinks about it, then writes out: *Have a good Christmas mate. Thanks for Devlin and that.*

Kyle sends Banjo a picture toasting a glass to his pool. *Christmas came early. Finally done a deep clean. No parties ever again.*

Banjo laughs at that. And his smile stays on his face as he tiptoes back to dinner and finds Alena declaring the end of some terrible Christmas cracker joke, *a mince spy!* Julie and the grandparents laugh. Carlos groans and Jace covers her face.

Finlay comes out the kitchen and finds Banjo standing at the doorway. He catches Banjo's eye and Banjo looks back at him. They hold one another there, smiling. It feels like there's a hand cleaning his split chin, pressed against a wooden drawer, hovering inches over his own, at the other side of a door.

We made it. That's what the look says. *We fucking made it.*

*

Earlier that day, Banjo and Finlay left the café together at closing time. When they rushed down the hill, the birds came up over the trees. They took one hand off their bikes and stretched out to each other, laughing. Like two little kids on their way home. Like they were re-enacting some childhood tradition. Bridging the gap between two beds. Only this time there was nothing in the way.

Acknowledgements

For my agent, Rachel Petty, who championed Banjo and Finlay from the very first day and has been there ever since.

For Alice Swan and Ama Badu, my truly awe-inspiring editors whose vision is nothing short of genius and whose passion for *Glasgow Boys* knows no bounds.

For Jenny Glencross, Jessica White and Sarah Barlow, who elevated *Glasgow Boys* through their incredible talents.

For the amazing team at Faber: Leah Thaxton, Bethany Carter, Natasha Brown, Hannah Styles, Sarah Connell, Sarah Davison-Aitkins, Louise Brice, Emma Eldridge, Simi Toor, Lizzie Bishop, Jack Bartram, Sarah Stoll, Lauren Robertson, Hazel Thompson, Hassan Ali, Catherine Daly, the fantastic sales team and anyone who ever worked on *Glasgow Boys*. I will genuinely never forget a single kind thing you said nor all of your exhaustive hard work.

For Jonathan Pelham and the stunning cover design that captures so much.

For John Radoux, who offered his expertise on the subject of foster care and child services.

For Ania Bas, who gave insight and guidance into the Polish immigrant experience.

For the wonderful Creative Writing and English Literature departments at Strathclyde and Glasgow University, particularly Colin Herd, Matthew Sangster, Andrew Meechan, Rodge Glass, Elspeth Jajdelska and Eleanor Bell.

For my incredible readers (and equally incredible friends) who saw almost every version: Amy Jo-Fowler, Lara Van Lin, Domenika Grabovska, Kristýna Blažková, Seán Farrelly, Sam Scifres, Brecht Van Winden, Kameron Bourgeois, Mimi Chau and literally anyone I ever spoke to on Archive of Our Own.

For my parents, Catherine McDonald and Robert McDonald, who gave me everything.

For my siblings, Joseph McDonald and Caitlin McDonald, who shaped me.

For my very best friend in the whole wide world, Jamie Thorburn. Words actually fail, but you're on every page.

For everyone on this particular page – *Glasgow Boys* is as much yours as it is mine.

And for those who see themselves in Banjo or Finlay, I hope you find the people you deserve to navigate this life with.

Scots Glossary

Aboot – about

Ae – of

Aff – off

Ah – I

Ah'll – I'll

Ah've – I've

'At – that

Am – I am

Aw – all

Aw'right – all right

Cannae – cannot

Dae – do

Didnae- did not

Dinnae – do not

Doesnae – does not

D'ye – do you

Fae – from

Fucken – fucking

Fur – for

Gimme – give me

Gie – give

Gonnae – going to

'Hanks – thanks

'Hink – think

Jus/jist – just

Kidden – kidding

Kindae – kind of

Nae – no or not

Naw – no

No' – not

Nuthin' – nothing

Oan – on

Oot – out

Some'dae – somebody

Tae – to

They – the

Wan – one

Wae – with

Wasnae – was not

Wannae – want to

Whit/whut – What

Wrang – wrong

Willnae – will not

Wis/wus – was

Wisnae – was not

Wouldnae – would not

Wusnae – wasn't

Ye – you

Yer – your

Yersel – yourself